ALL THE WRONG CHORDS

ALL THE WRONG CHORDS

CHRISTINE HURLEY DERISO

Mendota Heights, Minnesota

First Edition
First Printing, 2017

Book design by Jake Nordby
Cover design by Jake Nordby
Cover images by dextroza/Shutterstock Images; Paul Lesser/Shutterstock Images; vladimirderdyuk/Shutterstock Images
Interior images by Paul Lesser/Shutterstock Images

Flux, an imprint of North Star Editions, Inc.

Library of Congress Cataloging-in-Publication Data
Names: Deriso, Christine Hurley, 1961- author.
Title: All the wrong chords / Christine Hurley Deriso.
Description: First edition. | Mendota Heights, MN : Flux, 2017. | Summary: "Dealing with the death of her brother, teenager Scarlett Stiles joins a rock band and falls hard for the band's lead singer and local 'bad boy'"-- Provided by publisher.
Identifiers: LCCN 2017031806 (print) | LCCN 2017044093 (ebook) | ISBN 9781635830118 (hosted e-book) | ISBN 9781635830101 (pbk. : alk. paper)
Subjects: | CYAC: Bands (Music)--Fiction. | Dating (Social customs)--Fiction.
| Death--Fiction. | Grief--Fiction. | Grandfathers--Fiction. | Brothers and sisters--Fiction.
Classification: LCC PZ7.D4427 (ebook) | LCC PZ7.D4427 All 2017 (print) | DDC
[Fic]--dc23
LC record available at https://lccn.loc.gov/2017031806

Flux
North Star Editions, Inc.
2297 Waters Drive
Mendota Heights, MN 55120
www.fluxnow.com

Printed in the United States of America

To Jules and John, who lived this experience with me scene by scene, note by note, and chord by chord.

And to Dane and Emmy, who make my heart sing.

CHAPTER ONE

"Keys, please?"

Grandpa narrows his bright-blue eyes into the hot glare of the midafternoon sun, then sucks in his lips and grudgingly tosses them to me as we approach his Mercury in the driveway.

"I've gotta practice, remember?" I say cajolingly.

This is one of a dozen or so white lies my parents and I rehearsed before they dropped me off to spend the summer with my eighty-six-year-old granddad in Oakboro, Georgia.

"Don't let him drive you *anywhere*," Mom had told me with the intensity of a president handing over the nuclear code on his last day in office, and she'd reinforced the message once we'd arrived: "Dad, remember, Scarlett will be heading off to college in the fall, and we need you to supervise her driving every chance you get."

I think he smelled a rat from the get-go. I'm a week into my summer-long visit, and he still can't break the habit of heading to the driver's side every time we go to the car.

Or maybe it's not a habit. Maybe it's his stubbornness kicking in, even at the expense of a granddaughter who, my parents would have him believe, still hasn't mastered basic driving skills by age eighteen. Or maybe it's his suspicion that he's being played. I hope not. Grandpa may be old, but, whoa, that man is sharp. The smartest man I know, I think, and that includes my brother, who holds the record for the highest-ever SAT score in our high school.

Held, I mean. I've got to break the habit of using present-tense verbs for Liam.

Anyhow, I hate patronizing Grandpa, and I *really* hate the idea that he might suspect he's being patronized. Besides, I hate our driving arrangement as much as he does. Nothing makes me feel more warm and fuzzy than memories of sitting in the passenger seat while he drove me to the store or tennis courts when I was younger, whistling along to "In the Mood" or "Pennsylvania 6-5000." (Scoff not; those Depression-era swing bands were fierce!) Grandpa would tap his wedding band to the beat against the metal part of the steering wheel, occasionally even going full throttle, both hands whaling like drumsticks.

Which, now that I think of it, doesn't sound particularly safe. Add cataracts, bad hearing, and slowed reflexes to the mix and, well, I guess my parents have a point—a point they probably could have made without throwing my driving skills under the bus, but whatever.

Still, I miss snuggling into the passenger seat of Grandpa's car, savoring the musty, asthma-inducing aroma of the newspapers stacked in his back seat, and listening to Benny Goodman slay the clarinet.

Grandpa insists on *no* music when I'm driving. Whether or not he's buying the ruse that my awful driving requires his vigilant supervision, he still takes very seriously his responsibility to be the most annoying backseat driver he can possibly be. When I'm driving, he tends to gasp a lot, or slam on imaginary brakes, or toss his hands in the air like he can't believe I just did whatever I just did. I guess after raising four kids, he's learned that startling body language is preferable to screaming or barking out orders. He would be wrong.

So here we go again: our fifth car ride in as many days. I've noticed that when Grandpa drives himself, he tends to stagger his errands throughout the day, heading off to the store in the morning for frozen waffles, for instance, then going back in the afternoon for milk. I think he started that a couple of years ago, after Grandma died, to make his days as busy as possible. But when *I'm* driving, he consolidates his trips. I guess our rides are just as nerve-racking for him as they are for me.

We settle in the car and fasten our seat belts.

"You don't need that, do you?" Grandpa asks as I crank up the air conditioning after starting the engine.

"Grandpa, it's eighty-seven degrees. I started sweating just walking to the car."

He grunts his disapproval, but if that's all the pushback I get, I'm sticking to my guns.

I start inching out of his driveway, Grandpa's neck craned so he can observe my progress. "The *children*," he always murmurs tensely as I back out. "The *children*."

This is shorthand, I guess, for "neighborhood children may dart into your path at any moment, so go even slower than your current speed of three miles per hour." But I haven't flattened anybody yet, so I wish he'd lay off the hypothetical children.

But wait—someone *is* darting into our path right now. It's Grandpa's next-door neighbor Mrs. Bixley. She's trotting through the Bermuda grass, her arms aloft as she waves us down. When Grandpa spots her, he clutches his chest as if a UFO has just landed on his roof. I stop the car and roll down my window.

"Hi, Mrs. Bixley," I say, my foot planted firmly on the brake.

"The *brake*, the *brake*," Grandpa murmurs, just in case I might be inclined to floor it and crash through his garage door, leaving Mrs. Bixley in the dust. He's still panting in alarm over her surprise appearance.

"Is that you, Scarlett?" Mrs. Bixley asks me in a sing-song voice, and I try to imagine a context in which the answer would be "No."

"Yep," I say gamely. "It's me."

"Oh my goodness! I can't believe how grown up you are! And look at you driving! When did you get your license?"

"Two years ago. I start college in the fall."

"Oh my goodness, how time flies! When did you get into town?"

"Sunday."

"The *brake*," Grandpa stresses under his breath.

"Yes, your grandfather mentioned you'd be here for the summer. Isn't that wonderful! You'll *have* to come to my house this weekend for a nice home-cooked meal."

"She's getting fed, Carol," Grandpa says. He's finally calmed down and is trying to sound good-natured, but the edge in his voice is unmistakable.

"Getting fed out of cans, I imagine," Mrs. Bixley says in the isn't-he-adorable tone that irritates the hell out of Grandpa.

"I imagine she'll survive," he says, the edge now edgier.

"Come over for dinner tomorrow," she tells me, ignoring Grandpa altogether, which annoys him even more. "Joe will cook hamburgers on the grill."

"Thank you," I say, pitching forward a little to block her view, just in case Grandpa is shooting daggers with his eyes.

"Six o'clock!"

Grandpa leans even farther over than me to inject himself

back into the conversation. "Thanks, Carol. We're in kind of a rush . . ."

"Of course! Of course!" she says, her fingertips fluttering.

"Bye," I say, waving as I begin to inch out of the driveway.

"Both hands on the wheel!" Grandpa barks.

Sigh. It's gonna be a long summer.

• • •

I tap my foot impatiently, then retrieve my cell phone from my jeans pocket and text my friend Varun: I'm standing in line at a bank. Seriously.

Your point? Varun texts back.

That it's still a thing, apparently. My grandpa must be the only person left on earth who still stands in line to complete hella-boring errands that everybody else handles online.

Then there wouldn't be a line.

Smart-ass, I text back, grinning. And this is after we just spent half an hour standing in line at the post office, mind you.

That grandpa of yours sure knows how to roll out the red carpet for his guests.

A couple of people jostle past me on their way out of the bank, shaking hands with Grandpa along the way. Everybody in Oakboro knows him.

"Whatcha up to there, Scarletta?" Grandpa asks me as I finish the text, each of us taking baby steps closer to the front of the line.

"Just texting Varun," I say.

"The young man I met at your graduation?"

"Right. The funny one."

"Ah. Where's he from again?"

"Four houses down from ours."

Grandpa's brow furrows, so I elaborate. "His parents are from India."

"That's right, that's right. His father's the heart surgeon?"

"His *mom*," I clarify. "But his dad works at the medical school, too. I think he's a radiologist."

Grandpa looks pleased, so I'm guessing these are boyfriend-screening questions.

"You two seem pretty close," he says, confirming my guess. "Will you be going to the same college?"

"Yep, but he's just a friend."

Grandpa looks unconvinced.

"He's gay."

"Ah." Grandpa nods noncommittally and gazes past me. I peek at him for a quick sensitivity check. Grandpa is surprisingly chill, especially considering his age, but I'm never quite sure when something will throw him.

He's been thrown a lot lately, so I change the subject. "Grandpa, you really should get a smartphone," I say, holding it up for his inspection.

"Eh," he says, waving a hand dismissively. "I'm too old for that kind of thing."

"You're *not* too old," I insist, flicking my ponytail off my shoulder. "It's like carrying your whole computer with you everywhere you go. As much as you love trivia, you'd get totally hooked. Any question that flitted through your mind? You'd have the answer right away. Doesn't that sound great? And we could FaceTime."

"That's the computer thing where everybody puts their snapshots?"

"That's Face*book*. FaceTime is like talking on the phone, only we can see each other."

He pulls his baseball cap more snugly against his thinning white hair. "Well, if you don't know what I look like by now . . ."

I wrinkle my nose. "You'd totally love a smartphone, Grandpa. Hey, I could spend the summer teaching you how to use one! Like I taught you how to play guitar. You picked that up so fast! And when you started playing racquetball when your knees got too achy for tennis? You learn things super quick."

"Mmmmm," Grandpa responds, then starts softly whistling, his none-too-subtle way of opting out of the conversation.

But that's okay. I love to hear him whistle; he's always so content when he's listening to music, whether it's coming from his radio, his guitar, his piano, or his head. I love how bright and twinkly his blue eyes look behind his glasses as his vibrato whistling floats through the bank. I haven't seen that look much since Liam died . . .

I bite my lip to stop my chin from quivering. God, I miss my brother.

As I slip my phone into my jeans pocket, a middle-aged man who's just walked into the bank approaches us. "Mr. O'Malley?" he asks.

"Yes. Hello there!" Grandpa says congenially, his mind no doubt scouring its databank for clues to the man's identity.

"Mr. O'Malley, it's so good to see you." The man shakes Grandpa's hand and peers warmly into his eyes. "It's been years. I live out west now, but I'm in town this week visiting my parents."

"Yes, yes!" Grandpa says, pretending this information has solved the puzzle. "Good to see you! This is my granddaughter, Scarlett."

"Scarlett. Hi," he says, then smiles broadly. "Wow, you look just like your mom. I went to school with her. Please tell her I said hello."

"Definitely," I say, wondering how I'll manage that, what with being clueless about his name and all.

Grandpa and I will laugh about this when we get in the car. He's always running into people he used to coach in baseball or serve with on some committee, or who carpooled with his kids when they were in sixth grade. "*I* haven't changed, but *they've* gotten a lot older," he'll joke.

We wait for the mystery man to fold back into the line, but he's not done yet.

"I was so terribly sorry to hear about your loss," the man says, his gaze shifting between Grandpa and me.

"Thank you, thank you," Grandpa says, lowering his eyes reverently. I dig my nails into my palms.

"He was, what, eighteen?"

"Twenty-one," I correct the man, then clear my throat to quell the tremble in my voice.

"Just a tragedy . . ." he murmurs.

"A real tragedy," Grandpa concurs.

"Heart failure, my mom said?" he asks.

"Mmmmm," Grandpa responds, giving an almost imperceptible nod.

I've been in town long enough now to know that "heart failure" is the Oakboro version of Liam's cause of death, thanks to Grandpa's *spin*. And technically, it's correct. I mean, when you fatally overdose on drugs, your heart definitely does fail. But it's kinda like blaming kidney failure when someone's been shot to death. Yeah, the kidneys go kaput, but so does everything else. Grandpa knows the broad strokes of Liam's drug addiction, but I guess you can't begrudge him a smidge of denial.

Either that, or he's embarrassed. I sure hope that's not it. Liam didn't make the world's most stellar choices the last couple of years of his life, but he doesn't deserve to be considered an embarrassment. A selfless guy who would walk homeless people to a diner and buy them a meal? Yes. A musician whose fingers looked like butterfly wings when he played his guitar? Yes. A brother who ran four blocks with me in his arms when I face-planted after wiping out on my skateboard? Yes.

But an embarrassment? Never.

I swallow hard. One of the hardest things about losing Liam was losing *everything* about him: the twinkly blue eyes that looked so much like Grandpa's, the long, slim fingers that caressed the guitar so gracefully, the dry delivery when he told a joke . . .

Losing him wasn't a single loss: It was a million losses, all at the same time.

"Well . . . I just can't tell you how sorry I am," the man continues.

"Thank you, thank you," Grandpa says. "I'll be sure to tell Celeste."

"Yes, please do. God. Life is short."

"Mmmmm." Grandpa and I say it simultaneously, both of us having wrung maximum duty lately from this all-purpose response to platitudes.

"Take care," the man says, patting Grandpa's forearm before slipping to the back of the line.

We're quiet for a moment before Grandpa breaks the silence: "You have any idea who that fella is?"

"Beats me."

"Mmmmm. You know, people pat you a lot when you're old."

I laugh, lowering my head.

Grandpa's taken a pounding lately, but he's a survivor.

I guess I am, too.

CHAPTER TWO

"You don't need that, do you?"

Grrrrr. Grandpa's grousing about the air-conditioning again.

"Grandpa, it's hotter now than when we left the house," I argue as I back out of my parking space at the grocery store.

"But it's a *five-minute drive*," he says.

"I know, but the doctor said humidity is bad for my acne."

There. Will *that* solve the air-conditioning problem once and for all?

Grandpa peers at me, no doubt inspecting me for zits. "Your face looks fine," he says.

"And don't we want to keep it that way?"

Silence. I guess my reasoning was foolproof.

It's epically difficult to have the last word when arguing with Grandpa, so I should be reveling in my victory. But, of course, my guilt kicks in, so I turn down the AC as a conciliatory gesture. (*Down*. Not off.)

"Oh, Grandpa, did you remember to put the milk in the car?" I ask as I pull out of the parking lot. "It was on the bottom of the cart, so I might not have—"

Grandpa gasps as I turn toward the back seat to inspect the

groceries, and I'm just about to plead with him to stop gasping, which, omigod, is so incredibly nerve-racking, when—

"*Watch out*!"

I slam on my brakes in response to Grandpa's bellow as a guy on a bike darts out of our path, veering so sharply that he crashes into asphalt.

I slap my chest with my palm, staring saucer-eyed at the guy I almost hit and wondering if my heart will explode.

"Stop the car! Stop the car!" Grandpa orders, and at first, I'm too stunned to process the words. What does he mean, *stop the car*? My foot's on the brake; we're not going anywhere. But then I realize he means to turn off the engine and oh, I dunno, maybe lend a hand to the guy who's splatted on the pavement thanks to me, the person who almost killed him. Oh my *God*!

My jaw drops. "Grandpa, I'm sorry, I'm sorry, I'm *so, so*—"

"Scarlett, pull over and turn off the ignition," he says, his voice steady.

I lock eyes with him. "Right," I say with shaky determination, swallowing the lump in my throat. I pull into the nearest parking space, then fling my door open and run toward the bicyclist. Grandpa is right on my heels, amazingly spry for his age.

"Oh my God! I'm so, so sorry!" I say as I approach the guy. "Are you okay?"

The cyclist—a tall, lanky guy around my age wearing cargo shorts and a T-shirt—locks his deep-set chocolaty eyes with mine as he stands up, wiping gravel from his knees.

"I'm fine," he says, then glances over at his sprawled bicycle. I follow his gaze.

"Your bike!" I say, rushing to stand it upright as Grandpa and a couple of bystanders help the guy to his feet.

"I promise, I'm fine," he insists to them. "Just scraped my knees a little."

As I prop his bike on the kickstand, the guy takes off his helmet and shakes his light-brown hair free. Grandpa and the others hover around him, inspecting him for injuries. My whole body is shaking as I rush back toward him.

"You're sure you're okay?" I ask in a trembling voice.

He waves a hand through the air. "I was hurt worse than this stubbing my toe in the shower this morning."

Grandpa is rustling through the pockets of his chino slacks. "I want to leave my name and phone number in case you—"

"I know who you are," the guy responds. "Mr. O'Malley, right? I'm Zach Spencer. My granddad plays tennis with you. I used to watch some of your matches when I was a kid."

"Yes, yes," Grandpa says in the same tone of voice he used for the stranger in the bank a few minutes earlier. "Your granddad . . ."

"Harold Carver," Zach clarifies.

"Harold, yes! How's he doing?" Grandpa asks. "I stopped playing a couple of years ago. Bad knees. But I need to meet him for coffee one day soon and catch up."

"He'd love that. He still plays now and then—mostly doubles these days," Zach says as the passersby discreetly disperse, their curiosity and compassion seemingly overridden by their realization that he's fine and that a boring conversation is unfolding. My heart is finally slowing its full-on gallop.

"I've been meaning to call Harold," Grandpa says. "How's your mother?"

Zach presses in his lips. "She's okay, thanks."

"Glad to hear it," Grandpa says. "Yes, I've definitely been meaning to catch up with Harold. Now, let us drive you home."

"No, no," Zach says. "I'm headed just right down the street."

"Work?" Grandpa asks. "We can come along and explain to your boss how we held you up. Maybe he'd let us run you home to get cleaned up . . ."

"No, I'm just practicing with my band," Zach says. "Those guys aren't particular about how I look. No dress code there." He smiles shyly, gesturing toward his asphalt-scuffed clothes.

"A band, eh?" Grandpa says, a hot breeze blowing past our cheeks.

Zach nods. "Some guys I went to high school with. We're all in college now, but we regroup during summers."

"What instrument do you play?" Grandpa asks.

"Guitar. You should come listen to us sometime; we play on Friday nights at Sheehan's." During the invitation, Zach's brown eyes switch from Grandpa's to mine, then back again.

"We'd enjoy that," Grandpa says. "This is my granddaughter, Scarlett. She's in town for the summer, and I'm sure she'd welcome activities that don't involve the geriatric set."

I blush, mostly because this guy now has a name to attach to the crazy person who nearly plowed him down five minutes earlier.

Zach laughs genially. "You'll both be right at home. My grandparents come a lot. They're kind of our resident groupies."

"Well, that'll be just the place to catch up with Harold," Grandpa says.

"Our first set tonight starts at 7:30," Zach says. "We'll be playing on the deck if it doesn't rain."

"Well, I'm sure we'll be seeing you soon," Grandpa says, extending a hand to Zach. "Again, I can't tell you how sorry we are for the mishap. But I'm sure glad I got the chance to see you again."

Zach nods as he shakes Grandpa's hand.

I wring my hands together. "I'm just *so, so* . . ." My voice trails off ridiculously.

"Really, I'm fine," Zach tells me. "Hope to see you both at Sheehan's."

I wave limply as he hops back on his bike and rides away. I stand there for a minute, blowing a breath out of puffed-up cheeks, then head back to the car.

But Grandpa stops me short. "Keys," he says.

I hesitate for just a second, then toss them to him.

No argument here.

CHAPTER THREE

My sister, Sara, stomps into the bedroom I'm using at Grandpa's house, her arms swinging like machetes by her side. "Why did you let him drive?" she demands, her hazel eyes bulging.

My parents and Sara met Grandpa and me at Casa di Pizza for an early bird dinner at our midpoint of Mooresville, a half-hour drive for both of us. Then Grandpa and I drove Sara back to his house for the weekend. Grandpa and I discreetly waited until Mom and Dad drove out of the restaurant parking lot after the meal, waving cheerfully at them before exchanging places so Grandpa could take the wheel. Sara looked confused from the back seat, but she kept her mouth shut at the time, I guess to avoid hurting Grandpa's feelings.

But we're back at Grandpa's now, and he's settled downstairs into his recliner for his daily dose of evening news and *Jeopardy!*, so the gloves are off.

I glance sideways at Sara from the desk where I'm pecking away at my laptop. Oozing indifference is something I've turned into an art form as the younger sister of a perfectionist. "You mean Grandpa?" I ask blandly, my eyes now back on the screen.

"No, I mean Brian from *Family Guy*," she sputters. "You

know Mom told you not to let Grandpa drive. I felt like I was in a parade on the interstate! Except instead of throwing us candy as we cruised at thirty-seven miles an hour, everybody threw us the finger instead."

"So we were, like, the float in the parade?" I clarify, just to mess with her. "If that's the case, then *we* would be the ones throwing candy."

I'm still typing—*peck, peck, peck, peck*—both because I can multitask (in this case, arguing with my sister while filling out a form for the lifeguard job I start on Monday) and because Sara's blood boils when she can't draw me into her drama. Is it my fault that watching her head practically spin off her neck in frustration is highly entertaining?

Sara *grrrrs*, squeezing her hands into fists, and plops on one of the twin beds in the room. "Grandpa is *eighty-five years old*, Scarlett," she says, leaning back with her arms crossed indignantly, squishing the mangy teddy bear laying on the pillow.

"Eighty-*six*," I correct her. "And he's *still* a safer bet behind the wheel than I am. Ironic, right?"

I can see in the mirror over the bureau that Sara is squinting at the back of my head. "What do you mean?" she asks nervously.

I sigh, hit *Save*, and swivel in my chair to face her. Might as well spill the beans, particularly since Grandpa will no doubt be chauffeuring us around all weekend. "I almost flattened some guy on a bicycle today."

Sara gasps, and I flap the palm of my hand to shush her.

"It's no big deal," I assure her. "He's fine. But Grandpa made me cough up the keys—I'm guessing for the entire summer. Don't tell Mom and Dad."

"Are you *crazy*?" Sara says, pitching forward. "Scarlett,

Mom and Dad have been through enough. Do *not* add another tragedy to their plate."

Okay, this is the point in conversations when Sara crosses the threshold from mildly annoying to seriously rash-inducing. Her prissiness (which I think she reserves solely for me, since she has loads of normal friends) sets my teeth on edge. And her condescension has been on overdrive since Liam died.

"So I *shouldn't* let Grandpa drive us off a cliff?"

Her hands fly in the air. "This is no joking matter! He has cataracts! And he won't wear his hearing aid! He has no business behind the wheel. Scarlett, that was a major reason for you staying here this summer, so we could wean him off driving."

Wean. Like something you do to an infant.

I stand up, plant a hand on my hip, and set my chin. "I'm not here to conspire against Grandpa. And I'm not letting anybody treat him like a two-year-old."

Sara eyes me evenly. "So," she counters, "you'd rather let him kill himself in a car crash than support a reasonable limitation for an eighty-six-year-old man."

Thunder churns in the distance.

"Yeah, well, people die, now don't they?"

Dammit. Tears have sprung to my eyes. My emotions are so unpredictable these days.

A tense moment passes, then Sara walks over and puts her arms around me.

"It's okay," she whispers in my ear as I swallow hard.

I hug her back, sniffling into her long, glossy, dark hair. This is classic Sara and me. She's prissy, and I'm snarky. Until we're not. Until we're best friends, fierce protectors, wagon-circling allies. These moments don't last long, but even during our worst fights, we always snap back to being the little kids who reach for each other's hands at the circus as we maneuver our way through the popcorn line.

"I miss him, too," Sara says softly as our arms untangle.

I nod, peering into her moist eyes. "How are Mom and Dad?" I ask. "I mean *really*."

Sara knows what I mean. I'm the youngest, so our parents are more vigilant around me about putting up a good front. Sure, I've seen them both crumble in tears more than once in the past six months. Mom's knees have actually buckled a time or two. But they're determined to put on their game faces for my sake. It's one of the reasons we all decided a summer with Grandpa was a good idea—fake cheeriness is exhausting.

They're more genuine around Sara, especially Mom. Mom does the shtick about loving all of us equally (*both* of us now, I guess), but she and Sara have a special spark that keeps them on the same wavelength. Like Liam and I used to be.

"They're good," Sara assures me, nodding for emphasis. She puts on her game face for me, too. "Mom finally started taking some of his stuff to Goodwill."

I try to hold steady, but my eyes suddenly flood with more tears. I'm not ready for strangers to start pawing through Liam's things. Sara holds me as I sob softly in her arms.

"Just some old clothes," she assures me soothingly, running her fingers over my hair. "Stuff he would have gotten rid of anyway."

But I can't stop crying. If Liam had gotten rid of stuff before, it would have been because he was replacing it with *new* stuff—not because he would never need stuff again.

It seems like every day brings a fresh wave of reasons to be heartbroken.

Sara guides me to the bed and gently lowers me to a sitting position.

"It's okay," she coos, and I love her for trying to console me when I know she's just as torn up as I am.

"I know," I tell her through my tears. "It's just . . . the guy I almost hit at the grocery store was about Liam's age."

"Well," Sara says, "that was no reason to try to murder him."

I study her face for a moment, then sputter with laughter. Sara's smartass side is so random that it always catches me by surprise.

Plus, even amid the suckfest of losing a brother to a drug overdose, it's impossible not to feel safe in this room. It's barely changed at all since Mom shared it with Aunt Margie growing up, other than the bubblegum-colored bedspreads fading to pale pink and the now-weathered teddy bear. Some puffy-sleeved prom dresses are stuffed into the closet that won't close because the door is off track, and board games with missing pieces are stacked on the top shelf. Our whole lives, Sara and I have been snuggling under the same pale-pink bedspreads, surrounded by the same throwbacks of Mom's childhood. Yeah, it feels safe in here.

Late-afternoon sunlight is streaming through the windows, and thunder is rumbling lazily in the distance. "Hey, speaking of the guy I almost killed," I say, "he told me he's in a band. They're playing tonight at Sheehan's."

"Sheehan's?"

"It's that new restaurant where the record store used to be. We should go."

Sara's brow furrows. "But what about Grandpa?"

"He can come, too," I say, rising from the bed and

tightening my ponytail. "The guy said his grandfather comes all the time, and he and Grandpa used to play tennis together."

"But *Jeopardy!*"

"Grandpa can miss it for one night. C'mon. Let's go talk him into it. It'll do him good to get out of the house."

"Last time you got him out of the house, you almost killed somebody," Sara reminds me, and I cut my eyes at her with a grudging smile.

"You can drive," I tell her.

"Duh," she says. Rubbing her arms, she adds, "I'm still smudgy from sitting in the back seat. Why does he keep all those old newspapers anyway?"

I shrug. "Obituaries, I think. He goes to lots of funerals."

An awkward pause follows. I didn't mean it as a joke; I think that actually *is* why he likes to have newspapers handy. But it came out jokey, and neither of us is in the mood to crack wise about funerals.

"Come on," I say definitively, pulling Sara off the bed. "We need a change of scenery."

CHAPTER FOUR

"You don't need that, do you?"

I smirk subversively in the back seat as cool air blasts into the car. The good news is that now it's Sara on the receiving end of Grandpa's apparent allergy to creature comforts. The bad news is that I'm the one now choking on newsprint dust in the back seat.

Grandpa's a little grumpy, both because Sara talked him into handing over the car keys (she pointed out that *she* hasn't flattened any pedestrians today) and because he's missing *Jeopardy!*

It was a hard sell to get him to come to Sheehan's with us, but when I pointed out he'd be making good on his promise to the guy I almost killed on *his* watch, Grandpa reluctantly agreed.

It's still light outside, though fireflies are already doing their slow-motion dance through the sticky evening air. The thunder never amounted to anything—false alarms in Oakboro are common during the summer—so the temperature is holding steady in the 90s. Grandpa has insisted on wearing a tie to the little pub-eatery where Zach's band is playing. Sara and I assured him that was overkill, but he wouldn't budge. At least he skipped the jacket. He grimaced when he saw the cut-off shorts I'd changed into, so I threw on some jeans instead.

I figured if he could skip *Jeopardy!* for a night, I could be flexible, too. Sara is her typical chic self in a lemony sundress with a leather belt that matches her chunky sandals. She even threw in some color-coordinated jewelry and a few spritzes of honeysuckle-scented hair defrizzer. My hair is in the same ponytail I've worn since this morning. If it's frizzing, I haven't noticed. And considering I now reek of newsprint, frizz is the least of my concerns.

Grandpa is swiveling in the shotgun seat, freaking out that kids are riding their bikes in the street Sara is backing into.

"The children! The children!" he murmurs frantically.

"Grandpa, you're making me nervous," Sara says. "Oh look! Grandma's dogwood tree is in bloom—"

"Watch where you're going!" Grandpa yelps.

There will be no scenery appreciation tonight, not on the heels of my near-miss.

"Grandpa, *please*!" Sara wails, and I smirk again, resting my elbow on the closest stack of newspapers. Hopefully I'm not smudging anybody's obituary.

Obituary. There's that word again. My stomach clutches as I glance down and see a couple of funeral announcements circled with Sharpie. Poor Grandpa. He must lose an average of one or two friends or acquaintances a month. But most of those people die old. And none of those funerals could have prepared him for the day Aunt Margie and Uncle Max, trembling and bleary-eyed, picked him up and drove him to our house so Mom and Dad could tell him in person that Liam was gone—found dead in the shower overnight by his college roommate. Sara and I were sitting in the adjacent den, still too numb to do anything besides stare into space. But Grandpa's wail jolted us back to reality. It was primal, as if his lifelong commitment to vigilance had been a sick joke and life had been exposed as the crapshoot that it was.

Grandpa, a child of the Great Depression who started supporting his mother and sisters in high school after his father dropped dead of a heart attack, has always lectured us about the importance of responsibility, preparation, maturity, and good choices. A lot of good that had done. Mom and Dad had to physically hold him up as he sobbed in our kitchen. Then they guided him to the den and lowered him, crumpled and defeated, onto the couch. All of this, just as he was finally starting to process Grandma's death.

Sara and I had rushed to sit on either side of him, then we all huddled there together for, I dunno, maybe an hour, like shipwreck survivors clinging to a life raft. I'll never forget the hopelessness in Grandpa's face.

In lots of ways, he's been more protective of us than ever since Liam's death—God knows he can't handle another tragedy. But deep inside, the light flickered out of his eyes that day. *Why bother?* his sad, hollow expression seemed to suggest.

Or maybe that's what *I'm* thinking, and I'm just projecting my stuff onto Grandpa. Whatever. I don't have the energy to try to sort it out.

But I *am* sure of one thing: Life's a crapshoot.

I wonder when I'll be able to think of Liam without feeling like I've just been kicked in the stomach.

Speaking of which, I don't know if tonight's trip to Sheehan's is really the best idea. I haven't pulled my guitar out of its case since Liam died, and I haven't been able to listen to any of the songs we used to play together. Will it be possible to enjoy a band without screaming silently to the heavens to give me one more jam session with my brother? My stomach twists as I imagine myself losing it in front of everyone, including the guy I almost flattened, who probably already thinks I'm crazy.

Once Liam taught me how to play guitar at age twelve, I never went more than eight hours at a stretch without practicing, preferring to skip meals if I had to choose between picking and eating. At times, I think I'd have chosen picking over *breathing*.

Liam was such a stellar musician, and even though my natural talent is firmly in the *meh* range, he made me better. I have a pretty good ear and a decent sense of rhythm, so I play mostly by ear. Sticking music in front of me is like putting a map in the face of a driver who already knows the way. So I can hold my own with an instrument or a vocal.

But Liam's talent was in a whole different dimension. He had perfect pitch and mad dexterity. He always assured me I was selling myself short, but I knew I had to raise the bar to be worthy of a spot in the Joneses, the band he started his last year of high school. So I practiced like crazy. Night after night, I'd play my guitar until midnight, under the covers if necessary to avoid Mom's hollers of "*Get to sleep*!" I'd practice scales over and over or reproduce riffs note by note, trying to step up my game.

And what do you know? It worked. What I lacked in natural talent, I started making up for in sheer persistence. When Liam invited me to join the Joneses, I felt like I'd been inducted into the Rock & Roll Hall of Fame. He still took care of most of the heavy lifting while I played mainly rhythm guitar, but my occasional licks were downright solid, if I say so myself. I somehow also emerged as the *de facto* lead singer. I guess my sole-chick status sealed the deal. Plus, I was weirdly fearless on stage and smiled a lot, mostly because I was so deliriously happy when I was making music.

In the two years I played with the Joneses, our adoring (actually, *indifferent*) audiences rarely numbered more than a few dozen. We played at parties, fairs, and the occasional wedding, but we could have been playing in front of a bunch of wax-museum dummies, for all I cared. I just had an insane, insatiable need to make music. And seeing Liam smile when I threw in a nice, nimble lick, making it sound easy even though it was actually the result of twelve zillion hours of practice? My heart just soared.

Our last gig was four days before he OD'd (God, he was so happy playing that night), and my guitar has basically served as a dust collector ever since. The calluses on my fingertips have long since smoothed over. Almost every association I have with music is all bundled up with memories of Liam, and I can't go there yet.

So, will the sight of a Stratocaster send me tumbling into a black hole? I guess we'll see.

But for now, Grandpa is distracting me with more mundane details. Now that Sara is cruising uneventfully past the pine trees and brick ranch houses that line his street, the neighborhood kids still intact, he's obsessing over the evening ahead.

"Will they expect us to buy food at this place?" he asks, which we all know is out of the question, since he already ate his early bird spaghetti-and-meatballs at Casa de Pizza.

"No, Grandpa," I assure him. "Maybe just order a beer."

"I can't have a beer," he scolds me. "I'll be driving."

"*I'll* be driving," Sara corrects him.

"Not in the dark, you won't," he says.

She sighs, no doubt making a mental note to cross that bridge when she comes to it.

Actually, she's crossing a bridge now.

"They've expanded this to four lanes," Grandpa tells her in his driving-instructor voice, and I wonder whether or not he thinks this is breaking news, considering the bridge leading into downtown Oakboro has had four lanes at least as long as I've been alive. In fact, I think Mom mentioned playing the flute for the high school band performance that commemorated the celebration when the bridge was widened.

Now that Sara has mastered the four-lane bridge, Grandpa is giving her detailed directions to Sheehan's, using lots of hand gestures for emphasis. No need. She and I know downtown Oakboro—all seven blocks of it—like the backs of our hands. The sleepy Southern town had 4,000 residents *tops* during its roaring textile days, and now that the mill has shut down (don't get Grandpa started on *that*), the town's population has dwindled by at least half. The family-owned businesses that once dotted its downtown—vendors for jewelry, shoes, clothes, root beer floats, and that sort of thing—have mostly shuttered as well (a Walmart is right off the interstate now), so lots of the storefronts are empty. Fortunately, now that a car manufacturer has opened a nearby plant, the area is starting to flicker with signs of life again, including the recent addition of Sheehan's.

Sara's pulling into the parking lot now, politely nodding along with Grandpa's superfluous instructions.

Grandpa straightens his tie. "Let's not stay too long, okay, girls?" he says.

"No problem, Grandpa," I promise, wincing against a blast of hot, moist air as I open my door.

"We're going to be outside?" Sara whines as we get out

of the car, noticing that the band is setting up on the deck. "My *hair*."

"I am never taking you two clubbing again," I mutter.

As we walk through the parking lot toward the deck, I watch the band members plug cords into amplifiers on a slightly raised wooden stage that faces a dozen or so teakwood tables and plastic chairs. There are three guys in addition to Zach, the one I almost hit. They're all young and skinny, wearing faded jeans and flicking tousled hair out of their eyes.

Zach catches my eye and waves. My chest tightens as I see that he's plugging in a Strat.

Stop it, Scarlett. Just relax and have a good time.

I swallow hard, then wrinkle my nose and wave back at him meekly, hopefully conveying that I'm still really, *really* sorry about that whole parking-lot fail. He's mouthing something and gesturing toward two old people at one of the tables, so I assume he's pointing out his grandparents.

"I think your tennis buddy is here," I tell Grandpa.

Grandpa scans the crowd and spots his friend. His face brightens. "Hello, Harold!" he calls out as we approach the deck. The old man stands up and motions us over. Looks like a rollicking Friday night is in store for us.

As we weave our way through the tables, Harold starts pushing an empty one against the one he's sharing with his wife. Zach sets his guitar on its stand and hops off the stage to help him.

"Hello, hello!" Harold says as we approach, waving his arm in the air. "Sit, sit!"

Zach holds out a chair for me, smoothing his Stones T-shirt, then holds one out for Sara as we join them. A gum-chewing waitress comes over and distributes menus, then drifts away again. The two grandpas shake hands and make introductions as they take their seats. We all murmur our hellos, with me making one more sheepish reference to the bike crash and Zach gamely waving away my apology.

"What's up with the shirt?" Sara, who tragically knows nothing about classic rock, asks Zach.

"This?" he asks, holding a palm against the protruding tongue on his chest. "It's a Rolling Stones album cover. *Sticky Fingers*."

Sara furrows her brow, and I resist the urge to roll my eyes.

"It's an old one," Zach says genially. "We're actually covering one of their songs in our first set. 'Satisfaction'?"

"Yeah, I think I've heard of that," Sara says unconvincingly.

I point faux-discreetly at Sara and mouth "lame" to Zach, who suppresses a smile.

"Why the 'Beastings'?" I ask him, nodding toward the logo on the bass drum.

"Our drummer, Kyle, got stung by a bee the first time we practiced together," Zach replies, tossing his head in the direction of a gangly strawberry-blond behind the drum set.

"Ah."

Notes plunk through the amplifiers as the Beastings tune their instruments.

"Well," Zach says, clapping his hands together, "gotta go get started. You folks enjoy. And hey, thanks for coming."

We all smile and wish him luck.

Zach trots back over to the stage, hoists himself up, and straps on his Stratocaster. His guitar is the same color as the cardinal that suddenly swoops from a nearby tree branch into a sky turned peach by the setting sun. I see cardinals at the damnedest times these days—always when I'm yearning for a connection to my brother. The day of Liam's wake, I noticed one right outside the window of the funeral home as I slipped a guitar pick into his casket, and another was perched on the hood of our car as we left the cemetery after his burial. I can practically feel Liam's arms around me at those moments.

"Hi, Liam," I say to myself now, smiling faintly as I follow the latest cardinal's path with my gaze. This night's gonna be okay. I'm gonna be okay.

While Grandpa and Harold chat about tennis and knee-replacement surgeries, his wife asks Sara and me about school. We're giving the requisite boring answers when the band strikes up, drowning us out. Thank Heaven. I dislike chitchat in general, but these days we're usually only one or two questions deep before someone mentions Liam, asking how he's doing if they don't know he died or oozing sympathy if they do. I'm not sure which I hate more.

Besides, I've suddenly grown very interested in the band. *Whoa*, the lead singer is cute. His skinny hips, sun-streaked blond hair, and awesome bone structure are jaw-dropping in and of themselves, but it's his *confidence* that's holding my gaze. Those skinny hips undulate rhythmically as he strums his Les Paul Deluxe.

"Sailing on, pushing past the shore," he sings. "Time to roll out with the tide. The past is gone, but I know there's more. I will see you there on the other side."

I've never heard the song before, but it's incredibly infectious—as is the singer's smile, I might add. I notice everyone around me swaying to the music, like we've suddenly all been transported to the beach and a breeze is blowing through our hair. God, I love music.

After the song, the band moves on to another upbeat tune,

again one I've never heard but is still catchy enough that I'm singing along by the second chorus. "You wanna free my soul? Better spare yourself the heartache. Don't throw me a rope. Better keep it for your own sake. You gotta save yourself . . ."

The band follows the song with a couple of covers, and I sing along, tapping my sneaker to the beat. The strawberry-blond drummer is flailing his arms like a fearless banshee, his pointy elbows punching the air with every whack on the snare, and I occasionally drum along on my thighs.

Harold's wife catches my eye, smiles sweetly, and hollers, hands cupped around her mouth, "You're really enjoying the band!"

I offer a thumbs-up, then glance at Sara, who's giving me a scolding look, probably grumpy that I'm not contributing enough to the screechfest of a conversation with old people. Tough.

The band moves on to a sweet ballad: "Your love has finally set me free. You knew all along, but it's new to me . . ." They keep the sultry vibe going with a blues song that seeps languidly into the hot, humid air: "You left my life in shambles," the singer croons, "and my words are only rambles. I guess I lost the gamble. Yeah, I'm shamblin' . . ."

Zach eases into a guitar solo that sounds like the wind moaning. He and the hot lead singer lock eyes occasionally and smile, both of them seeming to float on the music. The lead singer occasionally intermingles one of his own licks with Zach's.

I feel my heart beat faster. The singer is hot *and* a solid guitarist. *Whoa.* I'm feeling lighter on my feet by the minute.

I'm not exactly a pushover when it comes to guys. Yeah, I've dated here and there, but I'm pretty selective and always opted out of high school silliness like proms or keg parties. (I avoided feel-good substances even before Liam got addicted to pills; those episodes of *Intervention* that Mom hooked me on worked their magic.) I much preferred spending my spare time writing bad novels and playing gigs with the Joneses. I had the occasional crush on my fellow band members, but being the lead guitarist's little sister tends to have a chilling effect on romance, so I mostly concentrated on the music.

And I'm concentrating on the music now, gazing at the blond's face as his voice hypnotizes me, his jaw-length hair accentuating his cheekbones. He's mostly squeezing his eyes shut during this last chorus, but he seems to catch my eye a couple of times.

"I'm shambling," he sings, his voice throaty and plaintive. "You got me shambling, man, and I don't give a damn. I'm just doing what I can to shake you off. Yeah, I'm shamblin' . . ."

When the song is over, I feel so mesmerized that I'm motionless for just a moment before breaking into exuberant, adrenaline-fueled applause. The singer catches my eye and smiles, an electric moment that lasts just an instant before his eyes skitter away. He wipes his forehead with the back of his hand as Zach begins a guitar intro on the next song. The singer leans into the mic and reels off the tune's *rat-a-tat* rap:

> *I'm done with all the fakes and posers. Had it with the backdoor closers. Cutting off the cons and hosers. Looking for a peach.*
> *I'm through with artificial flavors, wannabes and soulless cavers, dirty deals and shady favors. Castles on the beach.*
> *No throwin' shade; the sun will shine. Your smile is giving me a sign that love can still be genuine. I hope that it's in reach.*

The second verse is just as fun:

Photoshop and avatars, autotune and air guitars, fake Havana cheap cigars: Make it go away.
Your smile's the only thing to make me think my future won't forsake me.
If I'm dreaming, please don't wake me; think I'd rather stay.

Zach plays a bright, crisp guitar solo, followed by the bridge, then the singer eases back up to the mic for the final chorus:

So pick a door; let's make a deal.
We'll step inside and get a feel for living life a bit surreal.
It's all good when we make it real.

I applaud heartily, even offering a pinkie whistle, then hold up hand-horns for the cover of "Satisfaction" that follows, just as Zach promised. I hope it's not obvious that I can't take my eyes off the lead singer, all cocky and snarly as he struts around the stage channeling Mick Jagger. God, he's sexy.

At one point, Harold's wife taps my shoulder. "Having fun?" she mouths over the din of the music.

I nod dreamily.

Yeah, as a matter of fact, I am.

This might be the most fun I've had in six months.

• • •

"Well, I guess we better get going," Grandpa says as the band wraps up its first set. He rises from his chair and reaches out to shake Harold's hand, our empty cola glasses dotting the table.

"We just got here, Grandpa," I protest, aiming for casual.

"It's almost dark," he argues.

I open my mouth to reply when I feel a hand on my back.

"Are you enjoying yourselves?"

I turn to face the person behind me. It's Zach, who's just hopped down from the stage.

"You're great!" I say, and the others nod heartily.

"*Really* great," Sara says. "This is so much fun!"

My heart skips a beat as I realize the lead singer has suddenly eased over to our table. "Then stay for our second set," he tells Sara, grabbing a nearby chair and sitting next to her.

"Definitely. Our second set's the best," Zach says, pulling up a chair himself.

A waitress breezes up to our table and refills our drinks, momentarily blocking my view of the hottie.

"I'm Declan," he's saying to Sara, extending his hand as the waitress finally walks away and unobstructs my view.

"Sara," she replies, shaking it.

My body tenses. I've gone through life watching Sara magically draw guys into her orbit without the slightest bit of effort. In fact, it's probably her *lack* of effort that attracts them. Her dazzling smile and size-four figure don't hurt either, I guess. But people often mistake Sara and me for twins, our eighteen-month age difference notwithstanding, so I'm not exactly hideous-looking myself. Plus, *I'm* chill, too, and guys don't come buzzing around *me*. Sure, Sara's way more stylish than I am, so fine, she gets a couple of bonus points for that. But does she really deserve a thousand times more attention than I get? One on one, I hold my own with guys just fine. But around Sara, I'm hopelessly outmatched. She pretends not to notice, but I think she secretly enjoys outshining me.

Whatever. I learned my lesson long ago by staking out my own territory and avoiding running in the same circles as her. But Sara and I are in the same circle tonight, and I'm being elbowed out of it. Declan is glomming onto Sara like the moths around us diving for the tiki torches that line the deck. She's lowering her chin and laughing lightly at whatever he's telling her—*her* exclusively, not *us*—tossing locks of honey-suckle-scented hair off her shoulder.

I'm trying to concentrate on the chitchat unfolding at the table (Zach is actually speaking to *all* of us), but I can't silence the roar of blood in between my ears.

"My granddaughters are musicians, too, you know," Grandpa is telling everyone. "Sara plays the piano, and Scarlett plays—"

Declan's ears perk up. "We need a keyboard player in the band!" he says, his eyes still glued to my sister.

Well, of course you do.

"I'm just in town for the weekend," Sara says, and Declan's shoulders actually droop in response. "But Scarlett will be here all summer."

"You play keyboard, too?" he asks me, somehow managing not to glance my way while asking me a direct question.

"Nope," I say in a clipped voice.

"She plays guitar, and she's really good," Sara says. "She's played in a band before. Oh, and she sings."

Declan processes this information as if he's just been given the latest update on the national deficit.

"That's great," he says in my general direction. "You should come hang out with us."

"I'm working this summer," I say tersely, digging my nails into my palms and hoping to cut off at the pass any more pathetic shout-outs attesting to my existence. Not that Declan is listening; he can't take his eyes off Sara.

"Where are you working?" Zach asks me.

"The Harmon Hills pool," I say. "I'm lifeguarding. I start Monday."

"Cool," he says. "I swim there a lot. And hey, we're practicing tomorrow at four. Kyle's dad lets us use his warehouse—a loft over the old foundry. You know where that is? Just a couple of blocks from where—"

"From where I almost killed you this morning?" I say, managing a cool smile despite the pain of digging my nails into my palms as Declan continues salivating over my sister.

"Yeah, something like that," Zach says, and we laugh. "You should come. I'd love to hear you play."

I murmur something noncommittal, then blush and lower my eyes after Declan catches me looking at him.

"You know, we really should be going," I say, then press my lips together.

"I don't like to drive after dark these days," Grandpa tells the group, and they nod their endorsement of this stellar philosophy.

"*I'm* driving," Sara mouths to the guys.

"Watch out for bikers," Zach says with a grin.

"You're sure you have to go?" Declan says pleadingly to Sara.

"Yep," I respond crisply, slinging my purse roughly over my shoulder as I rise to my feet.

My ego can't take any more pulverizing tonight.

Touché, Sara. You win again.

• • •

Sara eyes me quizzically as she walks into the bedroom while brushing her teeth. She's already changed into a T-shirt and flannel pajama pants, her long, dark hair pulled into the loose bun she always sleeps in.

"What?" she asks through a foamy mouth.

I roll my eyes and flop backward onto the bed, staring at the ceiling. "Nothing."

"It's not *nothing*," she lisps through the foam. "You've been weird since we got back from Sheehan's. What's going on?"

I hesitate, then decide, *What the hell.* It's really not fair to hate Sara for being a babe magnet. I sigh, prop myself up on an elbow, and say, "I kinda fell in love tonight, and oh, great news, so did the guy. But he fell in love with *you*."

Sara studies me silently for a second, then raises an index finger, signaling me to hold that thought. She walks into the adjoining bathroom, rinses her mouth, and rejoins me, smelling all pepperminty. She sits next to me on the bed, squeezing her knees against her chest.

"Declan, right?"

I give an exaggerated pout and nod.

"Yeah, he's really cute. *All* those guys are. I think the guy you almost killed is super hot—in a really sweet, understated way, you know? Those *eyes* . . ."

I curl a lip. "Well, just take your pick, won't you?"

"Not for *me*, doofus. For *you*. Zach seems much more like your type. You're sure Declan is the one you like?"

My jaw drops. "Oh, excuse the hell out of me! I forgot all the hot guys are reserved for you."

Sara rolls her eyes. "You really think I'm interested in Declan? He's already in love: with himself. Plus, he's an air-head. You usually have the world's best radar for—"

"God, you are so smug!" I wail, pitching forward and

shaking my fists in the air. "The only reason you're dissing him is to change the subject!"

She observes me coolly. "The subject being . . . ?"

"That you can't stand having a guy pay attention to anybody but you."

"God, you're so dramatic," Sara says drolly. "But just to be perfectly clear: *I am not interested in Pretty Boy.*"

"And yet, once again here we are: you sucking up all the oxygen in the room while I sit around like a potted plant. Rag on Pretty Boy all you want, but you know you love being Pretty Girl."

Sara crosses her eyes, her go-to move to gross me out, and I can't help but squeeze my eyes shut and laugh.

"Quit being a whiny baby," she scolds, her eyes resetting to their natural hazel gorgeousness. "You're the one who's here all summer. You like him? Go for it. And shut up about my looks. You look just like me. That old lady we were sitting with asked if we were identical twins, for Chrissake."

"My nose is crooked," I say sulkily. "And besides, it's not your looks; it's your *vibe*."

"Well," Sara says, doing a little shimmy on the bed, "get *your* vibe on. The band invited you to their practice tomorrow. Go."

I grab the one-eyed bear and hold him lightly against my chest. "I don't want to look obvious," I say, absently picking at the mangy fur. "Or worse, desperate."

"*Go*," Sara urges. "I told Grandpa I'd take him to the drugstore and get some prints made. He took a bunch of pictures at your graduation."

I roll my eyes playfully. "Who still gets prints made?"

"Grandpa and me," she responds. "But not you. You'll be

at band practice. Oh, but be back by six. Grandpa said we're going next door for dinner. Don't you dare make me sweat that one out by myself."

The ceiling fan whirs overhead, clicking lightly. "Did you notice Grandpa's friends took pity on us and didn't utter a single word about Liam?" I ask.

Sara smiles wistfully, hugging her knees tighter against her chest. "I don't mind talking about him. I don't want anybody to forget him."

Crickets chirp rhythmically in the backyard woods.

"Then you do the talking tomorrow night at the Bixleys' house," I say, purposely injecting a jokey tone back into the conversation. I can't manage more than one sentence about Liam without getting weepy.

And I know I won't be able to bear looking at Grandpa's graduation pictures. It took every ounce of energy I possessed to keep a smile plastered on my face while he huddled us into various groupings that night—groupings that didn't include Liam. Thank Heaven that Varun was by my side to serve up hilarious snark about anybody who happened to cross our paths. (Shelby Dixon, for instance, who replaced her graduation cap with her homecoming tiara for photo ops after the ceremony. That was epic!)

I'm so glad Varun and I are going to college together. Sure, I've cried on his shoulder plenty of times in the past few months. Hell, he usually cries *with* me. He says he can't see me cry without joining in. But more often than not, he makes me laugh, and I need a steady infusion of laughter to keep from falling apart.

"Hey," I ask Sara, "whatever happened to what's-his-name? That boring engineering major you were dating?"

She shrugs, and her eyes fall. “I haven’t really been in a dating mood. I kinda let that fizzle after . . .”

She doesn’t have to finish the sentence. I have a feeling the rest of our lives will be divided into Before and After.

I sneak a peek at her somber face. “Is it terrible that I’m sitting here babbling about some hot lead singer in a band just a few months after . . . ?”

She squarely meets my eye. “*No*. That’s exactly what Liam would want you to be doing.”

I nod sharply. “But only since the hottie also happens to be a decent musician.”

“Exactly,” Sara says. “Liam had his standards, you know.”

A long moment passes as the crickets continue their symphony.

“Go have fun tomorrow,” Sara finally says in barely a whisper. “Let’s lead fabulous lives and make our brother proud.”

CHAPTER FIVE

Creak, creak, creak go the old wooden stairs as I make my way up to the loft.

I'm walking in slow motion. I hadn't been nervous about taking Zach up on his offer to sit in on the band's practice until I got here. Now I feel excruciatingly self-conscious. I bite my bottom lip, pausing in midstep as I hear the Beastings practicing upstairs. Did Zach mean it when he invited me to stop by, or was he just being polite, assuming I wouldn't do it? I can imagine all the band members' eyes falling on me when I walk through the door. They'll be wondering, *What the hell?*

"This is ridiculous," I mutter under my breath, then sit on a musty step to rethink. I spend a minute kneading my fingers together, then retrieve my phone from my jeans pocket.

Help, I text Varun.

Can you be more specific? he texts back, and I smile. He's working in a pathology lab this summer, including some Saturdays, so how responsive he is depends on whether he's elbow-deep in formaldehyde when I text him. I'm glad he's available now.

I saw this local band play last night and fell in love with the lead singer, I type. They invited me to come watch them practice, so here I am. But now I'm hiding in the stairwell, feeling weird. Do I go in? This guy is super hot, if that informs your opinion. Oh, and his name is Declan. How nouveau-cool is that?

Declan, huh? Sounds like a kind of polyester, Varun writes.

I grin, the amplified *thump* of the music upstairs vibrating against the stairwell walls. So do I crash their practice or not?

What's your plan? Holding the hottie against his will?

I wrinkle my nose, then type, No, just sitting there while they practice, looking impossibly cute and charming.

As opposed to desperate and stalker-ish?

Exactly. That's the risk. But I can def pull off cute and charming, right? So go for it?

I dunno . . . What R U wearing?

My prom dress.

Did you borrow Shelby Dixon's tiara?

Duh.

Go for it.

K. I'll let you know if we end up eloping tonight. And hey, how's your "like life"?

It was during our sophomore year that Varun informed me that his love life, such as it was, was actually a like life. He's had a few crushes, but he decided when we were freshmen to swear off true romance until college. "Better options," he insists. But I'm still not convinced he's told his parents he's gay, so I'm thinking he might have ulterior motives for opting for a like life (friends with no benefits) rather than a love life. His social life consists mainly of watching Netflix and eating takeout with me. I worry about him, especially over the past few months. He just seems . . . lonely. I know things will pick up for him in college. He's absolutely gorgeous—glossy black hair, intense ebony eyes, weirdly angular yet oddly appealing bone structure—so I know he won't be single for long. But for now . . .

My "life like" is nonexistent, Varun replies.

C'mon, there must be one or two cute patholo–

"Hey, Scarlett!"

I suck in my breath and turn in the direction of the voice. Zach is standing at the top of the stairs, then trotting down toward me. He's wearing slightly tattered cotton shorts, a faded T-shirt, sneakers, and a backward baseball cap.

"Oh, hey . . ." I feel my neck grow warm as I stand up and tuck a lock of hair behind my ear. "I was just texting my friend . . ."

"I'm so glad you stopped by," he says. "I was just gonna grab a Coke downstairs. Can I get you one?"

"No, no thanks, I'm good."

He tosses his head toward the top of the stairs. "Head on up, and I'll be back in a second," he says.

"You're sure I won't be in the way?"

"Totally."

I open my mouth to respond, but he's already sprinting down the rest of the stairs. I blow a breath through puffed-out cheeks. No turning back now.

The creaks of my footsteps sound cacophonous now that the band is taking a break. Damn! It would have been so much cooler to slip in mid-song, smiling shyly when Declan looked up from a guitar lick to catch my eye. Now they'll just be sitting around when I walk into the loft, sharing confused glances and wondering what I'm doing there. But since Zach has seen me, I'm committed—for better or worse. Awkwardness, here I come . . .

Creak goes the last step, and I push open the heavy oak

door, revealing a loft almost empty other than instruments, amplifiers, and a few foldout chairs.

Three sets of eyes fall on me.

"Hi," I say, aiming for casual as the guys shift in their chairs to get a better look. "I heard your band last night at Sheehan's, and Zach invited me to stop by . . ."

Declan stands up and walks toward me, a small cloud of dust from the plywood floor puffing with each step. "Hi," he says, shaking the hair from his face with a quick toss. "You were there with your sister, right?"

Right. But sorry, I left the goddess at home.

"Right," I say.

"We're just taking a quick break," he says. "You've met the rest of the band, right?"

"I don't think so . . ."

The other two stand up and walk toward me, extending their hands. I shake them as the guys introduce themselves: Kyle, the strawberry-blond drummer, and Mike, the dark-haired bass player with a deep cleft in his chin and a cigarette in his free hand. I make a mental note that Sara was right: All these guys *are* cute, each in a very distinctive way. But only one looks like a jaguar with clear-blue eyes, and that one is now slinking back to his guitar in faded jeans that hug his hips. I love this view.

"Have a seat," he calls to me over his shoulder as he straps on his Les Paul.

"Okay . . . if you're sure you don't mind that I hang around for a while . . ."

"Hang around all you like—on the condition that you applaud wildly after every song," a friendly voice says from behind, and I turn around to see Zach walking toward us, a Coke can in his hand.

"Deal," I say, settling into a chair. I cross my legs and get comfortable as the guys resume their positions: Mike to the left on bass guitar, Declan in the middle with his Les Paul, Zach and his cardinal-colored Stratocaster to Declan's right, and Kyle behind them on the drums.

Zach murmurs a few words to them, then Kyle hits his drumsticks together four times to count off a song.

Declan leans into the mic to sing as the band accompanies him with the rockabilly rhythm of a song I've never heard before:

Back it up. Back it up, up, baby.
You can pack it up. Pack it up, up, baby.
'Cause I'm stacking up. Stacking up, up, baby.
All the reasons, they're a mile high,
That I'm a sayin' bye, bye, bye.
So back it up.
Yeah. Just back it up.

Zach breezes through a nimble, finger-flying guitar solo, and I grudgingly make a mental note that he's a better guitarist than Declan.

But Declan's just fine himself. He repeats the chorus after Zach's solo, locking eyes with me every once in a while. It occurs to me that it's awfully hot in here; a couple of fans on the floor are the only things standing between me and virtual incineration. I self-consciously run my fingers through my hair to smooth the frizz and hope my extra spritzes of Hawaiian Sunset body spray will camouflage my sweat. But, hey, the guys are sweating, too. Little pinpricks of perspiration dot their

T-shirts, and it's not bothering them one bit. They're totally lost in the music.

I try to unglue my eyes from Declan's face, but seriously, I just can't do it.

As the song comes to an end, I break into the requisite wild applause (I promised, right?) and bounce in my seat.

"That was great!" I say. "I love the song. I never heard it before."

"It's a Beastings original," Declan says, his hair grazing his shoulders as he slightly cocks his head.

"You *wrote* that?" I gush. "Geez, you're amazing!"

"Yeah, I wrote it," he says, wiping sweat off his brow as the other guys chortle. He laughs back at them.

My eyebrows knit together.

"Okay, fine, Zach wrote it," Declan finally concedes. "But we have kind of a Lennon-McCartney arrangement going on: No matter which of us technically writes it, we both take credit for it."

Zach laughs gamely, and Kyle says, "Interesting concept, considering he writes 100 percent of them."

"Still, it's a great song," I say, still gazing at Declan.

He blushes a little (at least I *think* that was a blush), then listens as Zach guides the musicians through a few specific bars of the song. They practice the chorus a couple more times, then move on to a new song, this one a bluesy ballad. Declan grips the mic until his knuckles blanch as he sings the chorus:

I'm dying. Can't you see?
'Cause it's not meant to be.
Wish love would set me free.
Yeah, time is wasting me.

Declan reels toward the end, as if the words have blown him off balance. His eyes stay closed for a long moment as the song ends. My eyes stay glued on him.

"Zach wrote that one, too," Mike tells me, and I jump a little at the sound of his voice, as if startled out of a trance.

"You're incredible," I tell Zach.

"Aw, shucks," he says, and I smile.

The band runs through a few covers of songs I know pretty well. I quietly sing along and bounce my shoulders to the beat, interrupting my eye contact with Declan periodically by letting my lids close dreamily.

God, this is fun. Who knew a summer with Grandpa had such potential?

But at the thought, my stomach clenches. I'm not spending the summer with Grandpa to have fun. I'm here to try and steady a fragile old man after the worst sucker punch of his life. He's trying to be strong for all of us, but Liam's death was like a body blow for Grandpa, especially since he didn't know about the addiction until after Liam was gone. Grandpa had to find out all at once: not only that Liam was dead but that he'd been hanging on by his fingernails for the past two years, ever since a doctor had prescribed pain pills for a shoulder Liam had dislocated during a basketball game. How's that for irony? My health-conscious brother was injured playing a game, and the treatment killed him. All Liam did was take the damn pills he had been prescribed. Only after dutifully following the doctor's orders did he realize he couldn't quit—not because the pills made him high but because they maintained the new status quo his brain demanded. Blaming him for that would be like blaming him for getting an infection after appendicitis surgery.

If only I'd known . . . but I had been almost as oblivious

as Grandpa, even though I'd overheard a couple of screaming matches between my parents and Liam on the weekends he was home from college. I knew it was kind of a problem, but I figured it was on par with maybe smoking weed occasionally: something that helped him relax but that he could walk away from any time, something my parents were clearly overreacting about.

What an idiot I was. If I'd understood what was going on, I could have helped him. I know I could have. Liam listened to me. How could I have been so clueless? And how could Liam have kept me in the dark? We told each other everything! Sometimes I feel so mad at him—and then so guilty about feeling mad—that my whole body starts to shake. A couple of times lately, I've screamed at him in my dreams, feverish rants that jolt me awake in a cold sweat.

I realize I'm shivering now, the shimmer of perspiration on my skin giving me a sudden chill in the stifling heat. I squeeze my arms together and take a deep breath. *Stop it, Scarlett. Stop thinking about it.*

The Beastings have moved on to a ballad to finish out the set. Declan has swapped his Les Paul for an acoustic guitar, and I sway dreamily, eyes closed, as he sings:

I'm waking up, I feel the sunlight shining through.
My eyes are open, now I see.
The words you whispered in my ear, they're all coming true.
Your love has finally set me free.
You knew all along, but it's new to me.

A quiet moment passes after the song before I clap softly.

Zach offers a little bow, then says, "Come sing a couple with us."

My brow arches. "Me? No, no . . ."

"Aw, c'mon. You can share a mic with me."

"No, really," I protest, but Zach walks over and gently pulls me up by my hand.

"Just a couple," he cajoles.

"And didn't I hear she plays, too?" Mike says.

"Suit 'er up," Kyle says breezily from behind his drum set.

Zach glances at Declan. "Mind if Scarlett plays one of your guitars?"

Declan pauses for a second, then shrugs. "Here, take this one," he tells me, pulling the strap of the acoustic guitar off his shoulder. As he hands it to me, he uses his free hand to retrieve the Les Paul from where he propped it on a stand.

"*Guys*, I haven't played in months," I protest half-heartedly, but I'm smiling. Who am I kidding? It feels amazing to have a guitar in my arms again.

"C'mon, knock us dead," Mike says, winking at me.

"No pressure there," I respond with a laugh.

"Just jump in whenever you like," Zach says, then cues Kyle to lead in the next song. Kyle hits his sticks together—*whap, whap, whap, whap*—and the band is off and running on the Beatles' "Drive My Car."

Zach locks eyes with me and nods, his smile coaxing me to join in. I can't help but smile back, feeling my cheeks grow warm. I play the chords while Declan sings the first verse. Zach leans into the mic for harmony on the line leading to the chorus, and suddenly, I'm singing along.

I watch Zach intently to nail the timing and add a higher harmony part. By the time we reach the "beep, beep, yeah," my strumming and harmony are on autopilot, and I'm bouncing lightly to the beat, Zach's warm brown eyes still prodding me along.

Whoa, this feels amazing! I haven't felt this exhilarated since the last time the Joneses were on stage. Back then it was Liam's eyes I was staring into, absorbing energy from the euphoria in his face, like I always did. I love Zach for easing me back into this.

After the second chorus, Zach lurches into a searing solo that sounds like a car engine revving. *Damn*, he's really good.

During Zach's solo, Declan is swiveling his hips and jerking his head rhythmically, flicking his hair around like honey-colored straw. I try to catch his eye, but he's swimming in the music, oblivious to everything but the music, punctuated by Mike's bass guitar bouncing off the brick walls of the loft and reverberating against our chests.

We're all having so much fun that Zach signals us to keep going for a few extra bars, then nods to Kyle, who whales full-on for the last two bars, Zach jumping in time with the last four beats.

Mike staggers around when the song is over, goofing like he's about to keel over from awesomeness.

"You were great," Zach tells me, and I drop my chin, looking up at him gratefully. "How long have you been playing?" he asks.

I swipe a lock of hair out of my eyes. "My brother taught me when I was twelve. I played in his band back home for a couple of years."

"Stellar," Mike says. "And you've got a great ear for harmony."

I'm tempted to deflect the compliments, but what the hell. I didn't practice riffs under my covers for hours at a stretch all those nights for nothing, did I? Maybe the stars have aligned to bring me to this exact spot at this precise moment in time. Maybe Liam is pulling some strings. And come to think of it, didn't I see a cardinal as I biked here a few minutes ago? So all I say is, "Thanks."

Zach rubs his chin. "You know, we've been wanting to cover a few songs that would sound better with a female singer. Do you know 'Light a Path'?"

"Sure."

"Let's do that one, guys," Zach says, "with Scarlett on lead vocal."

Declan shoots him a look, and I stand there awkwardly for a second. "I don't want to be in the way," I say.

"Let's just give that song a try," Zach says. "Strum along if you want, Scarlett. But I'm mainly interested in how we sound with your vocals."

Declan lowers his mic stand a few inches, presses his lips together, and says, "Blow us away."

Was that snarky? Is he pissed that I'm invading his turf? I push a lock of hair behind my ear and clear my throat nervously as Kyle counts off the song.

After the band plays the first couple of bars, I take a deep breath, start strumming along, and step closer to Declan's mic. I lean in and start singing:

I've sailed through stormy waters, and I've flinched against the waves.
I've stumbled through the hollows of some deep and dead-end caves.
I've scrambled up a mountain and felt hollow at the top.
I've screamed into the darkness for the loneliness to stop.
And then you came along to light my path . . .

My voice starts out quivery—my nerves are on overdrive—but as I ease my way into the song, my tone improves. By the time I reach the chorus, with Zach joining in on harmony, my vocals are full and strong. My muscles unclench halfway through, and I start moving to the beat. Zach leans into his mic for the chorus, and we lock eyes.

When the song is over, the last chord lingering in the air, I smile, drinking in the moment.

"Nice, Scarlett," Kyle says.

"Yeah, very cool," Zach says. "Hey, Declan, you mind tuning your D string?"

Declan looks coolly at Zach, who points his thumb down, signaling that it's sharp. Declan twists his tuning peg, then plucks the string until Zach nods.

"Thanks, man," Zach tells him genially.

Mike and Kyle share a brief but significant glance.

"I gotta grab a drink," Declan says, unstrapping the Les Paul and propping it against the amp. He walks toward the door in long strides, pops the door open with the heel of his hand, and disappears into the stairwell.

"Sure, I'd love a drink! Thanks for asking!" Kyle calls after him with his hand cupped around his mouth, knowing Declan can't hear him. He and Mike snicker.

"I did *not* mean to interrupt your practice," I tell them apologetically. "I'm just gonna go now . . ."

"Go?" Mike challenges, arching his brows. "I say you're hired."

CHAPTER SIX

"Hey. You got a minute?"

All of the band members except Declan have driven off, and I purposely stalled before hopping on my bicycle to head back to Grandpa's. Declan softened after returning to practice with his Coke, but he still seemed less than thrilled that the other Beastings wanted to sign me on. On the bright side, his wariness has given me an excuse to talk to him one-on-one, so this might work out okay after all.

"Sure," Declan tells me, keys in hand as he approaches his red Chevy pickup in the parking lot.

"Um . . ." I walk toward him, gently biting my lower lip. "I just wanted you to know, I did *not* come to your practice intending to horn in," I say.

"It's cool," he says, flicking his hair out of his face with a quick head jerk. "You blend really well with the group."

I wrinkle my nose. "I messed up the chords on a couple of songs. Maybe you could help me? I mean, if you have any spare time . . ."

His brow furrows. "Now?"

Damn. He looks like I've just asked him to help move furniture or something.

"No, no. I just meant, you know, any time. Not that I'll

have a lot of extra time. I start my lifeguarding job Monday, and it's pretty time-consuming to sit in the sun and stare into the abyss all day."

He chuckles. Ooh, I made him smile! Score!

"You should come," I say coyly, capitalizing on the new sparkle in his eyes. "To the pool, I mean, when I'm lifeguarding."

"So I can stare into the abyss with you?" he says playfully.

I cock my head slightly. "Yeah. Or, you know, I could save your life. Whatever floats your boat. Pun intended, I guess."

He offers an adorable grin. "Well, that *is* what they pay you for."

"Exactly. So come get your money's worth."

Okay, did that remark sound stupid? I'm not even sure what it means. Plus, I didn't realize until I blurted it out that it sounded kind of a prostitute-ish, and that's definitely *not* the vibe I'm going for. But I'm overthinking, right? Because Declan is still smiling; his eyes are still sparkling.

I'm smiling, too.

"You're on," Declan says. "But if you don't save my life, I want a refund."

"Duh," I say.

I shift my weight self-consciously. I'm not used to being this flirty. The guys I've dated before—Brian in eleventh grade, Marco last summer, Jake the first couple of months of my senior year—seemed more like projects than boyfriends. *Time to learn how to kiss; time to share bus rides with a fellow alto-sax player on the way to band camp; time for a study buddy who understands calculus.* Not that I was using them; they're all still friends, and I think Jake and I might have gotten some traction if my life hadn't nosedived when Liam died. But I was approximately as passionate about romance as I was about, oh,

I dunno, major-league baseball. Until now, it's been something I tolerated when my options were limited.

Varun would double over with his crazy seal laugh if he were a fly on the wall right now. He's used to me debriefing after dates about how I dealt with Marco's retainer during make-out sessions or whether Brian was full of shit when he claimed Barack Obama as a distant relative—stuff like that. Declan has nothing in common with those guys. Plus, something about the past few months has emboldened me.

Declan's eyes scan the parking lot, which is empty of everything except his truck. "Where's your car?" he asks.

I nod toward the lamppost, where I've secured my bicycle. "I rode my bike."

"Oh. Well . . . you want a ride? I can stick your bike in the back of my truck."

A breeze blows through my hair at that exact moment, which is apropos, considering that I suddenly feel like I'm two feet off the ground. Could this be going any more awesomely?

But just as I open my mouth to respond, I gasp a little and fling my fingertips over my mouth.

"Uh-oh, I just remembered . . ."

"What?" he prods.

"I'm supposed to be at the neighbors' house for a cookout at six o'clock. Do you know what time it is?"

We reach for our phones simultaneously, both reaching into our pockets.

"Six seventeen," Declan says, peering at his screen.

I wince. "My grandpa's anal about being on time. I gotta go."

"Unlock your bike, and I'll toss it in the back of my truck," Declan says, and I'm momentarily too rattled about being late to appreciate the awesomeness of how this conversation is unfolding. But then I do.

"You're sure you don't mind?" I ask.

"Nah, it's fine."

"Hey . . ."

Declan looks at me expectantly.

"Um," I continue, digging the toe of my sneaker into the asphalt, "you should come. I mean, you'll be there anyway, if you drop me off. Wanna come eat burgers with old people?"

I expect another chuckle, but instead, he looks a little nervous.

"No pressure," I assure him, squeezing my phone tighter in my palm. "I just thought you might be hungry—"

"Uh," he says, "lemme just check on a couple of things . . ."

He turns slightly at an angle and starts looking at his phone, first reading texts, then sending one, his thumbs flying over the keyboard. My heart sinks.

Well, of course he has a girlfriend, you idiot. You think a guy who looks like that sits home with his parents on Saturday nights playing dominoes?

How ridiculous I was to invite him for burgers at the neighbors' house. Can I even come back to band practice after throwing myself at him like some kind of desperate fool, making him scramble to figure out how to let me down easy? I am such a—

"Sure, I'll stop by," he finally says, looking up from his phone.

My eyebrows begin to rise, but I stop their ascent, forcing myself to play it cool. "Great," I say. "Let's go."

• • •

"I am *so sorry* I'm late."

It's only as I'm greeting Mrs. Bixley in her backyard that I realize I'm an etiquette disaster on several fronts. Not only am I half an hour late, but I've brought an uninvited guest. Declan hangs back as I give Mrs. Bixley a quick hug.

"And I hope you don't mind," I say as our arms untangle, "but a friend gave me a lift. We were downtown, and I had my bike, and I realized I was running late, so I asked if he could—"

"Of course, of course!" Mrs. Bixley says, and bless her for mercifully cutting short my overexplanation.

She extends a hand, and Declan shakes it. "Mrs. Bixley, this is Declan," I say.

"Declan Harris," he says, leaning into the handshake. "Nice to meet you."

"Declan," she says. "Irish?"

"Um, yes. I was named after my grandfather on my mother's side," he replies.

I raise my hand. "I'm Irish, too! My mom's an O'Malley."

Okay, why is my arm in the air, and why do I seem insanely exuberant about my mother's maiden name? *Chill, moron.*

I lower my arm. "Declan's the lead singer in a band," I tell Mrs. Bixley, ditching my pep-rally tone and aiming for cool nonchalance. "I stopped by today to listen to them practice. I play a little guitar myself, and the lead guitarist had invited me to drop by. Then—"

"Come fix yourselves a plate!"

Jesus. I should carry Mrs. Bixley everywhere I go. She's like the antivenom to the word vomit that spews from my mouth when I'm nervous.

She leads us through damp Bermuda grass toward her patio, where her husband is manning a grill in belted shorts pulled up high and loafers with tube socks snugly hugging his lily-white calves. He raises a spatula to greet us as we approach.

"Welcome, welcome!" Mr. Bixley says. "Just in time for a burger."

I smile at him apologetically. "Thank you for having us. I'm so sorry I'm—"

Declan interrupts me. "Sàra, right?"

I follow his gaze to the patio table, where Sara is sitting with Grandpa.

"Right," she responds to Declan.

Grandpa is rising to greet us, probably mortified that I've sprung an uninvited guest on our hosts. I get my etiquette stickler-ism from him.

"Sit, sit," I tell him. "We'll grab a drink and join you."

I walk toward the cooler and call to Declan, "What can I get you?"

Oh. Looks like he's already helping himself to what he wants. He wasted no time, I see, pushing his patio chair so close to Sara's that a debit card couldn't slip through the gap. I suck in my lips and try again. "Declan? Want something to drink?"

He looks up and says, "What's that?"

"A drink," I answer stiffly. "Want something to drink?"

"Oh. Sure. Anything. Whatever you're having."

Of course. The sooner I stop blathering, the sooner he can glom back onto my sister. Sara sits there coolly, adjusting her sunglasses and stretching out her long, skinny legs, crossing them at the ankles. She barely even glances Declan's way, just peering into the setting sun and idly fingering her necklace as he leans in closer and closer. She can probably feel his breath on her cheek.

Why didn't I anticipate this? Was last night's lovefest not

quite explicit enough for me? Damn. It's just that—well, I had such a blast at the Beastings' practice, and then I killed it on the guitar, and then I got invited to join, and then Declan was actually flirting with me in the parking lot, and then he gave me a ride, so I guess I thought . . .

Thought what? That the hottest guy I've ever laid eyes on actually might be interested in me? *Pfft*. He's probably only here because he wanted to see Sara again.

I yank two diet colas from the cooler—yeah, diet cola is my favorite, which I'm guessing won't exactly be Declan's first choice, but screw it, he said he'd have what I'm having, so he can deal with it—then carry the drinks back to the table.

"Come fix your plates," Mr. Bixley calls from the grill, but Declan is oblivious, totally engrossed in whatever he's telling Sara. Fine. He can starve for all I care.

I set down my drink, place Declan's in his general vicinity (not that he notices), then walk over to a long plastic table. I pick up a paper plate at one end and work my way down the line of buns, condiments, and chips. Grandpa and Mrs. Bixley inch along behind me, and Mr. Bixley plops burgers on our buns when we reach the end of the table.

"Come and get it!" he calls to Sara and Declan. From the corner of my eye, I watch Sara rise to her feet and Declan follow along like a lovesick puppy. My stomach muscles clench.

Once we return to the patio table, Sara lingers before taking a seat, surveying the yard and commenting on Mrs. Bixley's hydrangeas. After Declan reclaims his original seat, Sara sits across from him, then glances significantly at me and nods toward the empty seat next to him.

Okay, this is just adding insult to injury.

But whatever. The seat's vacant, so I head that way.

But, oops! Declan just realized he wants more ketchup, and wouldn't you know it? Sara brought the ketchup bottle along with her, so he has no choice but to shimmy back over by her side and settle into the adjoining seat so they can share the bottle. Oh yay. They're nice and cozy again.

Sara casts me an apologetic glance, but I barely have a chance to process the humiliation, because Mr. Bixley is proving to be quite the chatterbox. He makes himself comfy in Declan's abandoned chair, then leans in and starts yammering to me about all the things he's an authority on. Luckily for me, turns out he's an authority on, well, *everything*, so the conversation gets more fascinating with every bite of my burger. When he finds out I'm planning to major in journalism, he explains somberly that print is dead and I'm doomed for disappointment.

"Okay, then," I tell him agreeably, "I'll major in English."

"Heavens, no!" he responds emphatically, explaining that the only thing I could do with an English career is teach—I don't want to teach, do I?—and even then I'd need at least a master's degree, if not a PhD, and haven't I heard that tenure is almost unheard of in college teaching these days?

And don't get him started on law school! Surely I'm aware that 93 percent of all recent law school grads are flipping burgers, so no need for me to so much as let that ridiculous notion flit through my mind . . .

Just when I'm about to suggest that chugging cyanide might be my best bet for the future, he decides it's time to refill his plate. How in the world he finished his first serving amid his torrent of career advice is beyond me, but I heartily endorse his plan for second helpings. Maybe I can break through Declan's trance now that Mr. Bixley has cut me loose.

But no such luck, because as I'm picking the perfect

moment to ease into Declan and Sara's conversation, Mrs. Bixley decides to pick up where her husband left off, commandeering me into the discussion she's having with Grandpa.

"Isn't that right, Scarlett?" she asks me, and I have no choice but to ask her to repeat whatever she just said that I didn't hear and couldn't care less about.

Then she's off and running about the upcoming mayoral election or the library fundraiser or the what-the-hell-*ever*. She's doing that Oakboro thing of mentioning somebody I've never heard of, and when she sees the blank look on my face, she mentions thirteen other people I've never heard of to try and offer a frame of reference. ("Anyway, it was such a nice cruise that Carol Funderburk told me she's going to—oh, Scarlett, you don't know Carol? Sure you do, honey. She's Jane Whitfield's daughter. You know, Jane from the post office? Stuart's wife? Stuart Whitfield, the Methodist minister?") Et cetera, et cetera, *ad nauseam*. It's like playing "Six Degrees of Kevin Bacon" in Hell.

And *omigod*, what's that Sara's doing while I'm learning about Carol Funderburk's travel plans? She's showing Declan my graduation pictures!

I dig my nails into my palms as I notice from my peripheral vision that Sara has grabbed a pack of photos and is flipping through them one by one, giving Declan a little running commentary. I want to leap out of my chair to stop this madness. This is so bad, so wrong, on so many levels. In the first place, the stupid photos are reminding Declan that I'm fresh out of high school—an unsophisticated rube, unlike the college babes he hangs out with during the school year. In the second place, Varun is in a bunch of those pictures, and Sara doesn't seem to be clarifying that we're *just friends*. In the *third* place, who even gets pictures printed anymore, and I'm just now remembering that my stupid forehead was broken out when those pictures were taken, and who cares about my ridiculous graduation photos anyway, and—

"Well," Declan says, "I gotta run."

Oh great! Sara is running him off!

"I'm so glad you could stop by," Mrs. Bixley tells him.

Declan tells her how awesome the burgers were and that he's sorry he's got to eat and run, then glances over at me as he rises from his chair.

"I'll leave your bike on the porch, Scarlett," he says. "Oh, and don't forget practice tomorrow at 4 p.m."

"Yeah, what's our practice schedule again?" I ask to stall for time.

"Saturdays and Sundays at 4 p.m., then Wednesdays at 7 p.m.," he says. "But sometimes we'll throw in extras, like before a gig or something. Promptness optional."

I laugh.

"So," he says, rubbing his hands together, "thanks again."

Then he leaves.

Two burgers, forty-two graduation photos, and double digits of mosquito bites later, the sexiest stud in America has now officially ended our first date—a date he spent memorizing each individual pore on my sister's face. I'm tempted to jump up and walk him to the driveway, but how pathetic would that be, after he's made it perfectly clear he finds me as fascinating as I find Carol Funderburk?

And why in the world is Sara still flipping through my graduation photos, passing them around the table so everyone can contemplate my forehead acne? Hasn't she done enough damage?

I think I'm gonna be sick.

• • •

"What the hell was that?"

Sara looks at me blankly from the twin bed she plopped onto when we returned to Grandpa's house.

"What was *what*?"

I plant a hand on my hip, standing in the doorway of the bedroom. "Why did you monopolize the conversation with Declan?"

Her eyes pop open. "Are you kidding? We were all sitting around a patio table, talking."

"Wrong," I say, my voice steely as I move into the bedroom, closing the door behind me. "Declan was talking to *you*. Just like last night."

Sara pitches forward to face me as I plant myself on the other bed with my arms crossed.

"We were all just talking," she says, enunciating every word.

My muscles tense. I get a little crazy when she patronizes me. "You know I like Declan," I say in the creepily lowered voice I use when I feel like screaming my head off is the only alternative. "Why couldn't you have let this be my moment?"

Okay, "my moment" sounds a little dramatic, but Sara responds to dramatic.

"Scarlett," she says, her eyebrows weaving together, "I don't know what I did wrong or what I could have done differently. From where *I* was sitting, it looked like nobody could get a word in edgewise in your conversation with Mr. Bixley."

My jaw drops as I rise indignantly from the bed. "I was talking to a hundred-year-old man who wears tube socks with loafers!"

She shrugs. "I heard him mention globalization, and I tuned out."

My hands fly in the air. "So you didn't think, *Hmm, Scarlett is clearly trapped in the world's most boring conversation, and here I am sucking up all the attention of the guy she likes, and maybe, just maybe, I should—*"

"I tried to switch seats with you! I showed him your graduation photos!" Sara protests. "I was trying to get him focused on you!"

My heart sinks at what a sad commentary this is: Sara trying to get a guy focused on her loser sister.

I guess Sara sees this in my face, because she stands up and takes my hands. "Scarlett, you are beautiful. You are smart. You are funny. If a guy isn't paying attention to you, then one, he's crazy, and two, who needs him? You are going to *slay it* in college."

She stares at me insistently until I return her gaze, then sigh. I know, I know. Sara didn't do anything wrong. It just feels so good to be mad at her. Until it doesn't.

"He's probably going to ask you out," I say softly, still grumpy but no longer homicidal.

Uh-oh. Sara's averting her eyes.

My mouth falls open. "Omigod. He's already asked you out."

She sucks in her lips, and I groan.

"What did you say?" I ask suspiciously, our hands falling apart.

"I turned him down, of course! A., I'm only here for the weekend; B., I don't really feel like dating anyone right now; C., I know you like him; and D., he's not my type. And as we've already established, for what it's worth, he's not *your* type either."

"You're such a snob!"

Sara shrugs. "He's a player."

"Why in the world would you think that?" I ask.

"I just get that vibe."

"Why?"

She waves a hand through the air. "I dunno. He's nice enough. But you can tell he's full of himself."

I shake my head briskly. "I didn't get that at all. He's been totally nice to me . . . if you don't count hitting on my sister."

"Then fine, date him. You're here all summer. Go for it. But those other guys in the band seem a lot nicer."

I cross my arms again. "So you think Declan is out of my league."

She huffs. "No. I think *you're* out of *his*. But do what you want. Geez!"

I consider her words, then fall backward onto the bed. "I want the hottie for once," I moan, then give an exaggerated pout, staring at the ceiling.

Yes, I realize how revoltingly superficial I sound, and yes, I hate myself for it. But still.

"You know what you should be thinking about?" Sara asks, and I brace myself for more condescension.

"What?" I ask warily.

"That they invited you to play in the band. That's so cool! Are you gonna be able to squeeze everything in? I mean, with the lifeguarding job and all?"

"Yeah," I say, "I'll work weekdays at the pool, so it's actually kinda perfect." The busier I am these days, the better I like it.

Sara smiles. "I'm so psyched for you. I mean, they're really good. And *you're* really good. You'll have a blast, just like you did with—"

She stops in midsentence, but I nod to let her know it's okay. "Today is the first time I've played my guitar since Liam died," I say. "It felt weird in a lot of ways . . . but it felt good, too."

Sara nods, her eyes oozing love. "Of course it did. You're amazing."

I wrinkle my nose, still a little too pissed to completely defrost. That's Sara: She's my biggest competition, then she's my fiercest protector. It's hard to keep up.

"So," she says, "does your band get paid?"

I shrug. "Basically pocket change and free pizza. I'm thinking I'll buy a Lamborghini with my share."

"Oh, and a beach house," Sara adds. "Gotta work on my tan."

"You don't get to stay at my beach house. I'm sick of you getting all the guys."

She sticks out her tongue, and I return the gesture.

A quiet moment passes as I stare at my interlacing fingers, then I confess conspiratorially, "When I invited Declan to the cookout, I was actually thinking it was kind of a date."

Sara raises an eyebrow. "Girlfriend."

"I know, I know," I say with a sigh. "But maybe if you hadn't shown him those hideous graduation pictures . . ."

She giggles, and I giggle back.

Sara's right. I should just concentrate on the band and push Declan's hotness to the back of my mind.

Yes. That's the plan.

Hope I'm strong enough to follow it.

CHAPTER SEVEN

Creak, creak, creak.

Here I come again, twenty-four hours later, up the stairs to the loft. My steps are even slower than they were yesterday, because now I have layers of nervousness, as opposed to the thin sheen of awkwardness I had the day before.

Maybe the guys are rethinking inviting me to join the band, for instance. I mean, I played along on only a few songs, most of which were of the three-basic-chords variety that even the most mediocre guitarist could nail without breaking a sweat. Zach sent me an e-mail with MP3s of the songs he wrote, and I practiced them on the bathroom floor until three in the morning. (Sara vetoed a midnight concert in the bedroom we share at Grandpa's, opting for sleep instead). Then I practiced some more after church, opting out of lunch with Sara and Grandpa to nail the chords and timing on a couple of the trickier songs. I was feeling pretty confident until I got to the loft. Now, I'm freaking out that I'll look like a poser. The Martin guitar I've got slung in a gig bag on my back suddenly feels like it weighs three tons as I walk up the steps.

Then there's Declan. The last time I saw him, he was studying my forehead acne in the graduation photos. Did I adequately convey an *oh-by-the-way, no-big-deal* vibe when I invited him to the cookout? Or did he get that I was basically throwing myself at him? If so, how in the world do I play it cool around him now, particularly since his reaction was to throw me back? Will I look like the most pathetic loser on earth when I trudge into the loft? Did he maybe even snicker with the rest of the band about my pitiful attempt at flirting?

Plus, although I hear a little rustling around upstairs, I realize I'm way early for practice. I got here at three forty, just to make sure the guys know I take this seriously and that I'm not some flake who will waste their time. But twenty minutes is *really* early. Do I look overeager? Will I cramp the guys' style? They're probably enjoying a few spare minutes to shoot the breeze and, I dunno, tell raunchy jokes or whatever guys do when girls aren't around, so if I show up now, will I spoil the mood?

I squeeze my eyes shut, stop in midstride, and do the same thing I did yesterday: take my phone out of my pocket and text Varun.

I'm at band practice but feeling chicken about going in, I text.

Last night, I gave him a broad-strokes version of my day, whooping triumphantly about being asked to join the band and whining relentlessly about mandatory attendance at an old-people cookout. But I strategically skipped the part about inviting Declan to the cookout, then having him blow me off for the next hour. I can tell Varun almost everything, but that was too epic a fail to share.

Why are you chicken? he responds. You're great.

I sigh. I'm not great. I'm just okay. I faked it yesterday, but my okay-ness will become apparent very soon. Blecht.

How did autocorrect deal with "blecht"?

It made it "bleacher."

Well, bleacher grimy frown off your face. Get it?

I grin and roll my eyes. Not your best work.

And why again is it that you're frowning? Varun texts.

Because I suck. What was I thinking, joining a decent band when my brother's not around to cover for me?

Stop it. You're very good. I don't know why you never give yourself enough credit. They wouldn't have asked you to join if they didn't think you were good enough.

Maybe they were just being nice.

You almost flattened the guitarist on his bike. Explain his motivation to just be nice.

I smile. I dunno. But I'm still thinking this might be a big mistake. Maybe I've just been deluding myself.

How did autocorrect deal with "dunno"?

It made it "Sunni." Hey, isn't that your religion?

Not even close. Regarding your existential crisis, methinks you're protesting too much. Fishing for compliments, maybe?

Nah. Granted, Varun knows me really well, and any other day, his assessment might be spot-on. But he's clueless about how my ego just got crushed, so I really am feeling shaky.

And didn't you say there's a really hot guy in the band? Varun continues. The one whose name sounds like a kind of polyester?

My stomach clenches. Yeah, but that's a no-go.

A moment passes, and I assume Varun is waiting for me to elaborate. But that's really all I have to say about that.

I'm sensing there's a story there? he presses.

I purse my lips. Ah, my dearest boy, that is a story for another day, I say, poking him with the ultra-formal language his parents use. It works better in person, when I can apply my bad Indian accent to the impression, but whatever. I've gotten jokey, which means it's time for him to shut down the probing.

I'll wear you down, Scarletta, Varun texts.

My family gives me lots of nicknames: Scarletta, Scarlotta, Scarlina, and whatever else suits their mood at the moment. At some point over the past few years, Varun overheard and followed their lead.

Maybe, I respond. I gotta go. Wish me luck.

He signs off with an emoji of a watermelon slice. Varun always signs off with a random emoji.

I take a deep breath. I guess I've got to scale this staircase eventually, unless I really *do* end up flaking on these guys, and I might as well power through now.

I jostle my Martin higher on my back and keep climbing. *Creak, creak, creak.*

I open the door to the loft and see Kyle and Mike sitting casually and talking. They jump up from their folding chairs when they see me. *Sigh.* I really *am* cramping their style.

"Hi, guys," I say with a little wave. "Don't get up on my account."

But they're already walking toward me, overly polite smiles pasted on their faces.

"Hey, Scarlett!" says Mike, the dark-haired one with the cleft in his chin.

"Hi," Kyle echoes, running a hand loosely through his strawberry-blond hair.

"I guess I'm early," I say apologetically. "Just wanted to make sure I didn't keep you guys waiting . . ."

"No chance of that," Kyle says. "Declan feels strongly about arriving fashionably late. If we ever started on time, you'd probably have to revive us from shock."

"Really?" I say, aiming for casual. "He doesn't seem like the type to be inconsiderate. He gave me a lift home yesterday."

The guys *mmmmm* vaguely in response.

"Which was really nice of him," I continue, my heartbeat quickening, "considering it probably made him late to wherever he needed to be. I hope he didn't keep his girlfriend waiting or anything on account of me."

Okay, did I really just say that? Could I be any more obvious? And didn't I vow to step away from the hottie? What an idiot I am.

But it doesn't really matter, because other than Kyle and Mike sharing a quick, inscrutable glance, they aren't taking the bait.

"Can I help you with your guitar?" Mike asks me.

"I've got it," I say, relieved that my momentary lapse of sanity appears to have passed unnoticed. "Mind if I tune up?"

"Oh, you like your instruments tuned?" Kyle quips. "You're definitely going to have to lower your standards if you're gonna hang with us."

I smile and walk toward an amp, then retrieve my guitar from its gig bag.

"Zach's not here yet, either?" I ask the guys.

"He texted that he might be a couple of minutes late," Mike says as he and Kyle walk toward their instruments. "His mom . . ."

I glance at him. "What about her?"

"Just the usual."

My eyebrows knit together. "What's the usual?"

"Oh, you didn't know?" Mike says. "She has ALS."

"ALS?" I ask, strapping the guitar around my neck.

"I forget what it stands for," Mike says. "It's the technical name for Lou Gehrig's disease: that horrible deal where your body freezes up inch by inch."

I gasp a little. "Oh no . . . is it curable?"

Mike shakes his head, eyes lowered.

"It's awful on so many levels," Kyle says. "Not only is she everybody's favorite mom, but she's everybody's favorite doctor. Well . . . *was*. She closed her practice recently when she realized she was having trouble staying on her feet."

"Sweetest lady in the world," Mike says. "I can't tell you how many pancakes she cooked for us when we slept over on weekends—not to mention how often she tolerated us playing our music till three in the morning."

Kyle smiles wistfully. "Remember in tenth grade when I accidentally smashed her mailbox with my Honda?" he says to Mike. "I'd told my folks I was spending the night with Zach, but I didn't mention that I was stopping by Ryan Colmes's keg party first. Dr. Spencer was so cool about it. She told me it would be our little secret—if I'd lay off the beer and learn an instrument instead. That's when I started playing the drums."

"Dude, she bought me my first bass," Mike says, taking a drag on his cigarette. "She acted like she'd just happened to pick one up at a garage sale or something, but I'm sure she overheard me telling Zach how much I wanted to play. And she knew my dad had just been laid off."

"Damn," Kyle says in barely a whisper, staring at his fingers. "She's the one who encouraged me to major in pre-med. We shoulda named the band after her. The Madelyns. Yeah. That's the least we could have done."

"She knows how crazy we are about her," Mike says softly. "Zach's written a couple of songs about her since her diagnosis. 'Sailing On'? It sounds like a love song, but it's about her: 'I will see you there on the other side.'"

I swallow hard. "I practiced that song for two hours last night. I'll never be able to hear it the same way again."

Silence hangs in the air for a moment.

"So . . . how long can she live with the disease?" I finally ask.

The guys share glances. "A year?" Mike says. "Maybe two? And however much time she has left, her quality of life will be crappy. The disease makes your muscles weaker and weaker until you can't move at all. Nobody deserves that shit, least of all Dr. Spencer."

"Did you read the newspaper article?" Kyle asks him. "She was exactly like you'd expect her to be: totally chill and philosophical. She was like, 'However much time I have left, it's all good; I've had the greatest life and the greatest family in the world.' "

"No wonder Zach's so awesome," I say. "And you'd never know anything was wrong. I mean, I haven't known him for long, but . . ."

"Zach rolls with the punches," Mike says. "He just does what needs to be done."

"But how can he walk around acting like everything's . . ."

My words trail off. *Fine*. That's how Zach acts. That's how I act, too. If someone had told me six months ago that I'd be able to keep drawing air into my lungs after my brother dropped dead, I wouldn't have believed it. I would've been sure I'd spend the rest of my life curled in a ball. But life doesn't give you that choice. I wonder what's harder: the sound of your mother's screech at three in the morning or the *drip*, *drip*, *drip* of losing someone, as Mike said, inch by inch. I feel so terrible for Zach. I went eighteen years with barely a hiccup in my life, and only now do I realize that most people walk around horribly wounded in one way or another.

"Is there anything we can do for him?" I ask the guys, then flinch at how ridiculously presumptuous I sound. Mike and Kyle have been his friends for years; I've known him for a weekend. I'm not part of a "we."

But these guys are too sweet to issue a bullshit alert. Instead, Mike says gently, "I think the band is just the diversion he needs. He's always happiest when he's making music."

Just like Liam was. I wish it had been enough. I wish that so badly.

The door to the loft creaks open, and we look over at Zach as he walks in. He keeps his guitars in the loft, so he's empty-handed other than a light backpack dangling from his shoulders. He's wearing jeans and a plain white T-shirt.

"'Sup, bro," Kyle greets from his drum stool.

"Ah, she's back!" Zach says, beaming at me as he walks over to us and grabs a guitar. "I thought for sure we scared you off yesterday."

I smile back. "Scared me off because you're way too good for me?"

He laughs. "Just the opposite: scared you off with our mediocrity."

"Are you kidding? You guys are amazing. I love your songs, by the way. Have you been writing long?"

"Awhile," Zach says, plugging his guitar into an amp.

"He was especially prolific in our calculus class, as I recall," Mike tells me, his eyes squinting as he takes a drag on his cigarette. "Nothing like differentiables to get the creative juices flowing."

"What can I say? Differentiables have always inspired me."

Zach plunks his guitar strings one by one, twisting the pegs to get them in tune, then offers to tune my guitar, as well. I gladly hand it over, what with my ear no doubt being much less discriminating than his. It never mattered how meticulously I tried to tune my guitar around Liam; he always ended up wincing during the first song we would practice, then grabbing the guitar from me and tuning it over again.

"So," Zach says as he hands it back to me, "since Declan's not here yet, why don't we start with some of the songs Scarlett will sing lead on?"

Everybody agrees, and I swallow hard to push past my nerves. *Just sing, stupid.*

Kyle counts off a song, and after we play the opening bars, I lean into the microphone to sing it:

You played me. You slayed me. You made me a wreck.
Your arms tightened up like a noose 'round my neck.

My voice is a little shaky at first, but after the first couple of lines, I feel myself loosening up, then squeezing my eyes shut as I channel Adele:

You swore I meant more, but you tore me apart.
I caved, and you gave me a hole in my heart . . .

Zach leans into his mic to sing harmony on the chorus, and this is where I really come alive. It's always the harmony that buoys me, and my voice sounds fuller and more vibrant as I lock eyes with him, smiling. He smiles back, and we hold our gaze until he launches into a solo after the chorus.

I'm on a high by the time we finish the song, but our last chord is still resonating as Zach starts gently critiquing our performance. He asks Kyle to slow the tempo just a tad and suggests that Mike walk down the bass after the bridge. Then we practice patches of the song—the bridge here, the chorus there—until Zach's eyes close contentedly and he nods with a smile.

We play it again from the top, seamlessly this time.

"Great job," Zach tells me. "Do you know 'Open Up My Heart'?"

I nod. "It's one of my favorites."

"Let's do it."

Kyle counts us off, the band plays the opening bars, and I fall right into the soulful ballad. Zach leans into his mic to sing harmony on the chorus. His smooth, supple harmony combined with my melody makes our voices sound like they're drifting on air:

And just how long can this go on,
The spell you've got me under?
Eternity sounds good to me.
I'll turn the key and open up my heart.

I feel so light on my feet right now. My grief is still raw, but it occurs to me that I'm finding comfort feeling connected to my brother through playing music again. I remember when Liam was teaching 'Open Up My Heart' to me during a practice with the Joneses, and I kept playing an A minor instead of A major on the channel. After my fifth or sixth time through playing the wrong chord, he snapped at me. It was no big deal; he just kinda snarled and told me the band didn't have all day, or something like that. If anyone else had said the same thing, I'd have brushed it off and moved on. But *Liam*, Liam had never snapped at me until that moment. Maybe on some subconscious level, I was aware that Liam was doing more and more things out of character those days: losing his cool with me, fighting with my parents. . . . But it never occurred to me to blame the pills. I blamed my parents for not getting off his back. I blamed myself for being obtuse. So when he snapped at me, I did the most uncool thing ever: I started crying. Not bawling or anything, just blinking back tears and trying to keep my damn chin from trembling. The other guys pretended not to notice, and we moved on pretty quickly, but I was mortified. We finished the practice, and with anybody else, that would have been the end of it. But not Liam. When I went to bed that night, I realized he'd sneaked into my room at some point and flooded my pillow with Smarties, my favorite candy. And on top was a homemade note: One side had a close-up photo of his hand playing an A-minor chord on the guitar with the heading "A Minor Deal," and on the back was a picture of his comically remorseful face with the heading "A Major Heel."

That was Liam. Pills or no pills, his sweetness always shone through.

Right now, at this moment, I'm wildly happy that I discovered the Beastings, or they discovered me, or whatever. Who needs a hot guy?

By the time we're practicing our fourth song, I'm so exhilarated that I'm no longer self-conscious about facing Declan for the first time since the cookout. And speaking of Declan . . .

We've just launched into our fifth song when he strolls through the door. I've got to admit, my heart skips a beat. His hair is damp, like he just got out of the shower, and it bounces loosely on his shoulders with every sinewy step he takes. I try to avert my eyes, but just as he's leaning toward an amp to reach for his guitar, we exchange glances and he smiles. God, he's cute.

But I guess the guys are less appreciative of his gorgeousness than I am, because when our song is over, Mike mutters, "Nice of you to join us."

Their eyes lock, but Zach is genially pushing past the tension. "Hey, Dec. Wanna go over 'Shamblin' '? We still haven't quite nailed that bridge."

"Sure," he says coolly, letting his eyes linger on Mike for a second longer.

I swallow hard, lower my chin, and take a step back, trying to make myself as unobtrusive as possible. Kyle counts off the song, and the band eases into its bluesy, sultry intro. It's one of several I practiced on the bathroom floor. It's in the key of D—nothing complicated about it—and I'm accompanying them passably on rhythm guitar.

Declan has been playing along, too, but by the chorus, his guitar hangs limply around his neck while he wraps both hands around the mic, caressing it like the back of a neck—the neck of someone he's leaning in to kiss with his full, moist lips. My knees feel weak.

Zach leans into his mic to sing harmony, and I start swaying dreamily to the beat.

"You left my life in shambles," they sing, "and my words are only rambles. I guess I lost the gamble. Yeah, I'm shamblin' . . ."

We move into the third verse, and I'm feeling relaxed enough by the second chorus to lean into Zach's mic with him. I listen to Zach's backup vocal, then join in on the higher harmony part, and watch his eyes closely to nail the timing. He offers an easy smile to prod me along.

It's at the bridge that Zach stops the band, directing us to go over a couple of bars a few more times. Declan isn't quite nailing the syncopated rhythm, and Zach wants to hammer away until he gets it just right. Stop, start, stop, start. Declan acts annoyed by the third or fourth time (his dimples look amazing when he purses his lips, by the way), but he hangs in there until Zach is satisfied.

By the last chorus, we're all on autopilot again, singing and playing in a woozy, bluesy trance.

When the song is over, I try to catch Declan's eye so we can bask in the moment together, but he doesn't glance my way. Zach, on the other hand, gives me a thumbs-up.

Mike reaches over, jostles my arm, and says, "You sounded really good. You pick things up fast. And your voice . . . you've got kind of a Stevie Nicks vibe going."

"Thanks," I say. "I practiced Zach's songs for hours last night. They're so good."

"You know," Mike responds, "I'd love to hear that song with you singing lead."

I blink a couple of times. "No, I think Declan sounds great," I stammer softly.

"Sure he does," Mike says unconvincingly, "but it doesn't hurt to change things up now and then, right?"

A tense moment hangs in the air, then Mike says, "Whatcha think, Zach? Think we should try it with Scarlett singing lead?

Zach rubs his chin lightly. "I wouldn't mind giving it a try. We might have to change the key . . ."

"No, really," I insist, my eyebrows weaving together. "I think it's better to just keep it like—"

"That's cool with you, isn't it, Declan?" Mike says, eyeing him evenly.

Declan holds his gaze, chin jutting out slightly, then jerks his head to loosen a lock of hair from his eyes. "Smoke break," he says in a tight voice. He roughly unstraps his guitar, tosses it against an amp, and strides toward the door, his damp hair bouncing with every step.

We're silent as the wooden door thuds shut and Declan's footsteps descend the staircase.

"So. That went well," Kyle says drily from his drum stool.

I squeeze my eyes shut. "*Guys*," I say, then turn to face them. "I don't want to mess up what you've got going. Declan sounds great!"

"Yeah," Mike agrees. "He's a legend in his own mind."

Kyle snickers, but Zach presses his lips together. "C'mon," he says quietly to Mike.

"Guys, please!" I say. ""I don't want Declan thinking I'm trying to replace him or anything—"

"Yeah, that would be tragic," Mike murmurs.

"Yes!" I agree, pushing past his sarcasm.

"Look," Mike says, talking only to the guys now, "Scarlett is clearly our solution."

Zach averts his gaze.

"It's time," Mike tells them.

Zach stares at his feet a second longer, then looks up, rubbing his chin again. "I vote we keep things the way they are, at least for the time being. Let's not let personal stuff mess up a good thing."

"*Personal*?" Mike thunders. "He was half a goddamn hour late today! Per usual! And you know he's gonna flake on at least half of our jobs this summer. I say cut him loose."

I run my hand through my hair, my heart pounding against my T-shirt. "If this is about me, I do *not* want to be the reason that—"

"This isn't about you," Zach assures me. "We've had some issues for a while."

"Except that it *is* about her," Mike says, "in that she's a far better musician than Declan—"

"No, I'm not!"

"And I'm guessing she'll be approximately a thousand times more reliable."

I give him a frantic glance, and Mike says, "Scarlett, sorry to put you in the middle of this. But hey, you're a better musician than Declan." He glances pointedly at Zach. "Nothing personal about that."

I open my mouth to object again, but Zach is waving his arms over his head to shut this down. "Look," he says, "we've got two gigs next week. That's what we should be concentrating on. We've got our band—including a great new addition—and it's all good. Let's just stay focused on the music. If we need to make adjustments along the way, we will."

He scans our faces. "Deal?"

I nod quickly, then Mike and Kyle join in grudgingly.

"Good," Zach says. "Let's get back to the music."

• • •

My stomach is still in knots as I prop my bike on its kickstand on Grandpa's front porch, then walk in the house.

Sara, lying on the living room couch reading a book, glances up. "Have fun?"

I groan as I let my gig bag slip off my back. I prop it in a corner, then fall into Grandpa's scratchy wingback chair and throw my head back. "I think I'm creating an incident."

Sara closes her book and sits up. "Details?"

I sigh and tell her what happened—including the fact that Declan never came back to practice after his "smoke break."

"Nobody's sure if he's still in the band or not," I say, nibbling a nail. "And if not, is he holding me responsible?"

I know, I know, I pledged to stop thinking about him,

but not only am I still hung up on his hotness (sue me, I'm human), but now I'm wondering if his indifference toward me at the cookout last night was actually hostility. Did he sense from the start that the band was trying to edge him out? Does he blame me?

Well, duh. Who wouldn't? You don't exactly embrace your replacement with open arms.

But that's never what I intended.

"Should I call him and explain that I—"

"Scarlett!" Sara pitches forward. "You've never chased a guy in your life. Stop obsessing over Declan."

My jaw drops. "Uh, in the first place, I am *not* obsessing over him. I'm simply trying to clear up a—"

Both of us look at the front door as Mom walks in. Her face brightens when she sees me.

"Hi, baby girl," she coos, then leans down to hug me, clinging to me and sniffing my hair.

"Hi, Mom," I say, my voice muffled by her embrace. "I didn't hear you pull in the driveway." Mom takes a deep breath as she finally pulls away.

I swallow hard. She's always been a touchy-feely kind of mom, but before Liam died, it was in a breezy, incidental kind of way. Now she hugs me the way you hug somebody who's just been wheeled into the ICU after a car accident. Poor Mom. She's getting better; she plans to return to her classroom in the fall, and I noticed shortly before leaving for Grandpa's that she's finally scribbling in her crossword books again. But her eyes still look sad all the time, no matter how many smiles she forces.

"How are my girls?" she asks, scooting next to Sara on the couch and putting an arm around her.

"Scarlett's obsessing over a guy."

"Sara!" I squeal, tossing a throw pillow at her.

"Sad but true," she tells Mom. "I haven't seen her this out of control since Mr. Fields."

I try to stay indignant but can't help giggling.

"Remember when you thought Mr. Fields was sending you subliminal lust messages while he was discussing mitochondria?" Sara asks.

"Shut up," I protest, still giggling.

"There was just something about the way he rocked those clip-on ties . . ." Sara says, staring dreamily into space.

Now we're all laughing, and yeah, I'm willing to take one for the team to make Mom laugh.

"So who's the new guy?" Mom asks, hazel eyes sparkling.

"Well," Sara says, warming to the subject, "we went to Sheehan's with Grandpa on Friday night and saw this band playing. They invited Scarlett to come to their practice, then they asked her to join the band."

"I thought you were lifeguarding," Mom says to me.

"That too," I say.

"And the lead singer is smokin' hot," Sara continues, "and she invited him to a cookout last night at the Bixleys' house, and—"

"And surprise! He fell in love with Sara," I tell Mom. "Will you alert the media, or shall I?"

Grandpa ambles in from the den—the baseball game he was watching on TV is still blaring at full volume—and smiles at our good humor. "Sounds like I'm missing a good story," he says.

Mom jumps up to hug him (her hug lingers with him, too), then settles back in her spot on the couch as Grandpa sits in the chair opposite mine.

"I was just telling Mom about Scarlett's new bandmates," Sara says. "One in particular . . ."

I wrinkle my nose at her, then say, "Hey, Grandpa, you know the lead guitarist? Mr. Carver's grandson, Zach?"

He narrows his eyes nervously, seemingly wondering where this is heading. Oh. Now I realize why he's edgy: We swore each other to secrecy about my near-miss, mostly so Grandpa could retain his leverage in forcing me to turn over the car keys. A lot's happened in the past two days.

"Yes?" Grandpa responds, and I talk quickly to put his mind at ease.

"Did you know that his mother has Lou Gehrig's disease?"

"Of course," Grandpa says. "We spent half an hour talking about it with his grandparents at Sheehan's on Friday night."

"Oh." I feel my cheeks flush with the realization that I had been fixated on Declan and totally oblivious to the old-people chatter. I hope I didn't seem ridiculously insensitive. It's just, well, Harold started talking about his titanium knee, and I figured it wasn't going to get any more interesting, so . . .

"It's awful," Mom says. "And Madelyn is such a great person."

"You know her?" I ask.

Mom nods. "She was the valedictorian in the class ahead of mine. Super smart. We all thought she'd end up winning a Nobel Prize for curing cancer or something. Everyone in town talks about what a great doctor she is."

"She had to close her practice," I say. "Her son is a really nice guy. He's the one who invited me to join the band."

"So he's the one you have a crush on?"

I roll my eyes. "I don't have a crush on anyone," I say,

enunciating every word, but even as I say it, Sara is telling her, "It's Declan, the lead singer."

"What's this about a crush?" asks Grandpa, and we all laugh. His hearing impairment seems to disappear when the conversation turns juicy.

"No crushes," I say firmly.

"What about that nice young Indian boy?" he says.

"I told you: He's gay."

"Ah." Grandpa looks disappointed all over again.

"Hey, speaking of Varun, have you talked to him lately?" Sara asks, fingering a lock of hair.

"Sure. We talk all the time. Why?"

"Just wondering. So he's doing okay?"

Mom purses her lips and pats Sara lightly on the thigh. They exchange a quick glance.

My eyes narrow. "He's fine. Why do you ask?"

"I was just wondering," Sara says, but her eyes drop when I try to hold her gaze. Weird. Since when is she interested in Varun?

Mom claps her hands together. "Well," she says, rising from the couch, "we gotta get going."

"Yeah, for sure," Sara says, hopping to her feet as well. "I've got to get back home. A big test is coming up in my online course."

They start bustling about, gathering their purses and the overnight bag Sara has already transferred to the foyer. They hug Grandpa and me and make plans for their next visit, with Mom reminding me to wear sunscreen at work tomorrow.

Grandpa and I walk out to the porch with them, then wave as they start up the car and drive off.

"So your mom seems good, right?" Grandpa asks me, resting his hand on my back as we walk inside.

"Yeah, she does," I agree, still vaguely distracted. I'm sure it wasn't a big deal, but what was up with that look Mom and Sara shared about Varun?

Weird . . .

• • •

"So now I'm freaking out, wondering if Declan thinks I was conspiring to take his place in the band."

"Hmmm."

I hear Varun clacking on the keyboard as I fill him in over the phone. I'm sprawled on the bed as crickets chirp outside in the darkness. I'm supposed to be at the pool at nine in the morning, so I'm calling it a day, even though it's not quite 10 p.m. yet.

"Are you paying attention?" I ask Varun.

"Yeah, sure," he responds absently, the keyboard still clacking. "The hot guy has found out that you're planning a hostile takeover."

"I am *not*," I say, giggling. "But speaking of hot guys . . . how's your 'like life'?"

"Still nonexistent. Thanks for giving me the opportunity to reinforce that information on a regular basis," he responds. "How about you? Are you gonna go for it with the hot guy?"

"The one who hates me?" I respond, hugging the one-eyed bear against my chest. "I'm thinking not." Again, I'm skipping the part about inviting Declan to the cookout and watching him come on to my sister. Varun has shepherded me through various humiliations over the years, but I'm nursing this wound solo.

"Well, keep me posted," he says. "Oh, and hey, I wanna come hear your band."

I bite my bottom lip. "Hold that thought, okay? If I crash and burn next week, I'd prefer to do it with as few spectators as possible."

"You'll be 'ingenuous,' " he wisecracks, referencing Shelby Dixon's yearbook announcement that she couldn't wait to start her fashion career and put all her "ingenuous" ideas to work.

I snicker, then say, "Come see me in a couple of weeks. And pray the band doesn't implode between now and then."

" 'Kay. In the meantime, knock 'em dead."

"That," I tell him, "is an *ingenuous* idea."

CHAPTER EIGHT

I adjust my sunglasses and peer into the sparkling blue water.

The pool opened at ten, and by 10:02 a.m., at least three dozen kids were tearing through the gate and diving into the water. My boss had gone over a list of my duties with me when I'd arrived at nine, but there really hadn't been much to say. I'd already gotten my Red Cross certification, and it took all of nine seconds to learn how to check the chlorine levels in the water. This was going to be an extremely low-maintenance job.

As in *achingly dull.*

I weave my fingers together as I scan the crowd from my raised chair, the smell of my coconut-scented sunscreen wafting through the air. I blow my whistle periodically to tamp down on horseplay or stop a kid from running on the cement, then resume my dull gaze.

I was hoping to at least be able to pop in my ear buds and listen to music, but my boss kept stressing how important it was to minimize distractions, so whatever. I hate that all this monotony is giving my mind free rein to ponder—yeah, you guessed it.

I can't help wondering if Declan might show up. I was supposed to save his life so he could get his money's worth at the pool, right? I'll remind him of that if he shows up, and we'll laugh (awkwardly, since I'll be six feet higher than him in my super-high chair), then I'll casually ask, "Hey, what was up with Mike at practice yesterday?" and Declan will explain some long-running feud that has nothing to do with me, and we'll laugh about how anal Mike is about being on time, then we'll pick up where we left off.

And where exactly was that? Let's see . . . the vast majority of the time I've spent around Declan has consisted of his hitting on my sister or his sniping with band members. None of this bodes well for our future. I get that. Still, what an adorable meet-cute story it would turn out to be if we could push past it (when we tell it, he'll insist that he was never hitting on my sister; he was just really shy around me because he liked me so much), and we'll end up as a couple. ("Hey, Varun, my like life is turning out to be pretty awesome after all," I'll report by, say, mid-July.)

God. Sara was right. I really am delusional. Even when Marco dumped me for Kimberly Clay at the lake on our last day of summer vacation last year, I sniffled for all of five minutes before Varun and I moved on to the vital business of making snarky remarks about the precious couple behind their backs. Never, *ever* have I chased a guy, and never have I sat around obsessing about one. What am I, a seventh-grader at a boy-band concert? This is *so* not me.

So why can't I stop thinking about him?

I blow my whistle and make a time-out sign to a kid who's whacking a girl with a noodle. What is it with boys wanting to turn everything into a weapon?

Well . . . not *all* boys. I smile lightly as I recall swimming when I was about ten, diving into the shallow end and banging my head on the bottom. Liam had me in his arms within seconds, shouting for Sara to bring a towel that he could press against my bleeding wound. He leaned close to my ear as he ran me to the first-aid station and told me everything was gonna be fine, just fine, that he had me and wouldn't let me go. My teeth started chattering—chattering from pain, fear, something—and Liam pressed his cheek softly against my mouth to make them still, running all the while. His sprint couldn't have taken more than seven seconds, but I remember the feel of his cheek against my chattering mouth like it was yesterday. I wonder now how he managed it: running with me in his arms, pressing a towel against my wound, and holding his cheek against my mouth all at the same time. How I wish he were here to ask.

"Scarlett? Is that you?"

I gasp a little, startled, and look down. "Zach . . . hi. What are you doing here?" I ask.

He smiles sheepishly and holds out his arms. I laugh and roll my eyes as I look over his swim-trunks-clad body.

"So I'm ruling out snow skiing," I say.

"I'm actually here with my mom," he says, glancing over at a pretty brunette who looks much too young for the walker she's holding on to. Several people are talking to her, and she's smiling brightly.

"Oh," I say, studying her from behind my sunglasses, trying to ferret out clues of her disease. But other than looking a little stooped . . . nothing. She just looks like a normal, healthy person dropping by for a swim.

"Hey, my mom knows your mother," I tell Zach. "They went to school together."

"Yeah, Mom mentioned that when I told her about you."

My eyes narrow. "Which part did you tell?" I ask playfully.

He laughs. "Only the good stuff. I skipped the near-death experience."

"Thanks," I say, wrinkling my nose.

I scan the pool, then nod toward the right side. "Those three lanes are reserved for swimming laps. All the kids are in the play area, so the lap lanes are empty."

"Yeah, we're headed that way."

"Do you need a kickboard or something? Maybe a noodle or a float?" I'm not sure if he knows I'm up to speed about his mother's ALS.

"We'll be fine," Zach says. "I'll be right by her side."

I nod. "I'll keep an eye out," I say, then wonder if that sounds excruciatingly patronizing. Still, I'm the lifeguard, and I feel like I should do *something*, so I keep blathering: "If you need anything, just wave, and I can be there in no time. Oh, and she can grab one of those buoys if she—"

"Thanks. We'll be fine, I promise. We do this a lot."

I lick my lips. Of course they do. This is their life. How stupid I must sound with my ineffectual little suggestions and babbling about rushing to their rescue. Right. Zach's got at least half a foot on me and looks like he could run a marathon. Do I ever look anything but ridiculous around this guy?

But Zach's eyes always look so kind. "Hey . . . I'm really glad you joined the band," he says.

I smile gratefully. "You think Declan will be back? I'm so worried I screwed everything up."

"Oh, he'll be back. He and Mike go at it pretty regularly, but they pull it together when it matters."

"What's up with them?" I ask.

Zach considers his words, then says, "Well, Mike does have

some legitimate gripes. Dec's a little . . . looser . . . than the rest of us. But he usually comes through."

I impulsively decide to probe deeper. "It seemed kinda . . . personal."

Zach waves a hand through the air. "It's always something, right? But everything's cool. I promise. Listen, I gotta get back to my mom."

"Sure, sure. Hey, just wave if you need me, okay?"

He smiles, gives a thumbs-up, then trots back to his mother's side. They chat for a couple more minutes with the people she's been talking to, then Zach carefully leads his mom to one of the swimming lanes. She holds on to the walker, her gait a little shaky.

I still can't wrap my head around her disease. Maybe there's some mistake. Surely she can't actually be dying. Maybe with enough exercise, she'll get stronger rather than weaker. Maybe they'll find a cure. Isn't ALS what all those ice-bucket challenges were about a few summers back? They raised millions for research, right? Some breakthrough might be just around the corner.

I wonder if Zach has the same thoughts, and if so, whether they help or hurt. I mean, you've got to have hope, but I don't want him to set himself up for disappointment, either. I remember Mom and Dad insisting, once they'd finally had no choice but to tell me about Liam's pills, that people recover from addictions all the time. Maybe they were just trying to convince me, but it seemed like they really believed it themselves—that this was just a phase, a rough spot, a blip in Liam's life. Mom and Dad stressed that they knew lots of people in their own circles who were sober after years of abusing booze or drugs. And it seemed like practically every family we knew came up to us at Liam's memorial service to tell us they knew what we were going through—that one of their kids, or a niece, or a cousin, or whoever, was going through it, too.

But all those people are still alive.

Maybe it would have been easier on Mom and Dad if they'd faced facts and prepared themselves, at least a little bit, for the possibility that Liam's addiction could be an endgame. Because the shock when we got the call was like a magnitude ten earthquake. The ground shook violently, then crumbled beneath our feet. You've got to be a little realistic, have at least a minimal dose of pragmatism, to be able to absorb life's shocks when everything goes straight to hell, right?

I don't know. Maybe nothing would have lessened the shock of that phone call. Maybe nothing Zach does now can brace him for how he will feel once his mom is gone. Maybe the best thing, the only thing, to do is hang on to hope. What else can he do? He must feel like a sword is hanging over their heads twenty-four hours a day.

But as I watch Zach and his mom now, I see real joy in their faces. They're swimming laps together in adjoining lanes, with Zach carefully monitoring his mom's progress along the way. When she slows down, he slows down. When she stops, he stops. I can't hear their conversation in between laps, but they're smiling and laughing. I'm still watching the other swimmers, still blowing my whistle now and then, still shutting down noodle assaults, but my gaze keeps drifting back to them. I hate what Zach's mom is going through, but she's clearly got a great family, caring friends . . . and right now, she looks like she doesn't have a care in the world.

I can't help smiling as they push off for another lap.

CHAPTER NINE

Creak, creak, creak.

Okay, I thought I was nervous the *first* two times I climbed these stairs. This time, I feel like a pool of jelly.

Zach keeps assuring me everything is cool. I've seen him every day this week at the pool with his mom, and he's always smiling. But three days have passed since the near-coup—this is the Beastings' first practice since then—and I don't know what to expect from Declan. I haven't seen him (no, he hasn't yet made it to the pool), and if Zach has any inside information, he hasn't coughed it up. There's no telling what I'm walking into.

But whatever. No seeking out last-minute pep texts from Varun today; we've got a job tomorrow night, my first performance with the band. Granted, we'll be white noise at a bar (Zach managed to get me an underage pass from the owner, provided I stay away from the booze), so it's not like anybody's gonna be flicking lights in our direction. But I still need every available ounce of gray matter devoted to the music. Also, I timed myself practically to the minute for this practice, arranging to walk in precisely at four. I don't want to be early—I've already surpassed my quota for awkwardness this week—but I definitely can't be late. I glance at my phone as I scale the last two steps. 3:58 p.m. Close enough.

I blow out a breath and push open the heavy oak door. "Hi, guys."

Zach and Mike are plugging their instruments into amps, and Kyle is settling into his stool at the drum set. No Declan.

"Hey, Scarlett," Zach says, slinging his guitar over his shoulders. "Long day on the noodle patrol?"

I laugh. Zach's witnessed enough of my noodle confiscations this week to be up to speed on the grittier aspects of lifeguarding. "An eight-year-old almost decapitated his sister this morning before I unarmed him," I say, unzipping my guitar from its gig bag.

"Yikes," he responds. "I guess the first-aid kit woulda been put to the test on that one."

The oak door creaks open, and we all look up and watch Declan walking in.

"Right on time," he mutters to no one in particular, ambling toward us with that slinky stride of his. "But who's keeping track?"

It's really insane how good-looking he is. I know, I know, I'm moving on. But his hotness is seriously distracting.

He doesn't meet my eye as he grabs his guitar and plugs it into the amp, but then, he's not making eye contact with the others, either. I'm still unsure whether he associates his rocky status in the band with me. But hey, he's here, and that's a good sign.

Zach is passing around copies of our set list for tomorrow night. I scan it anxiously. Okay, good. I've practiced everything that we'll be playing. Songs I know, combined with an audience full of drunks, will make for a winning combination, right?

"Who's singing 'Shamblin' '?" Declan asks, sounding only mildly interested.

"You," Zach responds. "Everything's just like normal, except for the new songs we've practiced with Scarlett singing lead."

Declan grunts noncommittally, and I notice Mike and Kyle exchanging a quick glance.

"Okay," Zach says quickly, "everybody tuned up?"

We all plunk our strings one at a time and twist the tuning pegs. I strum a couple of chords.

"Your G string is sharp," Declan says without looking at me.

"Oh."

I fumble with it some more.

"Now it's flat."

"Oh, sorry . . ."

I'm adjusting my tuning peg, fully aware that Mike and Kyle are sharing another significant look.

I play an E chord and wince. Now, it's more out of tune than ever. I fiddle with it some more. "Sorry, guys."

"It sounded fine the first time," Mike says under his breath.

"Bite me," Declan responds without looking at him.

"Okay, moving on," Zach says. "Scarlett, play your G string one more time?"

I do, and he bounces his thumb up, up, up. Still flat. I twist the peg, play the string again, and Zach nods.

"Count us off, Kyle?" he says.

Kyle hits his drumsticks together four times, his strawberry-blond hair bouncing with every thwack. *Whap, whap, whap, whap.*

And now we're making music together.

I guess we'll see how long this lasts.

• • •

Our practice ended up being relatively uneventful, but the tension never dissipated. Declan sang his songs pretty mechanically—no hip-swiveling or mic-caressing this time—and he barked a couple of grouchy observations about Mike's bass-playing. Mike narrowed his eyes at Declan when he wasn't looking, and Zach kept pushing ahead, trying to minimize downtime. I bit my lip between songs, hoping no sparks would fly. It was exhausting.

When it's over, Zach offers to give me a lift home, but I pass, hoping the bike ride will soothe my shot nerves. I secure my helmet, then head off into a muggy tailwind, my hair riding the crest of the breeze. Shorts-clad downtown shoppers and diners at outdoor wrought-iron café tables dot the sidewalks as I pass, and I wave at a few semi-familiar faces. A couple of them offer pinched smiles. "That's the girl whose brother OD'd," I imagine them whispering in my wake. How ridiculous for me to have thought I could leave the pinched smiles in the dust when I moved in with Grandpa. They're everywhere—a realization that somehow comforts and devastates me at the same time.

As I pedal across the bridge in the bike lane, I see a cardinal, and my heart momentarily soars. The bird swoops through the air, then settles on a barrier rail as I pass by. I could reach out and touch it. The river below shimmers in the sun. I bite my lip. Before Liam died, nothing was less complicated than feeling happy. Now, nothing's *more* complicated. *Sigh.* I smile at the bird with misty eyes and keep pedaling.

Once I get to Grandpa's house, I steady my bike on its kickstand on the porch. The aroma of butter and cheddar wafts through the air as I step into the foyer.

"Want a grilled-cheese sandwich, Scarlina?" Grandpa hollers from the kitchen.

I let my gig bag slide from my back onto the burgundy sofa in the living room, then join him in the kitchen and peck his cheek. The blue flame from the gas burner is glowing on his ancient stove. He smiles and flips a sandwich in a cast-iron skillet with a spatula.

"Hope you're hungry," he says.

I offer a weak smile. "Not really. I think I'll go lie down for a while. Thanks, though."

He glances at me, startled. "You've never turned down one of my grilled-cheese sandwiches before."

His face falls, and my heart sinks. Should I gulp one down for Grandpa's sake? That's another thing I've learned about grief: At the same time you're trying to deal with your own shit, you're also hypersensitive to your family's sadness, which just makes you sadder.

"I'm really bushed," I say. "Mind if I pass this time?"

"No, no . . . But are you feeling all right?"

I nod. "Yeah. Just tired."

His bright-blue eyes crinkle with worry. "Well . . . I'll keep the skillet on the stove. Let me know if you change your mind."

I smile. "Will do. Thanks, Grandpa."

His sad eyes follow me as I walk out of the kitchen. Damn. I should've eaten a sandwich for his sake. Surely I could have faked a little perkiness for just a few minutes, right? But I'm tired of faking stuff. *Grandpa will survive this devastating blow,* I tell myself. *I should quit trying to save everybody.*

I walk upstairs into my bedroom, close the door behind me, and collapse on the faded pink bedspread.

My lashes flutter, and pretty soon, I'm having one of those incredibly vivid nap-time dreams. I'm screaming at Liam, telling him it's time for school and that he's making everybody late, that he's screwing up our day. When he doesn't respond, I scream louder, then start shaking him, but I can't rouse him. "*Don't you hear the alarm*? *You're ruining everything!*" I screech.

I wake up in the real world to the sound of my ringtone trilling. I open my eyes, startled and disoriented, and squint into the late-day sun streaming through my window. I pick up my phone.

"Hi, handsome," I tell Varun groggily as I answer the call.

"Have you been *sleeping*?" he responds. "It's seven o'clock."

"Sue me. Just had an epically awkward band practice."

"Polyester Guy?" he probes.

Okay, *that* conversation's not happening.

"I just had the weirdest dream," I tell him instead, my voice still froggy. "Liam was making us late for school, and I was screaming at him to get up. I told him he was ruining everybody's life."

I wait for Varun's response, then keep waiting. And waiting. What the hell? Did he hear me? Is he judging me for being incredibly insensitive? Is he anti dream-sharing?

Then I realize that he's sniffling lightly on the other end of the phone.

"Varun?" I say warily.

Another moment passes, then he says in a fake-hearty voice, "Yeah, I'm right here."

God, what an amazing friend he is. I've lost count of how many times he's cried with me since Liam died, like he's literally feeling my pain.

"Isn't it weird that I scream at him in my dreams?" I say wistfully. "I don't think I ever screamed at him a single time in real life."

Another pause.

"So," Varun finally says, "elaborate about your awkward band practice. I need details."

I narrow my eyes, confused. "Okay, *that* was a *non sequitur*."

"Your dream was the *non sequitur*," he reminds me. "I want details."

I twirl a lock of hair in my fingers. "It was no big deal," I say. "I got there, and—"

I hear a knock on my door.

"Come on in, Grandpa," I call, then say into the phone, "Gotta go. Talk soon, okay?"

We end the call, and I sit up on the bed as Grandpa walks in.

"I need to run to the store, Scarlita. Wanna come along?"

I glance anxiously out the window. It's almost dusk. "Mind if I take the wheel this time?"

He hesitates.

"Grandpa, you said yourself it's harder for you to see in the dark than it used to be."

He ponders my words, then reluctantly nods. "But no homicides this time?"

"Deal." I get up, grab my purse, and follow him out of the room, down the hall, and out the front door.

Grandpa moves slower these days, a little stooped from arthritis and more deliberate with his steps. Just a couple of years ago, he was still flying around the tennis court, so this new normal is an adjustment. I also have to raise my voice when I talk to him. He tried a hearing aid a while back but didn't like it—"too tinny"—and he lacked the patience to hang with it. Or maybe it was the *motivation* he lacked. As kind as he is, Grandpa hates small talk and might consider it a plus that he's no longer expected to expound on the weather or the latest mayoral election or whatever. He generally disagrees with the majority opinion around here anyway and doesn't like to drill down on his opinions with anyone except family and close friends. I noticed when the Bixleys got started on national politics Saturday night, Grandpa segued pretty quickly. He's so smart and well-read that I think he's worried about coming across as a show-off if push came to shove. So yeah, he probably considers his hearing loss a net gain.

We put our seat belts on in the car, and he starts cautioning about "the children" again.

"I'm watching, Grandpa, I'm watching," I assure him, but yeah, I get that his vigilance will be on overdrive from now on, what with the near-miss. I make a show of craning my neck dramatically as I back out of the driveway, squinting my eyes to convey maximal concentration. I leave the AC and radio untouched, a considerable sacrifice on both counts. The faster I earn his trust back, the faster I can take back the wheel on a regular basis.

"So was that your mother on the phone?" he asks me once we're coasting down the street.

"Varun. We were talking about Liam," I say, surprising myself by dropping his name so casually into the conversation.

I feel Grandpa's eyes studying my face. "Honey, you don't talk to your friends about how he died, do you?"

"They know how he died," I say simply.

I can tell without looking that Grandpa's hands have tensed into fists.

"I think we need to be careful what we put out there."

I press in my lips. "I'm not ashamed of Liam, Grandpa. I'm proud of him."

"Of course you are! We all are. But we wouldn't want anyone to get the wrong idea . . ."

See, this is what drives me nuts about Grandpa. He's so incredibly smart, so wise, so uninterested in others' opinions . . . and then, *bam*, he says something like this.

"I wouldn't mind your explaining that he had heart failure," Grandpa adds quickly. He always spills out a rush of words when he doesn't really want to talk about something but only wants you to get with the program and move on. "I just think some of the details aren't really anyone's business outside of the family."

"The details."

"Yes. The details."

I pause, bouncing his words around in my head. Then I say, "Grandpa, do you understand how Liam got hooked on—"

"He wasn't hooked on anything," he mutters impatiently. "He was taking medicine. It was just that he never should have been prescribed that medicine in the first place. Damn doctors . . ."

He turns his face abruptly toward the passenger window.

I drive silently. Grandpa hardly ever curses in front of me. I think he's gone as far down this road as he's willing or able to go, at least for now.

"Hey, Grandpa," I say after a few moments, aiming for a lighter tone, "did I tell you I have my first gig tomorrow night with the band?"

"Oh, do you now?"

Good. Sometimes he shakes things off quickly; other times, his funk can linger. I'm glad he's pushing past it.

"I'd like to come hear you," he says.

"Uh. . ." I push a lock of hair behind my ear. "The place

we're playing tomorrow night will be a little . . . loud. Maybe you can come back to Sheehan's on Friday night and hear us there? Then you could sit with your tennis friend again. "

"And where is this concert tomorrow?"

Sigh.

"It's not a concert, Grandpa, just a . . . you know, a gig. It's at a place called Frosty's."

I take a quick sideways glance to gauge his reaction.

"That's a bar, isn't it?" he asks warily.

Darn. I was hoping Grandpa wouldn't be up on the bar scene.

"Yeah, but we'll only be playing for a couple of hours, not hanging out or anything."

Pause.

"Honey, I'm not a prude," he finally says. "I know what's required of a musician. You know, I played with a few bands myself when I was younger."

See? Grandpa can be all over the map. It's pointless to try to anticipate how he'll react to anything.

"I just want to make sure you're safe," he continues. "A beautiful young lady in a bar . . ."

"I promise I'll be safe, Grandpa," I say. "I'll be with the band the whole time."

"Harold's grandson will be there?"

"Yes," I say firmly. "Zach will be there. And I won't be drinking, of course."

He lets that sink in, then pats my knee. "I love you, Scarlina," he says softly. "I know what a smart girl you are. It's just . . . if anything ever happened to you . . ."

I nod. "I know, Grandpa," I say in barely a whisper. "I know."

CHAPTER TEN

"Writing me a love letter?"

I look up and peer through the gauzy dimness at a guy hovering over my booth.

He leans closer and reaches for my iPad. I pull it away, flashing a conciliatory smile at the last second. He *is* part of my audience, after all. No need to lay the groundwork for second-set heckling, if I can avoid it.

"Just . . . homework," I say, hoping it's a boring enough answer to keep him moving.

The first set at Frosty's went really well; I loosened up after the first couple of songs, particularly since hardly any of the couple-dozen bar patrons were paying much attention to us. We got some light applause after each song, but I'm guessing if we all played in different keys, nobody would have noticed or cared. The pressure's off. It's a nice way to ease in with the band.

Except that as soon as the first set was over, Declan walked to one corner of the bar with a scowl while Mike and Kyle walked to the opposite end. Zach lingered on the stage, making technical adjustments.

I'm glad I thought to bring my iPad. Might as well work on my summer essay, a prerequisite for incoming University of Georgia freshmen, during the downtime. I'm writing about

Liam, of course. I'm sure Grandpa will be thrilled that my professor will be the next to get up to speed on our "family business."

But Mr. Wonderful—a twentysomething guy with a bland face and ruddy cheeks—scoots next to me in the booth.

"Really gotta finish up," I say, still trying to convey a hint of friendliness.

"That's no homework," he says, bending closer to peek at my screen, though I've already X-ed it out. "Tell me the truth, beautiful: You're writing a song about the best-looking guy in the bar. Show me my song, baby."

I recoil at the smell of liquor on his breath and lean away from the arm he's trying to put around my neck. "I'm busy," I say, dispensing with the friendliness.

"You sure looked sexy on that stage," he tells me, leaning so close that I'm practically doing a backbend to avoid our noses touching. "You gonna play me my song when the band cranks back up?"

"Hey, Scarlett, sorry to bother you, but we've got to go over a few things for the next set."

The redneck and I both look up at the same time, and my tensed muscles instantly relax as I see Zach standing there.

"No problem," I tell him.

The redneck is still staring at Zach, but his arm is now dangling around my neck. He isn't budging.

"You mind?" Zach asks him, keeping a genial tone in his voice but subtly setting his jaw. The drunk grudgingly disentangles his arm.

The booth is a semicircle, and as Mr. Wonderful gets out on his side, Zach slips in on the other. He scoots protectively close to me as the redneck gives me one more ogle.

"Scarlett, huh?" the man grunts. "Well, I tell ya one thing: Frankly, Scarlett, I *do* give a damn."

He lingers a second to let his stab at sexiness sink in, then walks away in a tipsy swagger.

"Never heard that one before," I murmur to Zach as we share furtive smiles. "Thanks for saving me."

"You can't sit by yourself in a bar between sets, goofball," he scolds me lightly, tapping my forehead with his knuckles.

"Yeah, from now on, you're my boyfriend," I agree playfully.

"Deal."

"So . . . how do you think it's going?" I ask him, wrinkling my nose. "Am I doing okay?"

"Okay? You're epic. That guy fell in love with you after six songs," he says, motioning toward the redneck. "Wait till he hears you singing the blues. He'll be proposing after the second set."

"*Really*," I say, weaving my eyebrows together. "Are you sure I sound okay with you guys? If not, all you have to do is—"

"You're doing an amazing job," Zach says, holding my gaze.

I sigh. "But Declan . . ."

"Dec's doing fine," he says simply. "We're holding steady. It's all good."

Two pretty girls walk up, a blonde and a brunette. The blonde smiles and offers Zach a fist bump. "Sounding stellar, bro," she says.

"When did you get here?" he asks her.

"A few minutes ago." She looks at me and waves.

"Scarlett, this is my sister, Claire," Zach tells me, "and her friend, Callie."

I smile. "Hi. I'm Scarlett."

"You sounded great up there," Claire tells me. "Your harmony blends really well with the band."

"Wait till you hear her in the next set," Zach tells her. "She'll be singing lead on a couple of songs."

Claire raises an eyebrow. "How's that going over with Slick?"

"Who?" I ask.

She locks eyes with Zach for a moment, then shakes her head and looks at me again. "So, how do you like the Beastings?"

"I'm having a blast."

"Hey, you should join us," Zach tells Claire teasingly, considering she and her friend are already scooting into our booth.

"So, are you from around here?" Claire asks me.

"Right outside of Atlanta," I say. "But my mom grew up here. I'm staying with my grandfather this summer, then I start college in the fall."

"Is your grandpa sick or something?" Callie asks.

"No. I just . . . needed a change of scenery."

The bass line of a country song playing on the bar's sound system thrums in the air. "Well," Callie says, scanning the bar, "this is about as exciting as it gets in Oakboro."

"It's fine," I say, tucking my hair behind my ear. "I'm just stoked to be able to play with the Beastings. And I lifeguard during the day, so I maybe I'll see you guys at the pool. I've seen Zach a few times already."

"He swam a hundred meters in sixty seconds his senior year of high school," Callie says, leaning into the table, her eyes sparkling. "Fastest in the state."

"*Region*," he corrects her softly, staring at his folded hands on the table and blushing.

I turn toward Zach. "*Whoa*. Impressive!"

Callie nods. "He swims on his college team, too, and he's already broken a record for—"

Mike walks up to our booth and clears his throat. "Sorry to bother you guys," he says, then nods toward the girls. "Hi, Claire. Callie."

"You guys are sounding fierce tonight, Mike," Claire says.

"Please, no autographs."

She laughs at him, then Mike turns to Zach. "My guitar cable is shorting out. Can I borrow one of yours?"

"Sure." Zach slides out his end of the booth. "Steer clear of your buddy over there," he tells me as he rises to his feet, nodding toward the redneck a few feet away.

I hold up my palm. "Promise."

I giggle as Zach points to his eyes with V-shaped fingers, then points at me, mouthing, "I'm watching you."

My eyes follow him as he walks toward the stage with Mike, Kyle joining them halfway there. Then my eyes drift to the barstool where Declan is nursing another beer. He's been in the same spot throughout our break, talking casually to a girl who sits to his right. Not that I'm noticing.

I turn my attention back to Claire and Callie. "Your brother's so sweet," I tell Zach's sister. "He's been to the pool every day this week with your mom. I heard about her condition. I'm so sorry."

Claire nods, lowering her eyes. "Thanks. It's been rough."

"She looks like she's doing really well. I'm amazed at what a strong swimmer she is," I say. "I mean, if I didn't know she was sick . . ."

Claire absently traces a design on the table with her index finger. "Mom was always a really good athlete. But she's already struggling to stay on her feet. We've got a wheelchair ready when she needs to make the transition. That'll be a tough day." She swallows hard, and Callie squeezes her forearm lightly.

"I'm so sorry," I say again.

"Hey," she says, looking up at me, "if you have any pull with Zach, talk him into going back to school in the fall, will you?"

"Um . . ."

Claire looks at me expectantly for a moment, then shakes her head briskly. "Sorry. I didn't mean to put you on the spot. I just thought he might talk about it during practices or whatever."

"He doesn't," I say. "So he's thinking about quitting school?"

"Not quitting," Claire clarifies. "Just taking online courses, or taking a year off . . . whatever. He wants to be home with Mom next year, but she's freaking out, thinking her condition might disrupt our lives. That's the last thing she wants."

"Where does he go to college?" I ask.

"The University of Georgia."

"That's where I'm going."

"Us too," Claire says, nodding toward Callie. "We'll be rooming together in the freshman dorm. Well, unless *my* plans change. I want to stay with Mom, too, but Dad hit the roof when I even suggested it."

"You and Zach both need to just keep living your lives," Callie tells her. "You can come home every weekend if you need to."

"Or even commute," Claire says. "I can get to my classes in an hour."

"Claire, if you leave me stuck with a random roommate,

I swear to God I'll post our seventh-grade sleepover pictures on Facebook," Callie tells her.

Claire laughs, but then turns serious. "No matter what I decide, I'll be fine. But it's Zach's senior year. He's already got an internship scheduled with some big-shot engineering firm. I don't want him to lose any momentum. Plus, you know, Mom might live another two or three years . . ."

The words linger in the air, and we sit silently for a moment.

"Anyhow," she finally says, her voice firm again, "if you have a chance to mention to Zach that Mom really wants him to stay in school . . ."

I nod eagerly. "Sure. I'll be glad to do that. I can tell how close they are. It's so amazing watching them together."

"Zach's, like, one in a zillion," Callie says, and I nod.

He really is.

• • •

As we regroup on the stage to begin our second set, I notice Declan is still lingering at the bar. The girl he was talking to has drifted back into the crowd, and he's nursing another beer, gazing coolly into space. Zach catches his eye and motions for him to head back to the stage. Declan gives a slight nod, then slides off his barstool and works his way leisurely in our direction, slithering through the crowd and sharing smiles with every girl he passes.

"Really, whenever it's convenient for you," I hear Kyle mutter behind me from his drum stool—just another out-of-earshot dig at Declan. He and Mike share pissed-off glances.

Declan hops back onto the stage, hoisting himself up rather than walking around and taking the stairs, then ambles to the set and slings his guitar strap over his shoulder.

"Hey, guys, I'm thinking of changing up the set list, if you don't mind," Zach tells us, and we lean in for instructions.

"This is a pretty undiscriminating crowd, so do you mind if we swap out the last song for 'Sailing On'? The one I wrote last week?"

"Sure. I love that song," I say, then blush, wondering if I've piped up too soon.

But Mike and Kyle are nodding, too.

"For sure, man," Mike says.

"Uh, dude, you didn't print out the lyrics by any chance, did you?" Declan asks Zach, his voice slurring slightly.

"No, man, sorry."

"You sang it Friday night," Mike snaps at him. "Why don't you either memorize the damn music like the rest of us or lay off the booze?"

"Hey, I can call up the lyrics on my phone," I interject nervously, trying to defuse the tension. "I've still got the email Zach sent me."

"Yeah, that'll look epic, having our lead singer reading the lyrics off a phone," Kyle says, and my stomach tightens. True, Declan's not exactly the most conscientious member of the band, but I don't like seeing him ganged up on.

Declan tosses icy glares at Mike and Kyle, then turns back to Zach. "I think I can get through it," he says.

Mike pitches forward. "Don't fuck up this song," he tells Declan, spitting the words.

Declan stiffens and narrows his eyes to slits.

Okay, now my stomach is in full-blown nausea mode. Are these guys actually gonna start swinging fists?

Zach waves a hand through the air. "Chill, guys," he says in a soothing voice. "I'll sing the lead on 'Sailing On' tonight. Cool with you, Dec?"

Declan hesitates, glowering at Mike.

"We're cool, right?" Zach presses, and Declan grudgingly glances at him and nods.

"Yeah," he finally mutters. "We're cool."

"Great," Zach says, then before anyone else can throw in one last barb, he starts plinking his guitar strings one at a time, twisting his tuning keys. Mike, Declan, and I do the same with our instruments.

Tension still lingers in the air, but once again, Zach seems to have averted a blow-up. I wonder how much longer he can manage that before these guys smash their guitars over each other's heads.

Once we're tuned up, Kyle counts us off for a high-energy song that soon has the bar crowd clapping along and bouncing on their feet:

Back it up. Back it up, up, baby.
You can pack it up. Pack it up, up, baby.
'Cause I'm stacking up. Stacking up, up, baby.
All the reasons, they're a mile high,
That I'm a sayin' bye, bye, bye.
So back it up.
Yeah. Just back it up.

I break into a wide grin as the crowd (all thirty-two of them, give or take a couple) burst into finger whistles and raucous applause.

The energy only grows as we complete the set. Declan sounds better with each song, clearly loosened up by the beer, and a female bartender has made sure to keep him replenished, occasionally making her way to the front of the stage and handing him a cold one. As Declan swivels his hips and squeezes the mic, the girls go crazy. Whatever it is causing all the tension in the group, even Mike can't deny that Declan has the crowd, especially the girls, in the palm of his hand. I'm guessing that even if he just stood on stage and didn't sing or play a single note, he'd still have their complete attention.

He's actually putting that to the test now. We're down to the last song in the set, the one Zach wrote for his mom: "Sailing On."

Zach leans into the mic, and Declan basically just dances around clapping to the beat. Yeah, that works, too. The girls are still swooning.

But Zach—sweet Zach, with his soulful, chocolaty eyes and lilting voice—is attracting plenty of stares himself now that he's singing lead. He somehow manages to burrow his way into your soul, even on a song as fun and upbeat as this one. Mike's right: it sounds totally like a feel-good love song unless you know better. Leave it to Zach to add layers of meaning while still keeping the crowd on their feet.

And, *whoa*, are they on their feet. This crowd is epic. Or maybe we are. The energy of the whole band singing harmony on the chorus—"Sailing on, pushing past the shore"—leaves me breathless and exhilarated. Zach plays a mind-blowing solo after the bridge, and by the last verse, all of us are jumping up and down to the beat while Kyle slays the drums. I feel like a thousand volts of electricity are coursing through my body.

The guys and I all beam at each other, then Zach sweeps his arm in the direction of each of us individually so we can take a bow. By the time we all bow together, the walls are shaking with applause.

Maybe this is what Zach meant by everything sorting out. Once we're all caught up in the magic of the music, the petty stuff sloughs away. Hopefully this will clear the slate, and whatever is causing the tension will fall by the wayside.

"Thanks so much, everybody," Zach says into the mic, his arm outstretched for a final wave. "We'll be here again in a couple of weeks. Come back and see us, okay?"

He, Declan, Mike, and I pull our straps over our heads and start switching off the amps as the still-applauding crowd lingers to soak up the high.

As I lean my guitar against an amp, I feel arms around my waist.

"You were awesome," Declan says into my ear, and I turn around to face him.

I swallow hard, then gaze into his clear-blue eyes, which are a little bleary from the beer. I spontaneously wrap my arms around his neck and squeeze while Declan lifts me off the floor in a hug.

"God, that was fun," I say as we disentangle. His hair hangs limply with sweat, and his damp T-shirt hugs his narrow torso. My knees feel weak.

"Great job, everybody," Zach says from a few feet away as he crouches to unplug a cord.

I press my lips together, wait a second for my heart to stop thumping against my chest, then help the others start packing up the gear. The last half hour of a gig is always pure drudgery: carry heavy stuff outside, pack into van, repeat *ad nauseam*. But I was always eager to pitch in with the Joneses, not wanting anybody to think I was relying on a girl pass—or worse, a little-sister pass. And I'm happy to help now (well, maybe not *happy*, but willing), so here we go. We should be able to pack up quickly, what with five sets of hands. Plus, I'm still on an adrenaline high, so twenty-pound mic stands suddenly feel weightless. I take a deep breath to savor the moment: the music, the crowds, the hug . . .

Was Declan's hug just an in-the-moment burst of enthusiasm? I dunno. I'd almost nailed the *Forget Declan* mantra I'd been repeating the past few days, but that one hug seemed to reset my brain. I'm thinking now about his sweet smile, his challenge for me to save his life at the pool, his offer of a ride home that first night at practice . . . he even accepted my invitation to a neighbor's backyard cookout! These are all adorable things, right? So he spent a little time glomming onto my sister. So he shows up late occasionally to practice. So he and Mike aren't the best of friends. Some people just don't get along, right? It doesn't necessarily mean some big drama is unfolding or that either of them is a jerk.

"I'll get that," Zach tells me as I reach for a medium-sized amp, swooping past me to grab it. I open my mouth to protest, but he's already whisking it away, so I pick up a couple of gig bags instead. I carry them outside to the van, which Zach has backed up to the rear entrance of the bar. Declan is the only one standing outside. I load the guitars, then linger a moment.

"Gee, it's muggy out here."

Brilliant, Scarlett. When your imagination fails you, comment on the weather.

"Super hot," Declan agrees. "It's close to midnight, and it must still be eighty degrees. Brutal." He runs his fingers through his hair.

"Well, it feels a thousand times better than it did today at the pool," I reply.

He arches his brows. "That's right . . . you're lifeguarding this summer."

"Right. Four days down and no fatalities, so I must be doing something right."

He smiles and plants a hand on his hip. "So you say. I might just have to come see for myself, rather than take your word for it."

I drop my chin and laugh. "Any time. I plan to keep my streak going for at least another week or two."

He wrinkles his nose. "I'm a pretty crappy swimmer. I just might end your streak."

"Bring it," I say, smiling.

Our eyes stay locked as a moment passes.

"Well," I finally say, "better get back inside and help the others finish up."

"Right," Declan says. "Hey, by the way, did you ride your bike here?"

"Nope. Drove."

"Ah, darn." He studies me evenly. "I was kinda hoping you needed a ride home . . ."

I'm about to respond when the other guys walk out, each carrying the remainder of our gear.

"That does it," Zach says as they load it into the van. "Ready to do it all over again tomorrow night?"

"Hell, yeah," I say. "If a bunch of drunks liked us, I'm thinking we'll kill it at Sheehan's."

"Unless it's *because* they were drunk that they liked us," Kyle says, and we laugh.

"We'll set up tomorrow around six," Zach says. "That'll give us some time to go over the new stuff a couple of times. Does that work for everybody?"

We all murmur our consent.

My eyes flicker in Declan's direction, and I see him looking at me. I start to look away, but a sideways grin snakes slowly up his face, and I smile back, his eyes refusing to cut me loose. I blush and cock my head at an angle.

"Six o'clock *sharp* tomorrow," Mike growls, a cigarette dangling between his fingers.

Declan, still holding my gaze, mouths "Asshole," pointing at Mike discreetly. I suppress a grin.

"Everybody okay to drive?" Zach asks, trying to sound casual.

When all eyes fall on Declan, he narrows his eyes mischievously and purrs, "I'm golden."

Zach nods amiably but studies him nonchalantly. "Ya sure? I've got plenty of room in my—"

"I told you, dude, I'm golden," Declan repeats to Zach, but he's looking at me.

I lick my lips and lower my chin.

We say good night, and as we begin drifting toward our cars, I see that Declan is once again watching me coolly. I smile one last time, then turn toward Grandpa's Mercury. I hope it's not noticeable that I'm walking slowly, gauging his next move.

Because that *was* a move, right? He was definitely flirting . . . right? I'm still pacing myself as Zach, Mike, and Kyle slide into their cars and start their engines. It's just as they start to back out of their parking spaces that I click my door opener and reach for the handle. They wave from their cars as I open my door, still moving slowly. Their cars round the bend of the parking lot and cruise out of sight.

Which is when I feel Declan step up from behind.

"Sure wish you needed a ride," he coos in my ear.

And when I turn around to face him . . .

. . . he kisses me.

CHAPTER ELEVEN

Never before in my life have I fallen so eagerly, so effortlessly, so weightlessly into a kiss.

It doesn't even feel like there was a starting or stopping point. It feels more like a moment plucked from the heavens that was there all along, just waiting to be discovered.

Somehow, I'm not even surprised. I've felt an electrical current connecting me to Declan since the moment I laid eyes on him. This kiss doesn't just feel right, it feels inevitable.

My arms fold around his neck while his hands caress the small of my back, pulling me closer as our lips explore each other's, touching, tasting, probing. Suddenly, all my doubts and apprehensions have fallen away. All I know, all I care about, is that we're in each other's arms, and nothing could feel more natural.

Declan peers dreamily at my lips as he pulls away. Then his gaze slowly drifts northward until he's staring into my eyes. "You're beautiful," he says in a throaty whisper.

Looking into his eyes is like looking into a crystal—seeing everything, seeing nothing, blinded by sparkling light.

He leans in for another kiss, and this one seems to last an eternity. I'm lightheaded when he finally pulls away.

"Wanna go somewhere?"

I study his face for a second, momentarily disoriented. *Go somewhere*?

"Do you mean now?" I ask.

His mouth slides into a sideways grin. "Nah, I meant New Year's Eve. Yes, genius. Now."

Oh. Um . . .

"C'mon," I coo in a sultry voice, taking his arm and guiding him closer to my car. "We can sit in here." If he has more in mind than I'm willing to commit to, better to stay on my own turf.

I open the door and slip into the driver's seat while Declan walks around and gets in on the passenger side. I check my reflection quickly in the mirror and frown. My mascara's a little smudgy, and my hair's kinda matted against my face from perspiration. Oh well. Nothing I can do about it now, other than swipe my index finger under my eyes and toss a stick of gum into my mouth. Grandpa's car smells musty from the stack of newspapers in the back seat, but I'm grateful the front seat of his fifteen-year-old Mercury is a single unit rather than bucket seats, just in case we happen to fall into each other's arms again.

As soon as Declan shuts his door, he's leaning in again, this time pressing his palms against my cheeks as he kisses me. I run my hands through his hair, that beautiful sun-streaked hair that looks sexy even when it's limp from humidity. His salty lips taste of beer. We kiss a couple more minutes, pulling away abruptly when headlights flash nearby.

I look out the windshield, which is already starting to fog up, and see a bar employee pulling out of the parking lot. Another is walking toward her car, pulling her hair out of a ponytail. Oh God. Is this tacky? We'll be back here for more jobs throughout the summer. I don't want the staff thinking

I'm some kind of a bimbo. Still, when Declan pulls me in for another kiss after scanning the parking lot with only the most cursory of glances, I don't resist.

Finally, it's only our oxygen requirements that cause us to disentangle.

"You sure you don't want to go somewhere?" he asks.

I smile. "We *are* somewhere," I say, and he sucks in his lips.

"Let's talk," I tell him. "I want to get to know you better."

He pauses, then says tersely, "Whatever."

I stiffen a little. *That* was an awfully pissy reaction. But I'm being overly critical, right? I mean, of *course* any normal guy is gonna try to push things physically as far as he can. How many dudes are dying to "talk" in the middle of a make-out session?

Well, tough. Yeah, I'm loving the lip-locking as much as he is. But I really *do* want to get to know him better, a few things in particular . . .

I give him a sideways glance and ask, "What's going on with the band? What's up between you and Mike?"

He averts his eyes and cocks his head. "I dunno. He's always riding my ass."

I turn to face him fully. "But *why*?"

Declan pauses, seeming to consider his answer, then says, "His girlfriend dumped him, and he thinks I had something to do with it."

I swallow hard. "Did you?"

He snorts. "*No*."

I weave my fingers together. "But why would he think that if—"

"Who knows." He waves a hand through the air.

Crickets chirp in the woods behind the bar. "So . . . do you have a girlfriend?"

Declan grins at me and cups his hand behind my neck. "I dunno . . . do I?"

I smile back, then turn earnest. "Listen, Declan, when the guys asked me to join the band, I had no intention of trying to take your place or anything."

"It's cool," he says. "There's room for both of us."

"Exactly. I think Zach just liked having another harmony part."

"You're good," Declan tells me, his voice husky again. "And you're gorgeous."

He moves in for another kiss, but I pull back slightly, my eyebrows weaving together. "I just really don't want you thinking I'm sketchy or anything."

He studies my face and laughs. "You are way overthinking this."

"Yeah, I'm really good at that."

"You're really good at a lot of things."

He kisses me again, and after a couple of moments, I reluctantly pull away. "My grandpa will get worried if I'm not home soon," I say.

He purses his lips. "Right."

"But, hey . . . I'm really glad we had a chance to . . . clear things up."

He chortles, nodding toward the foggy windshield. "Is that what we've been doing?"

"Yeah," I say softly. "I think it is."

"Maybe we can clear things up again tomorrow night."

My heart thuds against my shirt. "Well," I say, "I don't know about you, but I'll be hanging out at Sheehan's."

He smacks himself lightly against the side of his head. "What do you know? Me, too."

"So . . . see you then? Or you can call me if you want . . ."

He hesitates, and my muscles tense. Was that too pushy? Too desperate-sounding?

But now he's pulling his cell phone out of his pocket. "Gimme your number," he says, and I do.

"Talk soon?" I say as he reaches for the door handle.

"Yeah. Soon."

• • •

"Aw, Grandpa. You shouldn't have waited up."

Grandpa closes his book and rises to greet me, tightening the sash of his plaid bathrobe as I walk in the front door and lock it behind me.

"I'd have been up anyway," he fibs, kissing my cheek. "How'd your concert go tonight?"

I smile, and we sit on the couch. "Not a concert," I remind him. "Just playing background music for a handful of people. But they actually got into it toward the end. It was fun."

I'm forcing myself to sound understated. I rolled down the window on my way home and let my hair blow in the breeze, cranking up the radio and practically shouting along with the lyrics, banging my head to the beat. I feel like I could run around the block a hundred times and still not deplete my excess energy. I can still taste Declan's salty, beer-flavored kisses on my lips. I feel like my heart might burst with exhilaration.

But no need to tip my hand to Grandpa. I totally get that my suck-face session with Declan may have been a one-time deal; we were both on a music high, after all, and he was definitely just a wee bit drunk, and we just happened to be the only people left in the parking lot. Still, there was no denying our chemistry. And that joke he made about wondering whether he had a girlfriend? Signals don't get much clearer than that, right? Still . . . who knows.

If Declan and I end up being, you know, a thing, I'm sure Grandpa would be cool with it. But I don't yet really know what we are. I just know what I want us to be.

I kick off my shoes and prop my feet on the coffee table, crossing my ankles. "I can't wait to play with the band again tomorrow night," I say.

Grandpa nods. "Honey, I'm proud of you for being so productive this summer."

I lightly finger a lock of my hair. "Thanks. It helps to stay busy."

A pinched look crosses Grandpa's face. He pauses, then leans closer. "Scarlett, I don't want what's happened to affect you. I want you to move forward and focus on your own life."

I sigh discreetly and squeeze my hands together. As crushed as Grandpa was by Liam's death, he was the strong one at the memorial service, slipping his arm behind Mom's back to steady her when she and Dad crumbled while hearing the steady stream of testimonials. At the reception after the service, he was in full host mode, shaking hands and greeting people in a clear, steady voice. He was like that at Grandma's funeral, too. I guess it's a coping mechanism—and clearly a good one. Grandpa has had plenty of practice rolling with the punches. Too much practice. But his resilience has kept him going, and he preaches it regularly to us. His platitudes came fast and furious on the heels of Liam's death: "Life is for the living," "Hope smiles from the threshold of the year to come," "A wounded deer leaps the highest," "The best is yet to be . . ." Blah, blah, blah.

I don't mean to be dismissive. I love how strong he is, and

I'm glad he's still around to help keep the rest of us strong. But sometimes, I wish he could just let us hang out with our sadness.

Or, as in this case, to at least allow us to make even the most fleeting reference to Liam without trying to shush us or jolly us back from the dark side.

"I can feel sad and move forward at the same time," I tell him quietly.

He opens his mouth to respond, but I opt to gently cut him off at the pass. "Hey, Grandpa, tell me again how you met Grandma."

Confusion flickers in his eyes. "How I met your grandmother?"

"Yeah," I say, burrowing deeper into the burgundy couch.

"Well . . ." He chuckles and peers into space. "I was the assistant manager at Davison's, and your grandmother had gone to a clerk, trying to return a scarf. She didn't have the receipt, and the clerk explained that she couldn't give your grandmother a refund without the receipt. Well, your grandmother just wouldn't take no for an answer, so the clerk referred her to me."

I smile, loving the easy cadence in Grandpa's voice.

"I offered her a seat in my office and explained just as politely as I could that rules were rules and that as much as we valued her business, we simply weren't in a position to break the rules willy-nilly."

I sputter with laughter at his Grandpa-speak, and he eyes me quizzically.

"What?"

"Nothing," I assure him. "Keep going."

"Well, your grandmother was indignant! She explained that she had bought the scarf only twenty minutes earlier and that the wind had blown the receipt from her fingers when she stepped outside. It was April, and as I recall, it *was* a particularly windy day . . ."

I giggle some more.

"And I expressed my sympathy, but I couldn't help but ask, 'Why did you buy the scarf in the first place if all you were going to do was march right back inside and return it?' Well, she bowed up like a prizefighter and said, 'That, sir, is none of your business!' "

Grandpa and I laugh together.

"I said, 'Yes, ma'am, it *is* my business,' " he continues cheerfully. "Even when a customer had the receipt in hand, we still requested a reason for the return. It was for the customer's own protection! If the merchandise was defective, why, we needed to know, so we wouldn't return it to the inventory. And your grandmother didn't even have her receipt!

"And *then*," Grandpa continues, clearly on a roll, "your grandmother turned on the poor clerk, insisting that Ethel—*Ethel*, my best employee!—should have put the receipt in the bag so it wouldn't fly away. Well, we had no such policy! And for that matter, why didn't your grandmother put the receipt in the bag herself?"

I'm giggling nonstop at this point, picturing Grandpa turning a ninety-seven-cent scarf into a matter of principle and imagining Grandma's feisty indignation at being shot down.

"Touché," I tell him through my laughter.

"Touché, indeed. Rules are rules."

Grandpa nods sharply, then leans in with a wink as he reaches his favorite part of the story. "So I took her out for a cup of coffee and a pastry instead."

"And she never got her refund?" I ask through my laughter, even though I've heard the story a thousand times.

"The coffee and the pastry were worth more than the scarf!"

We're both laughing now.

Grandma stayed feisty to the very end, threatening to sue the hospital if they put one more tube up her nose during her final hospitalization. Grandpa was usually the diplomat, the voice of reason, but as soon as he was clear on what Grandma wanted, he raised hell on her behalf. "She said no more tubes!" I remember him bellowing so loudly that the walls shook. I'm sure he scared the poor nurse half to death, but we were all relieved, grateful Grandma had such a fierce advocate. As much as we hated the thought of saying goodbye, none of us wanted her to linger like that.

I wonder if I'll have what they had: more than sixty years of devotion. I don't think about it much—I don't even want to get married until I have at least a decade under my belt writing in New York City after college (that's the plan, anyway). But God, did Grandma and Grandpa made it look tempting. How cool to be in love for so long. How cool to be in love, *period.*

I've still got a silly grin on my face, still tasting Declan's kisses on my lips.

I sigh contentedly. "I sure do miss Grandma." I say it lightly, spontaneously, but almost immediately regret it, fearing I'm triggering another glass-half-full lecture.

But instead, Grandpa keeps smiling and his eyes keep sparkling as he says simply, "I sure do, too."

That's Grandpa. He's always full of surprises.

• • •

"Well, *something's* definitely up."

I called Varun as soon as I got to bed. I was dying to talk

to him—adrenaline was still coursing through my veins—but with the same rationale I had used for Grandpa, I didn't really want to tip my hand just yet about Declan. So when Varun answered his phone, I played it cool, casually telling him I just felt like touching base. But he immediately sniffed out an agenda.

"Nothing's up," I assure him unconvincingly.

"It's Polyester Guy, isn't it?"

My chin drops. It's uncanny how transparent I am to Varun. "I bow to your superpowers, my friend."

"What the hell have you been up to?" he asks.

I grin and hug the one-eyed bear to my chest. "Declan and I kinda kissed in the car after our set was over tonight."

"Nothing tacky about *that*."

"It wasn't tacky," I scold, laughing.

"I guess it depends on how untacky his car is. What kind of wheels does he have?"

I cringe. "We were in Grandpa's car. It's a Mercury."

"Okay, ew."

"Yeah, that just occurred to me," I concede. "But it was just a kiss. Well, a kiss or two . . . or ten. Next time, we'll kiss someplace with no Grandpa associations, I promise."

"So you have a date?"

I bite my bottom lip. "Well . . . no. But I gave him my phone number. And we'll see each other all the time anyway. I mean, between band practice and gigs, we'll be hanging out together almost every day."

"Which will be totally un-awkward if things fizzle."

I huff indignantly. "You're such a pessimist."

"Just be careful," Varun says. "I'm not used to you being giddy."

"I am not giddy," I say giddily.

"Christ," he groans.

I twirl a piece of hair in my fingers and ask, "So what's up with you? Meeting any cute guys at your job?"

"Yeah. The scent of formaldehyde wafting through my pores brings 'em running."

"Seriously."

Varun sighs. "I work in a lab, Scarlett. A lab with a sixty-year-old pathologist who wears a polka-dot bowtie."

"Yeah, we've gotta step things up on your end. Wait till we start college. I'm gonna be, like, your personal matchmaker."

"Gonna ask you to pass on that plan, Scarletta."

I laugh, then turn serious. "Varun, are you really out to your parents? I mean, have you had an actual conversation, as opposed to just assuming they've figured things out by now?"

Pause.

"What does it matter?"

Uh-oh. There's an edge in his voice, but I push forward anyway.

"I think it *does* matter," I say, sitting up and gripping the phone tighter. "I think you're afraid to have a boyfriend because it would make it too real to your mom and dad. But I don't think you're giving them enough credit. And you're gonna have to get real sooner or later anyway."

Longer pause. "You handle your stuff, and I'll handle mine."

Ouch.

"We always handle each other's stuff," I say sulkily.

Varun sighs. "Okay," he finally says, sounding more conciliatory. "I'll handle your stuff right now: No more lip-locking Polyester Guy until he takes you on an actual date. And even then, take it slow. I want him showing up at your doorstep, opening doors for you, paying for your dinner—the whole nine yards."

Okay, now *I'm* a little peeved. "What makes you think he won't?"

"Not a thing. I'm just saying that if he *doesn't*, it's a deal breaker. There. Now I can cross your stuff off my list."

My stomach muscles tighten. Conversations with Varun are usually fun and effortless. When did this one go south?

"Guess I better go," I say.

He *tsks*. "Don't be mad. You're the one who started it."

"So you said that just to hurt me?"

He huffs. "No! I said it to *help* you. I'm serious. I don't want you hanging out with anybody who doesn't deserve you. Pay attention to whether he steps up. If he does, great. If he doesn't, shake him off before you get any . . . giddier . . . than you already are. That's all I'm saying."

"Yeah, I've really got to go."

"Stop," he says in a weary voice. "Stop being mad."

I want to stop. I'm not used to being pissed at Varun. I wanted him to share my high spirits, not douse them with ice water. I can't bear to feel distant from him. But for now, I just need to be alone with my thoughts.

"Talk soon," I promise.

I end the call, place my phone on the bedside table, punch my pillow, and hug the bear against my chest.

With all the noise swimming in my head, I have a feeling it's gonna be a long night.

CHAPTER TWELVE

Nothing.

I'm embarrassed to admit to myself that I've checked my phone approximately forty times since my lifeguard shift started this morning. All for nothing, of course, because I haven't received a single call or text from Declan.

Nothing. Nada. Nil.

I blow my whistle at a couple of kids running on the cement by the pool, making a time-out sign with my hands. They reluctantly transition to speed walking, pumping their arms like windmills, then glance at me for approval. I give them a thumbs-up.

Nice, right? Sitting perched several feet above everyone else and having them respond instantly to my commands is a nice departure from my usual bit-player role in my social life.

I always snicker at articles or blogs about girls "choosing" the wrong guys for romance, like this stream of studs is paraded in front of us, awaiting our approval. This may be true for girls like Sara, but not for me and not for the vast majority of girls I know. I don't feel like I've ever "chosen" a guy in my life. The guys I've dated—or, more accurately, hung out with—fell into my life mostly by default, generally due to circumstances like logistics or process of elimination. I don't feel like I ever "chose" a guy.

Until now. Dammit, I really like Declan, and I like him enough to go for it. Yes, I'm willing to take a risk, to take a stab for once in my life at "choosing" a guy. But as I glance at my phone for the forty-first time of the day, I see the downside to this empowerment. What if Declan doesn't want to be chosen? What if last night was just a one-time thing? What if Varun's insistence on stand-up behavior turns out to be less lame than I suspect?

Not that I don't consider Declan a stand-up guy. He's been perfectly nice. He gave me a ride home after our first practice! It doesn't get much more gentlemanly than that, right? And frankly, if he's a little looser, a little more casual, or even a little more, you know, *experienced* than Varun might like, well, that's fine with me. I just like him. Period. I don't want to overthink it. And who knows, maybe the reason he isn't calling or texting is because he's planning to stop by . . .

"Hey, Scarlett."

I jump a little, then look down and see Zach peering up at me, blocking the sun with his hand.

"Oh, hey . . ."

"Didn't mean to startle you."

"No, no . . . I'm just sitting here trying to keep kids from face-planting on the cement." I glance around. "Where's your mom?"

"Um, not feeling her best, unfortunately," Zach says. "But the guys came along today."

My heart skips a beat, and my eyes scan the grounds.

"Mike and Kyle just dove in," Zach says, pointing toward the lap lanes.

"Oh . . ."

"So did you have fun last night?" Zach asks, and I feel my neck grow warm. What does he mean by *fun*? Does Declan talk to him about, you know, stuff? And if so, does Zach know we made out last night? I don't know why I feel self-conscious about the possibility. In the first place, he probably *doesn't* know, and in the second, who cares if he does? It's not like Declan and I did anything wrong. Still, I wouldn't want Zach getting the wrong idea. And I don't want him thinking I'm not serious about the music. I think back to his solo last night—"I will see you there on the other side"—infusing such passion and energy into even the saddest of circumstances, and it occurs to me that his respect is very, very important to me.

"It was a blast," I say, then sneak a glance to gauge his reaction.

He's just standing there looking pleasant, a breeze blowing through his light-brown hair. If Zach knows what happened last night, he isn't letting on.

"God," I tell him, "when the crowd finally got into our music toward the end of the night . . . that was awesome!"

"Yeah, typically the drunker the audience, the better we sound."

I laugh. "That wasn't it. They were really loving it. Then, when we played your song at the end and brought the house down? That place was rocking." I tilt my sunglasses upward as I look him in the eye. "You're so talented."

Zach smiles. "Thanks."

He clears his throat, then says, "Tonight should be even better . . . more of a family crowd."

"Aw, you mean you won't be rescuing me from drunks between sets? That was half of the fun."

"I'll have reinforcements tonight. Hopefully our granddads will be on hand to keep everybody in line. We can enlist them as bouncers if necessary."

I nod. "Yeah. And if our music can get *them* on their feet with their titanium knees, we'll know we're solid."

"For sure."

I swish my ponytail behind my back. "Maybe your mom can come tonight, too. I mean, if she's feeling better . . ."

I'm never sure how much to probe about Zach's mom. He doesn't volunteer any information, and I don't want to pry, but I'd hate for him to think I wasn't interested or sympathetic.

"That'd be great," he says simply, then turns toward the sound of my name being called. Mike and Kyle have emerged from their swim across the pool and are waving at me as they jerk water from their faces. I smile and wave back.

"No horseplay, you guys," I call out playfully, and Mike responds by pretending to swamp Kyle. I point to my whistle, mock-threatening to call him out.

I turn back to Zach and squeeze my palms together. "If Declan were here, we could multitask and practice our vocals at the pool."

Zach smiles, but I feel my stomach clench. How stupid did that sound, injecting Declan into the conversation? Could I be any more obvious? But yet again, if Zach has a clue about my crush, he's not letting on. "Well," he says, "I guess I'll go get my laps in. See you at six at Sheehan's?"

"Right, six. Can't wait."

"Yeah, me too." He waves, walks to the side of the pool and dives in to join Mike and Kyle. My eyes follow them as they race across the pool, Zach easily leading the way.

Then I scan the pool and blow my whistle at another couple of noodle-whackers.

Just a couple of hours till my shift is over, then by the time I shower and change, it'll be time for the Beastings to start setting up.

I glance at my phone one more time, just in case I've missed any texts.

Nope.

Oh, well.

I won't have to wait much longer.

• • •

"Hot night, huh?"

Ooh, brilliant. Another weather comment.

Declan glances at me but doesn't respond, continuing to adjust the controls on his amp.

I lower my chin and lick my lips.

Declan was almost half an hour late getting here to set up. All the heavy lifting had already been done—unloading equipment from the van, setting it up on the deck at Sheehan's—so there's not a lot for Declan to do other than plug in his guitar and tune it up. Oh, and absorb the hate waves radiating from Mike's eyes. That must be a formidable job in itself.

A dinner crowd has already begun trickling in. Mike and Kyle are murmuring to each other, and Zach is busy tweaking the set list, scratching through a couple of songs with a pen and jotting replacements in their place.

I wish I could at least catch Declan's eye and offer a supportive smile or crack a witty remark or . . . *something*. Did Mike have to make such a big deal of Declan's being a half-hour late? Geez . . .

But we'll push past it. The night is just beginning. Once we're a song or two into our first set, everybody will relax and fall under the spell of the music, just like last night. By the last song, we'll be exhilarated and adrenaline-fueled. Then . . .

Then we'll see.

It took me ten minutes before leaving the house to convince Grandpa it was a good idea for me to ride my bike to Sheehan's. He didn't want me biking after dark, but I assured him it wouldn't be a big deal for me to catch a ride home with Zach or one of the others after we were done. *Or one of the others* being the operative words. I couldn't wait to tease Declan that I really *did* need a ride home tonight.

Zach starts handing out copies of the set list, going over a few last-minute instructions. As I sling my guitar strap over my shoulder, I look out into the parking lot and see Grandpa approaching, walking with Zach's grandparents.

"Looks like our groupies are back," Zach says, following my gaze.

I smile. "You know Grandpa's hardcore when he's willing to miss *Jeopardy!* But I'll have to run him off after the first set, before it gets dark."

I wave to the group as they make their way onto the deck, Grandpa adjusting his tie. He's cheered me on plenty of times before. He trekked to Atlanta semi-regularly to hear Liam and me play with the Joneses. I remember one sweltering day last summer when we were playing at a fair. When Liam got overheated and passed out, Grandpa was the first one on the stage, sprinting up like a teenager and cradling Liam in his arms. Liam was only out for a few seconds; once he drank some water, he was fine. But Grandpa sat pitched forward in the front row for the rest of the concert, ready to spring back into action if needed.

I shake my head slowly as my brain reboots for a reality check. Even now, in recalling that memory, I'm convincing myself that Liam was overheated, as opposed to high, when he passed out that day. Even Mom and Dad were clueless at that stage. But at least they faced reality eventually. Not me. If Liam hadn't dropped dead, I'd probably *still* be in denial, still begging my parents to get off his back, to give him some space, to stop making such a big deal about a few pills.

I just couldn't wrap my head around him being an addict. Granted, Liam had already started college by the time he got hooked, so I only saw him on weekends and holidays. But still, he always seemed fine to me: caring, sweet, and crazy conscientious, just like Grandpa . . . When we played in the band together, no matter what else was going on, Liam was always watching out for me, teaching me new chords or going over a harmony part, making sure I felt comfortable. And of course, he was super protective of me, routinely shooing away drunks or creeps who might get a little too friendly between sets.

So why wasn't I more protective of *him*? Why did I brush it off when Liam passed out on stage? Why did I take his side when Mom and Dad would pound him for getting his prescription refilled long after his injury had healed? Why did I take him for granted, letting him watch out for me without bothering to return the favor? I didn't think he needed looking after. I couldn't believe he was anything short of perfect, just like I couldn't believe he was really dead when Mom started screaming into the phone when the paramedics called at three o'clock in the morning. What an idiot I was.

I take a deep breath, and Zach guides us through a few notes and chords to make sure we're in tune.

"Sounding good," I tell Declan after Zach gives him a thumbs-up.

Okay, I seriously need to stop saying stupid things.

But this time, he smiles at me . . . just a quick smile, but we're connecting.

Yeah. We're connecting.

Maybe this night will turn out okay after all.

CHAPTER THIRTEEN

"Oh my goodness, you sound marvelous!"

I smile. "Thanks, Mrs. Carver."

As soon as our break began, Declan headed inside to the bar. My plan was to amble casually in the same direction, but Grandpa and his friends have cut me off at the pass. Right after I hopped off the stage, they waved me over to their table on the deck. I'd hoped for a quick stopover—saying hi, thanking them for coming, sending Grandpa on his way, then heading inside—but Grandpa is pulling up a chair for me.

"Seriously," Mrs. Carver says, the lines around her eyes crinkling. "You sound amazing!"

I wave away the compliment. "Zach's the amazing one," I say. "He's an incredible songwriter."

"He was making up songs before he knew how to read!" she trills.

"And playing the guitar by the second grade," her husband adds.

"He's super talented," I agree. "Hey, I'm getting to know your whole family. I met Claire last night, and I see Zach's mom with him at the pool a lot."

Mrs. Carver offers a pinched smile while her husband

lowers his eyes. "She looks great, by the way," I say. "Zach's mom, I mean . . . your daughter. How's she feeling?"

I know it sounds like the world's lamest question—"She's dying, thanks for asking"—but I don't know what else to say.

"She's hanging in there," Mrs. Carver says in a hushed tone.

I purse my lips. "I'm so sorry about what she's going through."

Zach's grandparents nod as my words hang in the air.

Finally, Grandpa claps his hands. "Well, Scarletta, as much as I've enjoyed this, I better hit the road before it gets dark."

He gives me a double take as he rises from his chair and adds, "You're sure you don't need the car?"

"Yeah, on second thought, I do, so if you don't mind hitching a ride home . . ."

Grandpa studies me for a second before I let him off the hook. "I'm kidding."

He wrinkles his nose playfully.

"I'm fine," I assure him. "Hey, thanks for coming. And drive safely."

I hop up to kiss his cheek. I think I can slip away gracefully now.

Oops. Not so fast. Zach, Mike, and Kyle have just walked over to the table and are pulling up chairs.

"You've never sounded better!" Mrs. Carver tells them as they settle in.

Zach sweeps an arm in my direction. "Our new secret weapon."

I feel my cheeks grow warm. "*Right*," I protest, smiling shyly.

"Wait till the second set," Mike tells Mrs. Carver. "She kills it on lead vocals."

"Oh, I wish we could stay for it, but we've got to be going, too," she says, pulling her peach-colored sweater tighter against her shoulders.

Her husband nods. "We're already up past our bedtime," he jokes.

He stands up, pulls out his wife's chair, and offers her his arm as she rises to her feet.

"I'll walk you to your car," Zach tells them.

We say good night and watch them walk out to the parking lot, Zach's hand resting lightly on his grandmother's back.

"So," I say to Mike and Kyle, "you think the first set went okay?"

Their eyes lock. "I think it could go better with a couple of adjustments," Mike says evenly. "But you were great."

I shift uneasily in my chair. I assume his comment was another Declan dig. But I don't want to know for sure, so I opt to change the subject. "So how did you guys get together? The Beastings, I mean."

The tiki torches lining the deck flicker in the dark, moths darting in and out of their glow.

"Let's see," Kyle says, resting his chin on his pale, bony knuckles. "I think we owe it all to Miss Caffrey."

He and Mike laugh.

"Zach was always writing songs in class," Mike says. "He scribbled one down in calculus after he finished a test, and when he passed it to me, our teacher thought he was slipping me answers."

"Her face was beet red," Kyle says, leaning back in his seat. "She was like, 'Zachary Spencer, what are you thinking, cheating on a test? You, of all people! I wouldn't have believed it if

I hadn't seen it with my own eyes. I am *deeply*, *deeply* disappointed.' " I giggle at his soprano imitation.

"It wouldn't have fazed her a bit if it had been Kyle or me," Mike quips. "But *Zach* . . ." He clutches his heart dramatically.

"So she starts reading the note aloud, and it's song lyrics," Kyle says, grinning.

"And not my best effort," Zach interjects wryly, rejoining us.

"Miss Caffrey reading it aloud was classic," Mike says as Zach sits down. "The distraction presented an excellent opportunity for the rest of us to *actually* cheat."

We laugh.

"So after she finishes reading it, Miss Caffrey says, 'Write a song about me, and I'll let you off the hook for passing lyrics during a test,' " Kyle continues.

"Okay, that could be interpreted as borderline creepy . . ." I tease.

"Nah," Mike says. "She's approximately 120 years old. I think she actually taught my grandparents. Anyway, Zach of course delivers the goods. The very next day, he hands Miss Caffrey her song."

"Sing it to us, bro," Kyle begs dreamily, leaning in for emphasis. "Sing us the song that put the twinkle back in Caffrey's eyes."

Zach drops his head and sputters with laughter.

"Yeah, let's add it to the set list tonight," Mike says.

"I'm up for it," I joke.

"How did that chorus go?" Mike says. "Something like, 'Miss Caffrey, can't you calculate my love?' "

We're all laughing.

"I think I managed to work the words 'partial derivative' into one of the verses," Zach says.

"Dude!" Kyle says. "I can't believe you wrote multiple verses. A single one would have sufficed. What a suck-up."

"It would have been impossible to express everything I felt about Miss Caffrey in a single verse," Zach explains earnestly, making us laugh harder.

"You guys definitely had more fun in calculus than I did," I say.

"Well, Zach did, at least," Mike says. "I noticed Miss Caffrey slipping him a Jolly Rancher from her candy jar every day from that point forward."

"God, and I actually had to work for my A," Kyle grouses.

"At least it took with you," Mike tells him. "You're the pre-med major."

"Ahem. Engineering major here," Zach reminds them. "Her legacy lives on in me, as well."

A waitress stops by and hands us all soft drinks from a tray. "Compliments of the house," she says, and we all hoist our glasses in gratitude.

As I take a sip, my eyes drift toward the door. I wonder if Declan will come out and join us.

Doesn't look like it.

But it's cool. I love drinking in all these good vibes.

It's been a while since I laughed like this.

• • •

"No, really, I don't mind."

Kyle has offered to carry one of the smaller amps to the van for me as we pack up our equipment, but I pull it closer to my side.

Our performance went just fine—not as electric as last night's, but then, most of the Sheehan's crowd was too busy licking barbecue sauce off their fingers to applaud. Still, they seemed pleased as they drifted off the deck after we played our last song.

I carry the amp off the deck, tugging at the humidity-dampened shirt clinging to my body. I wish I'd had a chance to duck into the restroom and towel myself off, maybe spritz on a little perfume. Declan's already at the van, so I'll finally have a chance to talk to him.

I walk through the parking lot and approach him as he loads up a couple of guitars. I wait for him to turn around, then offer a little wave.

"Hi," I say.

He runs his fingers through his hair. "Hi."

I hand him the amp. A few other people are milling around the parking lot, mostly servers and bartenders heading to their cars after finishing their shifts, but the rest of the band is still on the deck, and Declan and I have plenty of privacy.

"You sounded great tonight," I tell him.

"Thanks. You, too."

He starts walking back toward the deck.

"Um . . ." I say, hovering in the same spot.

He stops in midstride and looks back at me. "Yeah?"

"Uh . . ." I fumble with my fingers. "I guess we'll be finished loading up in a couple of minutes."

"Right."

"So . . . since it was such a great gig, we should totally celebrate."

He hesitates for a moment, and my stomach muscles

clench. But then he smiles, his lips pressed tightly together as a dimple burrows into his cheek.

"Totally," he says, his clear-blue eyes glimmering in the darkness.

I feel my muscles relax.

"Yeah," I say. "Totally."

He winks at me, then resumes walking back to the deck.

I exhale through O-shaped lips.

Chill, Scarlett, I tell myself. *Everything's fine. We'll be alone soon, and that's what matters.*

Still . . . I wish it had happened a little more organically. Did I come on too strong? But I shake the thought out of my head. After all, *he's* the one who came on to *me* last night.

I squeeze my hands together, then walk back to the deck.

The other guys are zipping guitars into gig bags and grabbing armloads of equipment.

"Right behind you," I tell them as they head to the van.

I watch them for a moment. Zach and Kyle are chatting while they walk. Mike's right on their heels, and Declan is a few paces behind them. I seize the opportunity to slip into the restroom. I walk inside and frown at my reflection in the mirror. My hair looks damp and matted. My makeup is a little smudgy. My shirt is still clinging to my body.

Oh well. This is how I looked last night, too, and that seemed to suit Declan just fine. Still, I think I can manage to spruce myself up just a little. I pull off my shirt, turn on the sink, moisten a few paper towels and dab them against my skin. Then I fan myself dry, reach into my purse and pull out some deodorant and perfume. I swipe the deodorant under my arms and spritz the perfume on my neck and wrists.

I put my shirt back on, run a brush through my hair, pop

a stick of gum in my mouth, rub tinted gloss against my lips, and give my reflection one last look.

Better.

I head back out, slinging my purse over my shoulder as the door shuts behind me.

I walk back to the deck and see Zach, Mike, and Kyle grabbing more gear. My eyes scan the area, first around the deck, then down to the parking lot. No Declan.

Weird. Maybe he ducked into a restroom, too.

I pick up a couple of mics and walk beside Kyle as he makes his way back to the van with another load.

"Your drums were awesome on 'Back It Up,' " I tell him.

"Thanks. I think it was a good call for Zach to end the set with it. It's one of those songs the crowd feels like they already know, even if they've never heard it before."

"Right? I actually heard people singing the chorus after the song was over. Hey, too bad we couldn't squeeze in the calculus song."

"Yeah, this crowd seemed like they were in the mood for math."

Now that we're in the parking lot, I see that Declan's truck is missing. Hmm . . .

"Wonder where Declan is."

"He left," Kyle tells me.

My muscles tighten. "Ya sure?"

Kyle nods. "He took off a couple of minutes ago."

"But we weren't even finished loading up yet—"

"Yeah, it's totally unprecedented for Declan to bail on his responsibilities."

He left? What the hell? Maybe he went to grab something,

then head right back? Or maybe he expects me to meet up with him somewhere?

But where might that be? And how would he expect me to know? I don't even have his phone number.

But he has mine. I quickly retrieve my phone and glance at the screen.

Nothing.

"This is the last of it."

Kyle and I look at Zach as he and Mike approach us with arms full of gear.

I step out of the way so they can load it up, then glance over at the bike I've chained to a post. I guess I'll be pedaling home in the dark after all.

What an idiot I am.

"Great work tonight," Zach tells us. "Practice tomorrow at four?"

"Yeah, about that . . ."

We all look at Mike.

"Declan was thirty minutes late tonight," he tells us, planting his hands on his hips. "I say we cut him loose. That's not personal; it's just good business."

Zach shifts his weight, considering Mike's words.

Mike nods in my direction. "We've got everything in the band that we need. Declan's weighing us down."

An anxious moment hangs in the air. I open my mouth to speak, then shut it again. What do I know about anything? I'm the moron who'll be biking home in the dark. Maybe kicking Declan out of the band is the best thing that could happen. Regardless, I definitely haven't earned a vote.

"Let's see how it goes at practice tomorrow," Zach says quietly. "Deal?"

Mike and Kyle pause, then murmur their grudging approval.

I squeeze my lips together. "Well . . . see you guys tomorrow," I say, then head to my bike.

I'm just a few steps away when I hear Zach's voice.

"Scarlett?"

I turn back around. "Yeah?"

"Need a ride?"

• • •

"Ya sure you're feeling okay?"

I glance at Zach as he drives the van and manage a smile. "Yeah, I'm fine. Just tired."

My elbow rests on the open window as a breeze blows through my hair.

"So," Zach says, rounding the hill that leads to the bridge, "do you have any thoughts about Declan?"

I glance at him anxiously. *Any thoughts? As a matter of fact, I do: he's an asshole.* But what exactly is Zach getting at?

"I mean about whether we should keep him in the band," Zach clarifies.

Oh.

I shrug. "I don't get a vote," I say. "I'm just grateful to be in the band. I'll support whatever decision you guys make."

"Sure you get a vote," he says. "You're part of the band, too."

"Yeah, but just barely. And you guys clearly have a history . . ."

Zach rubs his chin with one hand as he steers with the other. "I wish Dec were more reliable, but he really is a good musician," he says. "Plus, you know, he's a friend. I hate cutting anybody loose. And I was hoping that the personal stuff would blow over. But maybe not . . ."

"So, the personal stuff. Has it been building up for a while?"

Zach considers his words, then says, "Mike and Dec have never exactly been the best of friends. But things kinda came to a head last weekend, right around the time you joined the band, unfortunately. I'm not really clear on the details."

I suck in my lips. When Declan mentioned that Mike blamed him for a breakup, I gave him the benefit of the doubt, like maybe the girl had a crush on him that she couldn't shake. Nothing Declan could do about that, right? But maybe he led her on. Maybe more . . .

Whatever. Who the hell cares.

"I'm just so psyched to be playing with you guys," I say.

"So tell me about the band you played in before," Zach says, crossing the bridge.

I twirl a lock of hair in my fingers. "It was my brother's band. He died a few months ago."

I hadn't planned on saying that, but there it was. And I said it without my voice cracking. Maybe I'm getting stronger.

"I heard about that," Zach says softly, his eyes on the road. "I'm so sorry."

Stars are dotting the night sky.

"He was amazing on the guitar," I say, gazing into the breeze. "He did some songwriting, too. He wasn't as good at it as you are, but . . ."

"I'm sure he was incredible," Zach says. "Losing him so young . . . I can't imagine what that feels like."

I glance at Zach, wondering if I should mention his mom. Yes, he *can* imagine what it feels like. But what is there to say?

It sucks to be us? I wait a minute to see if Zach will elaborate, but he doesn't.

So I keep talking. "Liam dislocated a shoulder playing basketball and got hooked on the pills the doctor prescribed." I figure that if Zach knows I have a dead brother, he probably knows why. Grandpa prefers fact-fudging; I prefer context.

"That's really sad."

The streetlights pass by in a blur.

"I get upset with myself," I say, "because I kind of knew he had a problem, but I couldn't really face it. If hadn't had my head up my ass, I could have helped him. I feel like I failed him." Okay, *now* my voice is breaking, but just barely.

"You know that's not true," Zach says. "You loved him. That's all you can do . . . just love people while you have the chance."

I rest a nail against my bottom lip. "But he knew how much I looked up to him," I say, my voice steady again. "If he knew I was onto him, maybe he would've stopped, for my sake. And I should've known because . . . because I knew *everything* about Liam. We had this really special connection."

Zach glances at me, his deep-brown eyes warm and caring. "It's probably because he was so protective of you that you didn't realize how bad the problem was," he says. "I'm sure he did everything he could to hide it from you."

I turn toward Zach, warming to the subject. "I wish people wouldn't hide things," I say. "Keeping secrets just makes things worse."

"I totally agree," he says. "Even if you think you're protecting people, you're not doing them any favors by keeping them in the dark." He glances at me anxiously. "Not that I'm judging your brother . . ."

"No, of course not," I say. "And maybe I couldn't have helped him even if I'd known how bad his addiction was. But God, I would have tried so hard."

Tears spring to my eyes, and I blink them back.

"You know what's weird?" I say. "When I found out Liam was dead, I went a little . . . insane. I remember thinking, *Everybody quit crying! Stop wasting your energy being sad! Now that we know how bad this is, we can fix it. C'mon, everybody, all hands on deck! We gotta save Liam!*"

I watch Zach swallow hard. "I know the feeling."

"Talk about denial," I say absently. "I guess my mind is really good at trying to keep me clueless. You know what else is crazy? I remember thinking, *Okay, I've got to solve this problem, but I need Liam by my side to be able to think straight. If I can just be with him long enough to clear my head. . .*"

I'm staring out the window again, my hair riding the crest of the breeze.

"I've never told these things to anybody before," I say, more to myself than to Zach.

"I'm glad you told me," he says.

A long moment passes.

"It's the red brick one," I say, pointing to the left as he coasts down Grandpa's street.

Zach nods, then pulls into the driveway.

"Thanks so much for the ride," I say. "And thanks for listening. You're really easy to talk to."

He's turning off the ignition.

"You don't have to stop the car," I tell him.

"No problem."

"Zach, really . . ."

But he's already out of the van, heading to the back to

retrieve my bike. I get out as he pulls it from the van, trying to take it from him.

"I've got it," he says, then wheels it toward the porch as I walk by his side.

Once we're on the porch, I study his face for a moment. "My mom always called Liam her 'goodest boy,'" I say as crickets chirp in the yard. "You're the goodest guy, Zach. Just so you know."

Zach drops his chin and smiles. He steadies my bike on the kickstand, then walks toward the front door with me as I fish my key out of my purse.

"Got it," I say, holding it up for his inspection.

"Well . . . see you tomorrow at four?"

"Or at the pool," I say. "I'll be there till two."

He cocks his head. "So you basically work twenty-four seven?"

"Basically."

"Impressive. Wish I could hang out with you. But I've got to run a few errands tomorrow, so . . . four?"

I smile. "Right. Four."

I put the key in the lock and open the door.

"Thanks again," I say.

Zach nods, then walks back to his van.

I wave before shutting the door behind me.

The house is quiet and dark, other than the lamp glowing in the living room. Good. Grandpa didn't wait up this time. I take a deep breath, then hear my cell phone chirp.

I freeze in my tracks. Is it Declan texting? Maybe he really *did* have some kind of plan for meeting up? As much as I hate to admit it to myself, my heart is pattering at the thought.

I pull the phone out of my pocket and stare at the screen.

Tell me everything.

I sigh. It's Varun.

Damn. Why did I have to tell him about Declan? I am a world-class fool.

I'm really tired, I text back. Talk tomorrow?

Uh-oh. I'm thinking that means it either went really well or really bad.

I smile wanly. Nitey-nite.

Details tomorrow, he texts, then signs off with a dolphin emoji.

I stand there for a second, then toss my head back. "Catch a clue," I groan to myself.

I slog toward my bedroom. I've got to get up early for work. It's time to shake Declan out of my head and get some sleep.

Yep.

Time to move on.

CHAPTER FOURTEEN

"It's just a game."

I glare at the freckle-faced kid. "It's never okay to hold somebody under water, even for a second," I tell him, then glance around to see if his mom is anywhere in sight. I see her on a beach chair a few yards away peering at her phone.

"We were just playing around, right?" the kid prods his chubby friend, the one he was holding under water before I climbed down from my chair and went charging in their direction, blowing my whistle and waving for them to get out of the pool.

The chubby boy nods reluctantly, chlorine-scented water dripping from his hair.

I bend down until I'm nose to nose with the freckle-faced kid. "No holding people under water. Ever. Game or no game. If I see you doing it again, I'll throw you out of the pool. Got it?"

He scowls for a second but quickly lowers his eyes and mumbles, "Got it."

I start walking away, my bare feet padding across the cement while I adjust the razorback strap of my Speedo, then turn toward them again. "Don't ever let anybody mess with you and call it a game," I call to the chubby kid.

I climb the ladder back up to my lifeguard chair and lift my sunglasses long enough to lock eyes one more time with the freckle-faced kid: *I'm watching you.*

I've got no patience for bullies. I saw close-up the damage they do. My stomach clenches as I recall watching Varun catch hell for being gay, even before he was ready to admit it to himself. The worst was a spring day in eighth grade. Varun's goal all that year had been to bench-press 175 pounds by high school. He worked so hard at it, pumping iron in gym class and after school. His mom bought him one of those expensive home fitness contraptions, and every time I went to his house, he was in the garage, working out. He was so focused, so disciplined. That's Varun: give him a goal and *dare* him to come up short. Won't happen.

He was so proud of himself that spring day in the school gym. The dismissal bell had already rung, but lots of people were still milling around for after-school activities: baseball, soccer, cheerleading . . . and I guess word had spread that Varun—who had started the year as the skinniest, gangliest kid in middle school—was actually closing in on his goal, because by the time he hit the gym, a small crowd had gathered, maybe a couple dozen people. There was Varun, lying under the barbell, his ebony eyes crinkled into laser beams, staring at the ceiling as his bulging biceps started pushing upward. A few stray remarks floated through the gym at first, but everybody turned stone silent as Varun pushed the barbell higher, higher, higher, then straightened his arms. The arms lingered in midair for just a couple of seconds as the crowd cheered. People were applauding and stomping their feet as he lowered the weights back into place. I was jumping up and down, whistling with my pinkies on the sides of my mouth.

Varun rose from the bench and fist-pumped the air, his handsome, angular face beaming. The perspiration on his cheeks and forehead made him glow. I'd never seen him look happier.

That's when Justin O'Dell sauntered to the front of the crowd, a look of sheer contempt in his eyes. "You're still a faggot," he said with a sneer.

And just like that, Varun's moment was over. He didn't respond, but his face reddened and his knuckles blanched as he squeezed them into fists. Varun stopped lifting weights that day.

But I always had Varun's back, and he could usually slough off the morons, making snarky remarks in their wakes that would make us convulse in laughter. Who gave a crap what *they* thought?

But deep down, Varun *did* care. He still does. And so do I. That's why I have zero patience for brats who make a "game" of holding other kids' heads under the water. No bullying on *my* watch.

And my sleep-deprived night hasn't exactly done wonders for my patience. I eventually drifted off around 3 a.m., but I tossed and turned, dreading the thought that I'd have to face Declan again in a few hours.

Assuming he shows up for band practice, of course. I'm getting now that Declan's reliability is something of a coin toss. How could I have been so stupid? I'm usually a decent judge of character, but in Declan's case, my brain turned to sawdust. Why did I basically throw myself at him last night, only to give him a gift-wrapped opportunity to turn my ego into mincemeat?

Oh well. Even if he does show, the band just might fire his lazy ass. However it shakes out, I'll have to deal with it. Awkwardness is the price you pay for lip-locking a guy in your granddad's Mercury. (As Varun so eloquently put it: *Ew.*) I'll suck it up and play it cool.

Uh-oh. Now, the freckle-faced kid is shoving the chubby kid as they walk toward the deep end. I blow my whistle and give him a time-out sign. "Fifteen minutes out of the pool," I call to him sharply, pointing toward the pool chair where he'll be exiled.

"No fair!" he whines to me, throwing his hands in the air.

"And this is your last warning," I tell him. "Any more rough stuff, and you're outta here."

I hear a low whistle below me. "Man. You mean business."

I glance down and see Declan standing in plaid swim trunks at the foot of my chair.

I studiously keep my eyes peeled on the freckle-faced kid to ensure he makes his way to the chair. He does, but he's slow about it, glowering at me en route for good measure. His mom is still glued to her phone, oblivious.

I glance down at Declan. "Hi," I say coolly, not wanting to give him the satisfaction of knowing I give a shit that he blew me off.

"So those horseplay rules are actually enforceable," he says. "Guess I better not try any funny stuff."

I keep my eyes on the kids in the pool, peering through my sunglasses.

"So where'd you wander off to last night?" Declan asks me.

Oh please. I haven't had a ton of experience in this area, but I'm up to speed on guys who act crappy and then try to turn the tables.

I blow my whistle at an overzealous noodle-whacker.

"No hitting!" I call to her.

"Wow. You really *do* earn your paycheck," says Declan. "Maybe I won't need a refund after all, even if you don't save my life."

The freckle-faced kid is trying to skitter off the pool chair, but I lock eyes with him as he makes his move. "Ten more minutes," I call to him, and he sulkily sits back down.

"So, seriously," Declan says, "what happened to you last night? I thought we were gonna hang out. I mean, yeah, I had to go gas up my truck, but I thought . . ."

I thread my fingers together. "Maybe some other time," I tell him.

He shifts his weight. "Hey, you sounded great last night," he tells me.

"Thanks."

"Yeah," he continues, "I really liked the way you changed it up on—"

"Scarlett!"

I glance over at the gate and see Kyle walking through it, waving at me.

I smile. "Hi!" I call to him.

"Shouldn't you be getting off soon?" Kyle asks, pointing at the clock on the clubhouse wall.

I hold up five fingers. If Kyle notices Declan standing below me, he's not letting on.

"Wanna swim some laps when you're done?" Kyle calls. I give him a thumbs-up.

Julie, my coworker, walks to the lifeguard stand. "I just clocked in, if you want to take off now," she says.

I smile down at her. "Ya sure?"

She nods.

"Thanks."

I get out of the chair and climb down the stairs. When I reach the bottom, I nudge past Declan to reach Julie's side.

"That Williams kid is in time-out for five more minutes," I tell her. "Keep an eye on him, will you? He's been really aggressive today."

"Will do," she says.

I start to walk away but turn briefly toward Declan, still standing there. "See you at practice," I tell him casually, then slip my sunglasses into a drawstring bag and fling it over my shoulder. I head to the lap lane Kyle has dived into and toss my bag on a nearby beach chair.

"Race?" I ask Kyle after his head bobs out of the water, and he nods.

I dive in and race him across the pool.

When I'm the first to get to the other side, I pump my fist victoriously.

"You got a head start," Kyle complains.

I laugh. "Rematch?"

"Sure."

He leans closer to me. "Think we should ask Declan to join us?" he asks conspiratorially, nodding toward another part of the pool where Declan is swimming.

I wrinkle my nose. "Let's not and say we did?"

"Works for me."

We kick off the side and bound back into the sparkling blue water.

• • •

Kyle and I have just finished racing for the tenth or so time when we reach the end of the pool, look up, and see Mike standing there. I don't see Declan anywhere, but then again, who's looking?

"Hop in," I tell Mike. "But race me at your peril. I'm freakishly fast."

He smiles and dives in. When he comes up for air, Kyle tells him, "I think Declan's around here somewhere. Should we save him a trip to the loft and fire him now?"

I'm not sure if Kyle is joking or not; his tone is light, but the guys were definitely serious the night before.

"Maybe we better put that plan on hold," Mike says, slicking back his wet hair. "Zach had a pretty rough morning. I don't want to add any stress. If Declan shows up for practice, let's just let it ride for the time being. Suit you guys?"

"What happened this morning?" I ask.

"His mom," Mike responds. "She fell and needed twelve stitches in her jaw. But Zach texted me a few minutes ago and said they're home now. He'll make it to practice."

My muscles tense. How ridiculous of me to obsess about Declan flaking on me when Zach's dealing with stuff that really matters. "Is she okay?" I ask.

Mike nods. "I think. But it was a tough morning. The doctor recommended going ahead and transitioning her to a wheelchair. Plus, construction workers have been in their house for two weeks, tearing down walls and installing ramps and rails . . . it's like their world is literally crashing down on their heads."

I nibble a nail. All Zach and I talked about when he drove me home last night was *me*, even after his sister had asked me to help convince him to go back to school in the fall. That conversation had slipped my mind entirely. How self-absorbed could I be?

"Should we go over there?" I ask. "I mean, stop by his house and see if there's anything we can do to help?"

"I stopped by on my way to the pool," Mike says. "My mom made a casserole, and I dropped it off."

"Should we cancel practice?" I ask.

Mike shakes his head. "The band is like therapy for Zach," he says. "Gives him something else to think about, you know?"

Yeah. I know.

"I just feel so helpless," I say.

"Let's just aim for a drama-free practice," Mike says. "I'll do my best to keep my mouth shut about Declan."

Kyle gives him a guarded look, then asks, "Heard from Mia?"

Mike waves a hand through the air. "Mia who? Moving on, bro."

"That's the spirit," Kyle says.

My eyes shift from one of them to the other, then back again. But they're apparently done with that conversation. I tighten my wet ponytail and say, "I better get going. I've got to take a shower before practice."

"You've really got to stop raising the bar, Scarlett," Kyle teases. "Before you came along, even pants were optional."

I raise an eyebrow. "I might even wear pearls. Prepare to be dazzled."

"Oh, you dazzled us right out of the gate," Mike says, and I laugh.

"Gotta keep you guys on your toes," I say.

I wave to them, then hop out of the pool.

I collect my bag and walk toward the gate. Just as I'm about to leave, I hear a voice behind me.

"Hey. Going so soon?"

I turn around and see Declan, his hair dripping from his swim.

"Yeah," I say. "I've got to get ready for practice."

"Right. Practice."

He plants a hand casually on his hip.

"So," he says, lowering his chin and licking his lips, "didn't you say something last night about celebrating?"

Sigh. He's really going to remind me of that mortifying line?

"Let's celebrate by staying in tune at practice," I say, then reach to open the gate.

"Or," Declan says, lightly holding my forearm back, "we can think of some other way."

He lowers his head until we're eye to eye.

I press my lips together. "I don't think so."

Hearing what Zach went through this morning makes this whole ridiculous flirt-fest seem even more juvenile than it did before. And what is it with guys seeming interested only after girls write them off?

Because that's exactly what I'm doing: writing Declan off. My stupid little crush has officially run its course. But I might as well be polite. Declan and I will still be in the band together, after all, assuming the guys don't throw him out on his ear. And *I'm* the idiot who decided that a necking session in a parking lot signaled some kind of relationship. But I've officially reclaimed my sanity—and hopefully, my self-respect.

"See you at four," I say.

He opens his mouth to respond, but I've already reached

past him and opened the gate. I swing my bag lightly by my side as I walk out to the parking lot.

I think I hear him offer a reply, but I can't make out the words and don't feel inclined to slow my pace.

I'm moving on.

CHAPTER FIFTEEN

"Still not quite right."

Declan is again struggling with the syncopated rhythm of the bridge in "Shamblin'," and Zach is exhibiting preternatural patience in helping him.

Declan made it to practice on time—maybe he senses something is up—and we dove right into the music. Zach is as genial as ever, but he seems tired. I'm glad Mike and Kyle have spared him the chore of voting on Declan's fate.

"Play along with me," Zach says, strumming Declan's part on the bridge. Declan seems vaguely annoyed, but he strums grudgingly. They play it through a couple of times, and Zach nods as Declan starts to get it right. Mike is rolling his eyes behind him.

After a few more minutes of practice, we start it again from the top.

I feel a little stab in my heart as Declan's smooth, mellow vocals fill the loft. He's caressing the microphone and swaying rhythmically on his sinewy hips. This is Declan at his best. He has enough raw talent and soulful charisma to fill an arena. It's when Zach prods him to nail the details that he flakes, seemingly uninterested in knocking himself out. I have a feeling he's been able to passably fake his way through huge chunks of his life. No wonder the other guys are frustrated. But man, when he wraps his fingers around that microphone and purrs out a vocal, there's no denying he's golden. No wonder I fell so hard.

But that was then, and this is now.

Interestingly, he's the one who's been trying to catch my eye for the past hour. It probably slayed his ego that I refrained from falling at his feet earlier at the pool. Tough. Yeah, I fell for those ocean-blue eyes and sun-streaked hair, but I don't give people second chances to blow me off.

Besides, all I can think about right now is how sad Zach's eyes look. I hope I have a chance to talk to him after practice, to make it up to him that I monopolized the conversation last night, showing not even a sliver of interest in what he's going through. I've never asked him point-blank about his mom's condition before, but I want to do it now. I want to hear about his morning and let him know I want to do whatever I can to help. Plus, I'm eager to make good on my promise to his sister and try to talk Zach into staying in school. Yes, I've been a lovestruck imbecile for the past week, but the summer's just getting started. I have time to make this right. I want to be the kind of friend he deserves. And how much fun was it hanging out with Mike and Kyle earlier today? Whether Declan stays in the band or not, I have a feeling I'm finding my sweet spot with the Beastings.

Declan's just finished singing the first verse, so I'm leaning into my mic to sing harmony on the chorus. I jump a little, startled when I realize he's leaning into my mic as well, rather than continuing to use his.

"You left my life in shambles," we sing, "and my words are only rambles. I guess I lost the gamble. Yeah, I'm shamblin' . . ."

He's standing so close that I can feel his breath on my cheek, and I sense his eyes seeking mine. I resist at first, but by the end of the chorus, the vibe is so heady that I find myself meeting his gaze.

Yeah, I get it. You're adorable. Now get over yourself, will you?

He returns to his mic for the second verse, then Zach eases into a haunting, doleful guitar solo. By the following chorus, Declan has found his way back to my mic. We sing it together again, and this time, his gaze won't cut me loose.

We follow the chorus with the last few bars: "You got me shambling, man, and I don't give a damn. I'm just doing what I can to shake you off. Yeah, I'm shamblin' . . ."

By the end of the song, I feel a little lightheaded, and I rest my hand on an amp to steady myself.

Granted, that was intense.

But it doesn't matter.

I've learned my lesson with Declan.

• • •

"Hey, Zach?"

Zach turns around, his gig back slung on his back, and smiles at me. "Yeah?"

"Um . . ." I fumble with my fingers.

Okay, that was stupid. I have nothing to say. But Zach is rushing out the door after practice, and I don't want him to leave without having the chance to reach out to him.

"Just . . . I thought you sounded really good today."

Well, *that* was incredibly lame. But he's still in midstride out the door. It would be beyond awkward to holler out, "Sorry your day sucked, and sorry I've been such a sucky friend, and oh, by the way, I hope your mom is okay."

Zach smiles. "Thanks," he says. "You, too. Hey, sorry to rush, but I've got to get home."

I nod. "Oh, sure. See you tomorrow at four?"

"Right. See you then."

The other guys wave to him as they pack their gear.

Zach waves back, resumes his stride, then turns around again. "Oh, Scarlett, do you need a ride home?"

"No, no."

"You're sure?"

"Yes. Go. I'm fine. Thanks, though."

He hesitates for a second, but I wave insistently.

I swallow hard as I watch him disappear behind the door. It shuts with a *thud*, late-afternoon sunlight streaming through the windows of the loft.

Mike, Kyle, and Declan are flipping off amp switches. Kyle says something jokey to me about the pool that I don't quite catch. My eyes are still on the door.

"So is that a yes?"

I turn toward Kyle. "Sorry. What?"

He glances at Mike. "I think all that chlorine is marinating her brain."

I manage a smile, then turn off a mic. Declan reaches for the same switch and bumps my arm. "Sorry," I murmur.

"Uh, technically, *I'm* sorry," he says. I don't respond, even though he's trying to catch my eye.

"Well, I'm headed out, too," Mike says. "Scarlett, you're sure you don't need a ride?"

"Yeah, I'm sure. Thanks."

"Okay. See you guys tomorrow. Last one out, flip off the lights and lock up, okay?"

I open my mouth to respond, then squeeze my hands together. The thing is, *Zach* is usually the last one out. *He's* the one who quietly tends to every last detail and keeps everything humming. I guess he's got his hands full now keeping things humming at home. He got at least half a dozen texts during practice, which is unusual. I hope everything's okay—or at least as okay as things can be, considering the circumstances. Maybe his mom is bedridden now that she's fallen. Maybe someone needs to be with her twenty-four seven. Maybe she needs a prescription filled. Maybe those construction workers at his house messed something up. I bite my bottom lip. Zach must have the weight of the world on his shoulders.

"Wait up, Mike," Kyle calls to Mike, then catches up with him.

"Later, guys," he calls out in our general direction, and I wave.

I grab my gig bag and head for the door. I'm ready to go home, snuggle into Grandpa's couch while he plays the television set way too loud, and eat leftover chicken and rice off a tray. As I start walking out, I say to Declan, "So you'll get the lights?"

"No," he says, and I turn around to face him, my brow furrowing.

He gives me a sideways grin. "*We'll* get the lights."

I study him evenly for a second, then resume walking. Whatever.

"Hey," he says, trotting over to me and dangling my forearm in his hand. "Let me give you a ride home."

I stare at his hand until he lets go of my arm. "I'm good," I say, then keep walking.

But Declan bolts ahead, then turns to face me, blocking the door. "*Please* let me take you home?"

"No thanks," I say. "Gotta go."

He searches my eyes. "So you've got plans?"

I resist the urge to roll my eyes. "Yeah. I've got plans."

"The thing is," he says, studying his fingertips, "I'd really love to spend more time with you." He glances up. "Is that a possibility?"

I manage a tight smile. "Sorry. It's been a long week. I really just want to go home and crash. But I'll see you at practice tomorrow."

I push the door open and walk through it. It's as I'm walking down the stairs that I hear a boom of thunder. I walk down a couple more steps and hear a second thunderclap, then a third. Raindrops starts pattering on the roof.

Oh, great. I don't mind biking in a downpour, but I don't want my guitar to get wet. My gig bag is probably no match for a summer storm. I pause, then decide my best bet is to leave my guitar in the loft. I trot back up the steps, the rain falling harder now. I walk through the door of the loft just as Declan begins walking out.

He raises an eyebrow and points skyward, the rain pouring on the roof overhead. "Looks like you'll need a ride after all."

• • •

I glance anxiously behind me from the passenger seat of Declan's pickup as he hoists my bike into his truck bed. The rain is falling so hard that he's barely a blur.

Once the bike is secure, he ducks his head and dashes to

the side of the truck, then slips into the driver's seat as fast as he can, slamming the door behind him. His hair is dripping as his soaked shirt and shorts cling to his body. He swipes his wet forehead with the back of his hand.

"There's a hand towel in the glove compartment," he says. "Could you hand it to me?"

I fumble for it, feeling guilty that he's sopping wet on my account. The rain nailed me, too, but I was only in it for a few seconds. Declan looks like he's been tossed into a lake.

"I'm so sorry," I mumble as I hand him the towel.

He wipes off his face and neck. "No problem," he says, then tosses the towel on the floorboard.

He starts the ignition, backs out, and inches his way out of the parking space. The rain is coming down so hard that his visibility is near zero. He peers out the windshield as he makes his way down the block. I stay quiet, not wanting to distract him.

After a couple of blocks, the rain eases up a bit. Declan switches his windshield wipers from turbo speed to regular.

"So did you hear Zach's mom was in the emergency room this morning?" I ask.

"Was she?" Declan responds, sounding concerned.

I nod. "She fell. I think she's okay—she's home now—but she needed some stitches in her jaw."

He considers my words. "Zach didn't mention it," he says.

"He didn't mention it to me, either," I reply quickly, hoping I haven't said the wrong thing. "The others told me. Zach's always so steady; you'd never know he had a care in the world."

Declan crosses the bridge. "Yeah, that disease she has . . . what a bummer."

"You know her?"

"Sure. Zach and I have been friends since first grade. I've been to his house a thousand times. Plus, she was our whole family's doctor before she had to quit a few months ago."

The windshield wipers swish rhythmically. "So the four of you guys have been friends since you were kids?" I ask Declan.

He gives a sly smile. "Well, we've *known* each other since we were kids. But I'm not sure Mike and Kyle would call me a friend. They haven't exactly signed up for my fan club."

I smile. "I think they were just a little pissed you were late last night."

Declan shrugs. "They've always treated me like shit."

I glance at him from the corner of my eyes. Should I give him a heads-up that he may have pushed his luck too far this time and that the Beastings are considering canning him? No . . . of course I shouldn't. The last thing I want to do is make things any more complicated or awkward than they already are. Still, if the bad blood goes way back, I can't help wondering what's up with that. But I don't have to wonder for long, because Declan keeps talking.

"Zach and Mike and Kyle were the brainiest guys in high school," he says. "I barely squeaked by. That never mattered to Zach; he's never judged me. But once the three of them moved into AP classes, Mike and Kyle treated me like I was raw sewage or something."

"Did they, like, bully you?" I ask, thinking how unlikely that seems based on what I know about them.

Declan shrugs. "Not really. They just acted really arrogant and superior. I think they wrote me off as some world-class slacker. But I have dyslexia. Things don't come as easy to me as to them."

I direct him toward Grandpa's house, then hug my arms

together, chilled by my wet clothes. "I'm sorry," I say softly. "That sucks."

He waves a hand through the air. "It's all good. I never see them anymore except for summer breaks. And then I just tune them out." He grins at me, his blue eyes glimmering. "Pun intended, I guess."

I smile.

"If it wasn't for Zach," Declan continues, pulling into Grandpa's driveway, "I'd have left them in the dust years ago. But, you know, we earn a little money every summer, and I really like making music. So they trash-talk me behind my back, and I let it roll right off."

My hands squeeze my forearms tighter. "I hate that."

He puts the truck in park and turns off the engine.

"Oh, you don't have to stop the truck," I say quickly, but he's already opening his door. "Declan, really, I don't want you to get out in the rain again—"

Declan shuts his door and walks to the back of his truck, retrieving my bike. I open my door and rush back to join him. "I've got it, I've got it," I say, trying to take it from him as he walks it toward the porch.

"I'm gonna be a gentleman whether you like it or not," he says as raindrops spit against our cheeks.

When we get to the porch, he props the bike on its kickstand. "Come inside and let me get you a towel," I say.

"Nah," Declan replies, tucking a hand into the pocket of his soggy shorts. "Just . . ."

I search his eyes. "Just what?"

"Just . . . go out with me. I want to get to know you better."

Whatever expression I'm giving makes him lean closer. "Please?"

I pause, then shake my head. "I don't think so," I say. "Thanks, though. It's just . . . since we're in the band together, I think we should keep things professional."

He considers my words, then laughs. "Professional? So you consider the Beastings professional?"

I feel my cheeks grow warm, embarrassed. I guess Mike and Kyle aren't the only ones who can act arrogant and superior.

Declan leans closer still. "Are you blushing?" he asks, grinning.

"No, no . . ."

"You are! You're blushing."

"I just want to keep things simple," I say, avoiding his gaze.

"Then *simply* go out with me." He licks his lips slowly. "I loved spending time with you the other night. I wanna do it again."

I take a deep breath. Is there any really good reason to say no? I mean, maybe what happened last night really *was* a misunderstanding. And what Declan just told me about Mike and Kyle . . . well, that puts a whole different spin on things, you know? I hate that they make Declan feel stupid. Sure, I like Mike and Kyle a lot, but there's nothing cool about that. I feel a stab in my stomach as I wonder if that's how Varun and I made the Shelby Dixons of our school feel.

I swallow hard. "Okay."

Declan cocks his head. "Okay, you'll go out with me?"

I finally meet his eyes and smile. "Yeah."

He smiles and nods his head sharply. "I'll be back in an hour."

I laugh. "You mean tonight?"

"Yeah. I'm starving. Just lemme run home and take a quick

shower. I mean, unless you prefer the drowning-cat look, in which case we can go right now."

I size him up playfully from head to toe. "You weirdly pull it off."

He leans in and kisses me. It's just a peck, and it's so quick and effortless that I don't have time to respond. "So do you," he tells me in barely a whisper.

I fumble with my hands.

"You're blushing again."

I shake my head, smiling. "Cut it out."

Then he leans in for another quick kiss. "I'll be back in an hour."

I open my mouth to respond, but he's already darting back out into the rain, ducking his chin and running to his door. He turns around when he gets there and waves to me.

I wave back, wait for him to back out of the driveway, then blow out a breath through puffed-out cheeks as he drives away.

Looks like I have a date tonight.

CHAPTER SIXTEEN

I sputter with laughter as Declan pretends his French fry is a cigarette and apes the way Mike smokes, all squinty-eyed and purse-lipped.

True, I feel a little disloyal laughing at Mike behind his back, but Declan's really nailed it. Plus, it feels good to laugh. I felt like an idiot when Declan pulled into a burger joint for our date, realizing I'd way overdressed. But I hadn't known what to expect, so I'd opted for a halter top, flowy skirt, and wedge-heeled sandals, figuring I was striking a balance between dressy and casual. But wearing a skirt to a place where you stand in line to place your order is like, I dunno, singing opera at a rave or something. Declan changed out of his wet clothes for the date, but his shorts and T-shirt are just as informal as what he wore to practice. He's told me three times how gorgeous I look, but I still cringed when he pulled into the parking lot, hoping he hadn't pegged me as some kind of princess when he'd picked me up. At least this place is one step up from a chain; there's no dollar menu or bouncy house, so that's a plus. Still, I had to shout to the bored teenager across the counter to place my order over the din of shouting kids and screaming babies. While wearing heels.

So yeah, even though Mike is the butt of the joke, it feels good to laugh.

"Mike may be smart," I say through my laughter, "but he's stupid to smoke."

"See what I'm saying?" Declan says, spreading out an arm as the fry dangles in his fingers. "And people think *I'm* the stupid one."

"Hey, wait. You smoke, too," I say, laughing.

He considers my words, then grins. "Oh yeah."

We laugh together, then I lean into my elbows. "Hey," I say, turning somber, "no one thinks you're stupid."

"Oh please," Declan responds, blowing a lock of hair out of his eyes. "Mike probably thinks I'm too stupid to realize he's trying to get me thrown out of the band."

My muscles tighten, and I avert my eyes.

"Oh, so you're in on the conversations, too," Declan says, his voice still light.

I squeeze my fingers together. "What are you talking about?" I ask, and my effort to sound clueless is only making me sound phonier.

He gives a short, sharp laugh. "I'm late one time, and that asshole turns you all against me?"

I swallow hard. Technically, he's been late more than once, just in the short while I've been playing in the band, and Mike's not an asshole to object. But the last thing I want to do is get in the middle of this.

"You're blushing again."

I grab a fry to give me something to do with my fingers, and Declan laughs at me.

"It's okay," he says. "I'm not gonna make you rat out your buddies."

I swallow my fry and say, "Let's not talk about the band."

"You know," Declan says, "the irony is that I'm the band's biggest draw. They'd have a fraction of their fans without me."

This is actually quite plausible; it's hard not to notice the girls who practically salivate when he's singing. On the other hand, the Beastings aren't exactly filling arenas.

"So," I say, "tell me about your family."

He sips his Coke and keeps fingering the straw when he's done. "My family," he responds. "I've got an awesome mom, a loser dad, an annoying little brother . . ."

"Why's your dad a loser?"

"He's not around," Declan says offhandedly. "He left when I was a kid."

"So you never see him?"

Declan shrugs. "He blows into town once a year or so."

A couple of kids dart past us. The little girl accidentally runs into my leg, and I wrinkle my nose playfully as I steady her to quell the look of panic on her face. She smiles at me and resumes running.

"I'm sorry about your dad," I tell Declan. "That's awful."

He studies my eyes. "*You*, on the other hand . . ."

I laugh self-consciously as he drags out the sentence.

"Yes?" I prod.

"I bet *you* have the perfect family. The kind that plays board games and talks about current events at the dinner table."

I manage a wistful smile. If only he knew. Actually, Declan's description is pretty spot-on about my Before life. But my After life is the only one that counts now. *Drug addict. Overdose.*

Dead brother. That's my family life now. "I guarantee you, we're not perfect," I say.

"Yet you *do* play board games and talk about current events at the dinner table."

He's leaning into the booth, an eyebrow raised like a detective homing in on a breakthrough. "I knew it!"

"Not so much," I say through laughter. "We haven't broken out the Monopoly board in, like, days."

"And you have a cat and a dog," Declan continues. "No, two dogs. A lab and a terrier."

"One dog, and he's a mutt," I correct him. "And no cats. My dad's allergic."

"So," Declan says, leaning back and draping his arm across the top of the booth, "is your mom as pretty as you and your sister?"

"She has a mustache," I tease, pushing past my mild discomfort that Sara is still apparently fresh on his mind. "And a beard. But she has really good posture."

"No annoying little brother in your family?"

I stare at my hands as I ponder how to respond.

"I had a brother," I finally say softly. "An older one. Liam. He died." My words hang in the air.

"Oh," Declan finally says in a hushed voice. "Sorry."

I nod.

"So," he says, "how did he die?"

"Drug overdose."

"Ah."

Another awkward moment passes. "My dad's a druggie," Declan offers, and I nod, tensing at the word. I would use a thousand words to describe Liam before "druggie" came to mind. Maybe that's why Grandpa doesn't like to tell people how

Liam died. It's hard to see him reduced to a single detail—and a crappy one at that.

"I hope your dad gets better," I finally say. "I bet it's hard not to have him around."

Declan gazes past me and shakes his head. "Nah. It was having him around that was hard." He pauses, then claps his hands together. "Wanna take a drive?"

Oh. That was abrupt. I figured he'd ask when Liam died, or how old he was, or whether we were close, or . . . whatever.

But maybe this is better. The only thing more incongruous than wearing heels to a burger joint, I guess, is getting weepy between bites of fries.

"Sure," I say. "Let's go."

• • •

"So," I say when Varun answers the phone, "Polyester Guy took me on a date tonight, just like you wanted him to."

"Really."

I narrow my eyes, closing the bedroom door behind me. "Yes, really. Why is that such a surprise?"

He huffs. "Okay, you have seriously got to stop getting so defensive about this guy."

I sit in the desk chair and rub the back of my neck. "Sorry," I say. "I'm just tired. I baked all day at the pool in, like, thousand-degree weather, then we had band practice, which was really tense since—"

When my pause becomes overlong, Varun prods, "Since what?"

"Since—I dunno. It's just been a long day. Sorry I snapped."

Okay, that wasn't exactly smooth, but I realized too late I was venturing into territory I hadn't intended. I want to share my excitement about my date, not answer a lot of questions about why the guys want to kick Declan out of the band.

Varun hesitates a moment. He knows a dodge when he hears one, but then he lets me off the hook. "So where did Polyester Guy take you?"

Okay, here's another overlong pause. "Out to dinner," I finally say.

"*Dinner*," Varun says.

Now I'm the one to huff. "Why are you being so weird about this?" I ask him.

He laughs. "*I'm* being weird."

I moan. "I was just really psyched to tell you about my date."

He hesitates, then says sweetly, "Then tell me. Tell me about your date."

I lean back in my chair. "Well, we went to . . . dinner . . . then for a drive."

"A drive."

I tap my phone playfully. "Do we have a bad connection? Why do you keep repeating what I say?"

"Just following the story. You went for a drive. Do I want details?"

I giggle and twirl a lock of hair. "No details. We went to a place at the lake called Bristow Point."

"Mmmmm," Varun says, sounding concerned. "A make-out spot, I'm assuming."

"We mostly just talked," I stress.

"So no steamy windows?"

I smile. "I didn't say that."

He chuckles ruefully.

"But we just kissed," I add quickly. "And don't judge. Varun, you are seriously underestimating how hot he is."

He chortles. "And that has always been so important to you," he says sarcastically.

"Well, why shouldn't I enjoy his hotness? God knows I'm overdue. It's not like there are any hot guys back home. I mean besides you, of course."

He groans at my obligatory shout-out.

"You *are* hot," I assure him. "Speaking of which, update me on your like life. Any dates with cute lab techs?"

"Yeah, I'm actually engaged now to the sixty-two-year-old with the polka-dot bowtie. Hey, maybe your band can play at our wedding."

"Ooh, better idea: I'll be your best man, and Declan can play you down the aisle."

"Oh my *God*."

I laugh, stretching out my legs and kicking off my heels. "I know you're thinking Declan's not my type," I say.

"Am I?"

"But he's deeper than people realize. He really opened up to me tonight. I mean, he's got major stuff going on in his life."

"Yeah, hangnails are a bitch," Varun says.

"I'm *serious*. For instance, he told me he's dyslexic. Isn't that sad?"

"Tragic."

I huff, exasperated. "It *is* sad. He said it was really rough when he was a teenager."

"Yeah, you'll excuse me for not hosting a prayer vigil for what a gorgeous straight white guy had to endure in high school."

I bite my lip. I know Varun is joking, kind of, but I had a

front-row seat to the bullying *he* endured. He even got dragged behind the bleachers and beat up one day after junior-varsity track practice. By the time I reached him, he was wiping blood off his face as he rose unsteadily to his feet. He wouldn't tell me who'd beat him up—I swear to God, I would have made the scumbag wish he'd never been born—and he got mad when I pressed him for details, brushing me off when I tried to dab my finger against his bloody lip. So I let it go. But I kept an extra-close eye on him from then on, using my death stare to practically dare anyone to mess with him.

So I get that he's not exactly going to be sending a sympathy card to Declan. Still . . .

"Everybody's got their stuff, you know," I say softly.

Varun moans wearily. "Yes, Scarletta," he says, "I know that gorgeous straight white guys and beautiful straight white girls have their 'stuff.' "

I swallow hard. Did he really just throw me into the mix? "I lost Liam," I say. "You don't know what that's like."

"I know plenty."

I squeeze my eyes shut and pop them open. Where the hell is my sweet, empathetic friend?

"I'm *sorry*," Varun says quickly. "I didn't mean it like that. I just meant . . . I don't know what I meant."

"Losing a twenty-one-year-old brother isn't like losing an eighty-year-old grandmother," I say, spitting the words.

"I know, I know. I'm sorry."

My heart beats hard against my halter top. What is *up* with this? Varun and I went years without ever being so much as *annoyed* at each other, and suddenly we're having pissing contests about dead relatives?

I'm about to respond when my phone beeps. I glance at the screen and see that Sara is calling me on FaceTime.

"Sara's beeping through," I tell Varun. "I better go."

He sighs. "Don't be mad at me, Scarletta."

I take a deep breath. "Don't be mad at me, either. I love you times infinity."

He pauses, then says in a choked whisper, "Back atcha."

When I answer Sara's call, her eyebrows weave together. "Are you crying?"

I shake my head briskly. "No, no. It's just . . . Varun and I kinda hurt each other's feelings. That *never* happens."

"Talk," she says, sitting up straighter on her bed.

"Well . . ." Where do I begin? Telling her about my conversation with Varun will require telling her about my date with Declan. Do I want to go there? Sara's already told me that she thinks he's a player. Will I get as deflating a reaction from her as I did from Varun? I want somebody to share my excitement, not diss me for being shallow or naïve.

"*Talk*," Sara repeats.

Oh, what the hell.

I tell her how Declan and I kissed a couple of nights ago in Frosty's parking lot, then how we went on an actual date tonight. (I skipped the part about his blowing me off twenty-four hours earlier.)

"Where did he take you?" she asks.

"Just *out*."

"Out where?" Sara persists.

I huff indignantly. "Just some restaurant. Who cares? Anyway, we ate dinner, then we . . . took a drive."

She studies my eyes, which makes me roll them. "Nothing

happened. It was just a date. I don't even know why I'm telling you about it. That's what got Varun and me in trouble."

"What did Varun say?" Sara probes, sounding, omigod, so prissy that I feel like screaming.

"I was trying to tell him," I respond in a clipped voice, "that Declan isn't nearly as superficial as people assume, just because he's hella good-looking. I mean, like . . . he's got dyslexia, for instance."

Now it's Sara's turn to roll her eyes.

"Stop it! It's a real thing! What is it with you and Varun thinking you get to be the ones who decide which problems count?"

"Scarlett, Varun's a really good judge of character," schoolmarm Sara informs me solemnly. "And he really cares about you. I think you should trust his instincts."

My hand flies in the air. "You barely know Varun! And he's not exactly Mr. Perfect. He just got finished informing me that he gets how I've been feeling the past six months, because, you know, my twenty-year-old brother and his eighty-year-old grandmother dropping dead are, like, totally the same thing."

"Oh."

That's all Sara says in response. Just "Oh." And she's averting her eyes.

I peer at her suspiciously. "Why are you acting like you already know something about this?"

She glances at me impatiently. "I just said, 'Oh.' I don't know what else to say. People say the wrong thing sometimes, you know? It's not like I haven't lived it for the past six months, just like you."

"But that was *beyond* the wrong thing," I reply. "It was almost . . . mean."

Sara shakes her head, making the loose bun on her head flop slightly to one side. "I don't know why we're even talking about this," she says. "I want to hear about your date."

I study her eyes, wondering why this conversation feels so weird.

"Talk, Scarlett," Sara says. "Tell me about your date."

"We had fun," I say defensively.

Sara waits a beat, then makes a rolling motion with her hand.

Sigh. I'm less inclined to talk about this than ever. Is everybody in my life committed to raining on my parade? But since I'm the one who brought it up, I guess I'm stuck following up. "It was good to go have fun," I finally say, "because things have been really tense at band practice lately."

Uh-oh. Have I yet again boxed myself into talking about things I really don't want to discuss? It doesn't exactly reflect well on Declan that the band is trying to throw him out, and the last thing he needs is another strike in Sara's eyes.

"Why has it been tense?" Sara asks.

"Well . . ." I begin, searching for a way out of the trap I set for myself. "You know Zach's mother has that awful disease, and she fell this morning."

Zach. Now *there's* someone with stuff. How ridiculous for me to be obsessing about my date when he's going through so much crap.

"Zach must have the weight of the world on his shoulders, but he never lets on that anything's wrong. He just acts so strong and steady. And *sweet.* He drove me home the other night, and all I did was talk about Liam. Zach's really easy to talk to. I felt guilty afterward, thinking, *Idiot. You didn't ask him a single question about what he's going through.* But when you're around him, he makes you feel like you have 100 percent of his attention. He's just really . . . kind.

"Anyway," I continue, "two of the guys in the band—Mike and Kyle—they're kinda pissed about a couple of things going on, but they can never drag Zach into any kind of bitching session. He just won't go there. Oh, and did I mention Zach writes all this amazing original music for the band? He's incredibly talented. Even his catchiest songs have, like, layers of meaning. There's this one song he wrote for his mom . . . God, he's so sweet. But anyhow, there's some friction in the band, and things were kinda tense at practice, so . . ."

I pause to catch my breath. I'm not sure why I'm suddenly rambling on about Zach. It's just . . . God, what a great guy. He's so much more together than most people I know.

"So now I know all about how your date went," Sara says dryly.

I narrow my eyes. "What do you mean?"

Sara shrugs. "I mean I asked you about Declan. But all you seem to be talking about . . ."

She pauses before finishing her sentence.

". . . is Zach."

• • •

It's about five minutes after I turn off the light and pull my covers under my chin that my phone pings. I reach to my bedside table, pick it up, and read the text:

Sorry I hurt your feelings. I love you forever, Scarletta.

Varun signs off with a snowman emoji.

CHAPTER SEVENTEEN

"So, do you really believe in this stuff?"

Grandpa glances at me, startled. He almost never takes his eyes off the road when he's driving, so I know I have his attention.

I hadn't intended to go all existential on him, but as he drives us home from church, I just can't resist. This is the third Sunday I've been to church with him since I moved in for the summer, and I'm really curious how he feels about it. He's so smart that I'm tempted to believe he's just going through the motions, just keeping up a lifelong habit by going to Mass. On the other hand, Grandpa is honest to the core of his soul (assuming he *has* a soul, of course, ha ha), so I'm genuinely curious.

"What *stuff*?" he asks, but I know he's just stalling for time.

"The church stuff," I say. "The God stuff."

"Of course," he says, his bright-blue eyes once again staring intently ahead.

My hair blows in the hot late-morning breeze. (No AC on Grandpa's watch. *Sigh.*)

"I know you're spiritual," I clarify. "So am I. But the nuts and bolts: the virgin birth, the talking donkey, the ark . . ."

He waves a hand through the air. "I don't pay attention to any of that."

I narrow my eyes. "But shouldn't you? I mean, if you stand up every Sunday and say, 'This is what I believe,' shouldn't you kinda have to believe it?"

"The Apostle's Creed doesn't say anything about talking goats."

I giggle. That's Grandpa, homing in on a literal loophole. "I mumble my way through it," I confess conspiratorially.

He sneaks another glance. "Why is that?"

I shrug. "Mom has always told me to be true to myself, and I don't really believe most of what I'm saying at Mass. But I don't want to be disrespectful, either, so what the heck. I mumble."

Pause.

"Scarlita, I think you're overthinking this."

I laugh again. "I'm not *over*thinking. I'm just thinking. Wouldn't God want us to think and to at least make an attempt to be authentic and honest about whatever conclusions we draw?"

Grandpa considers my words, then says definitively, "The Sermon on the Mount."

I study his profile. "What?"

"The Sermon on the Mount," he repeats. "That's what I concentrate on. How we treat each other. How Jesus treated people. That's what's important."

I swipe a windblown strand of hair from my face. "Then why fool with the incense and the talking goats and all the rest of it? Why not just live your life treating people well?"

"Scarlett, the Bible devoted maybe thirty words out of a million to a talking goat," he says, exasperated.

Okay, I've pushed this too far. It's usually fun to pick Grandpa's brain about things. Get him started on politics or history or the economy, and he can rattle a thousand talking points off the top of his head, melding all of them into a really impressive case for whatever point he's making. But I guess the chilling effect he learned in Catholic school had staying power. He doesn't mind joking about religion or theology, but he limits his irreverence to a single quip or two. This conversation is pushing his limits, making him nervous.

"I just hope Liam and Grandma are okay," I finally say.

Grandpa tightens his grip on the steering wheel. "Of *course* they're okay," he responds. "Why wouldn't they be okay? Scarlett, surely you don't think that just because of Liam's problem, God would hold that against—"

"Of course not," I say emphatically. "If I thought that for a *second*, trust me, I'd never step foot in a church again. It's just . . . whatever is or isn't true about religion, I just hope Liam and Grandma are really in a better place. That's all."

I face my open window, my hair flowing in the wind.

"That's all any of us want," Grandpa says softly. "That's the point of the whole thing."

I turn and peer at him. What does he mean? Does he mean the God thing is just something we made up to give us comfort after our loved ones die and to keep us from freaking out about our own mortality?

No. I think Grandpa has way too much integrity to fake it.

So does he mean the only point of going to church is to reserve our place cards in Heaven?

No. Grandpa has way too much character to reduce religion to a quid pro quo.

I'm not sure what he means.

"I just want them to be okay," I repeat wistfully.

Grandpa reaches over and pats my leg. "They're okay, honey," he says, his voice gentle but firm. "I know they're okay."

I nod, gaze at the river as Grandpa crosses the bridge, then turn up the music he lowered when I started talking. It's a big-band CD I gave him for Christmas, and he resumes singing along: "And when he plays with the bass and guitar, they holler, 'Beat me, Daddy, eight to the bar'. . ."

His eyes twinkle as he starts tapping his wedding ring on the steering wheel to the beat.

"Now *this*," he tells me with conviction during the clarinet solo, "is music."

I smile and snuggle deeper into my seat, the smell of his musty back seat newspapers wafting through the air. "Yeah," I agree dreamily. "It is."

• • •

I gasp, startled, as someone grabs me from behind.

Band practice starts in ten minutes, and I'd been tuning my guitar, the first one to make it to the loft, when a string broke. I zipped out to the parking lot to retrieve a package of strings from the basket of my bike and have just reentered the stairwell. Right as I begin to climb the stairs, I feel someone's arms around my waist.

I turn around and see Declan.

"Hey, beautiful," he says, pressing me so close that I have to pull back a little to avoid our noses touching.

"You scared me to death," I say, my heart still pounding.

His eyes gaze into mine at half-mast, looking like clear-blue crescent moons. He leans closer, puts his palms on my cheeks, and kisses me. I hesitate at first, then lean in. His lips feel moist and smooth as our heads do a synchronized dance—mine tilting left while his tilts right, then vice versa. My loosely interlocked fingers press the small of his back, but as he kisses me harder, my hands drift upward and wrap around his neck. I feel like I'm swimming underwater in a heated pool, oblivious to everything except the silky warmth enveloping me.

I'm lightheaded when he finally pulls away. "I've been waiting all day to do that," he murmurs.

I smile, studying his tanned and chiseled face.

"Hold that thought," I say. "Maybe we could grab some pizza after practice?"

"Mmmmm," Declan replies. "I definitely work up an appetite around you."

Okay, was that a yes or a no? I'm not sure, but I push away the thought. I'm relieved that I feel excited to see him, especially after my conversation with Sara last night. Yes, I was talking to her about Zach, but hey, a lot is going on in Zach's life. He's a friend. Aren't I entitled to have friends while still enjoying the most adrenaline-fueled romance I've ever had?

Yep. Gazing into Declan's eyes is confirming my growing conviction that hotness can factor significantly in my life, with no apologies necessary. Sara's had plenty of hunks for boyfriends; why shouldn't I get a hunk boyfriend of my own?

Boyfriend. I'm still trying to be cautious; I haven't forgotten that Declan blew me off the other night, although I'm more willing than before to buy his excuse of making a gasoline run. After all, he practically begged me to go out with him last night. And just like Varun stipulated, it was an actual date. Declan clearly likes me. Why shouldn't I like him back? And how does Sara know what my type is, anyhow? It just so happens that this type suits me fine.

I've already told Grandpa to expect me home late tonight. I feel tingly just thinking about more alone time with Declan.

"Hey, do me a favor?" he says, his fingers still dangling behind my neck.

"What?"

"Um . . . this thing between you and me?" He winks. "No reason for the band to know about that . . . right?"

I stare at him for a moment, and his arms fall to his sides.

"What?" he asks nervously. "Did I say the wrong thing?"

"No, no . . ."

Still, my stomach clenches as I contemplate his words. In the first place, I hate being winked at. I know Declan looks adorable doing it, but it makes me feel, I dunno . . . patronized, or played, or . . . something like that.

And why doesn't he want the guys to know we're seeing each other? Frankly, that suits me fine, particularly considering how Mike feels about Declan. And I don't want Zach to know I'm seeing Declan because . . . because I have so much respect for him. I want him to respect me back and not assume I start up flings with anybody who crosses my path. Yeah. I definitely don't want Zach knowing.

But these are issues that apply to *me*, not Declan. What's up with him wanting to keep us on the down low? Sure, he's entitled to his own reasons. I just can't help wondering what they are.

"I just think . . . keeping things quiet keeps them less complicated . . . you know?"

"Sure," I say, my lashes fluttering. "Yeah. Less complicated, definitely."

We hear the door to the stairwell open, and Declan takes a step backward.

"Hi, guys," Kyle says, stepping into the stairwell with Mike.

"Hi, Mike. Hi, Kyle," I respond.

"Hi," Mike says, looking only at me. "Did you just get here?"

"No, no . . ." I straighten my T-shirt. "I just . . . I broke a string tuning my guitar. I had an extra pack outside, so . . ."

I pull the pack of strings out of my jeans pocket and hold them up for his inspection. "Better hurry up and restring my guitar so I won't hold you guys up."

I lower my chin, then trot up the stairs.

• • •

"It's okay. I promise, you're doing great."

I feel my cheeks grow warm as Zach—for the *third* time—walks me through a part for a new song he wrote. I usually pick things up pretty quickly, but I'm struggling with the harmony on the chorus.

Zach is singing the melody; Declan will sing it when we perform, but right now, Zach is just trying to teach us the song. It's pretty basic for the other guys, especially Declan, who's just playing rhythm guitar, but the harmony is definitely tricky.

I couldn't help but notice that when I botched it the third time, bringing the song to a screeching halt yet again, Declan sighed and shifted his weight, planting a hand on his hip. But Zach acts like he has all the time in the world to help me through it.

"I need you to hit the seventh on the third line," he says patiently, strumming his guitar as he sings my part to me again:

I see the hope back in your face,
And now I know just where to start.
Yeah, all the pieces are in place,
And I won't let you fall apart.

Then, we sing the line together, our eyes locked, and I finally get it right. Zach smiles.

"Nailed it," he says.

I smile back. "It's a beautiful song," I say, and the moment lingers in the air.

Declan claps loudly. "Okay. Let's get it right this time."

Mike snorts, and Declan gives him a sideways glance. "You got a problem?" Declan snarls.

Mike rubs a stubble-covered chin. "Just enjoying the irony."

Declan's eyes narrow into slits. "What the hell does that mean?"

Mike shrugs. "God knows we've had to wait on *you* enough times to get something right. So the first time Scarlett needs a little extra help, it's a big problem?"

I gulp and squeeze the neck of my guitar tighter.

"I never said it was a problem," Declan mutters, his voice a low hiss.

"Let's start it from the top," Zach interjects, aiming for a breezy tone.

We play it again, this time the whole way through:

You say that life has shook you up and knocked you down a time or two.

And I can see it in your eyes: you think I haven't got a clue.

Your heart is heavy, and the phantoms of your past have seared your soul.
But hold on tight, 'cause hope's in sight, and I'm about to make you whole.

I see the sorrow in your face,
And I don't know just where to start.
But all the pieces are in place,
And I won't let you fall apart.

I'll pick you up and gather all the shattered parts you left behind.
There's nothing missing from your bruised and broken heart that I can't find.

I see the sorrow in your face,
And I don't know just where to start.
But all the pieces are in place,
And I won't let you fall apart.

I see the hope back in your face,
'Cause now I know just where to start.
Yeah, all the pieces are in place,
And I won't let you fall apart.

Yeah, all the pieces are in place,
And I won't let you fall apart.

Zach holds my gaze the whole way through, his kindness and patience pulling me along as effortlessly as a gentle ocean wave as he sings the melody. I tense up during the chorus—I don't want to screw it up again—but I nail the seventh right on cue, and Zach smiles at me. I smile back.

Our eyes are still locked when the song is over, and the moment hangs in the air.

"Finally," Declan mutters.

"Oh, shut the hell up," Mike mutters back.

Declan spins and glares at him. "So it's gonna be a life sentence, huh?"

Mike rolls his eyes.

"Yep, that's what I thought," Declan continues. "You're gonna spend your whole life riding my ass just because—"

The moment seems frozen in time as we wait for him to finish the sentence.

"So you're finally going to admit it?" Mike asks him.

They hold their glares for a long moment, then Declan waves a hand through the air. "Let's just get back to the music," he says to Zach.

"Right," Zach says. "Let's take it from the top."

• • •

"You need a ride, Scarlett?"

I glance at Zach as I zip my guitar into the gig bag. "Um . . . no, thanks."

He nods. "Just a reminder that we're booked at Sheehan's on both Friday and Saturday night next week. Cool?"

"Yeah, cool," I say. "See you at practice on Wednesday. Have a good night."

"You, too."

I walk toward the door, hesitate, then pull it open and start walking down the steps.

I guess Declan's waiting for me in the parking lot, and I'm not sure I want to be around him. Maybe I'm making too much out of it, but he was really snotty when I was struggling with the new song.

Then, that tense moment between Mike and Declan . . . what was that about? Why wouldn't Declan finish his sentence? I don't know, but I'm going to ask him. I assume there's more to the story about Mike's girlfriend than Declan wanted to say—or than I wanted to hear. He might get pissed if I hold his feet to the fire, but you know what? At this point, I'm not sure I even care. Yeah, we had fun last night, but I'm tired of ignoring bright-red flags. Maybe tonight will go well, maybe it won't. I'm not sure which scenario I prefer at the moment. But if I'm going to spend the evening with him, I want to hurry up and get on with it. I don't want Zach seeing me ride off with Declan. Actually, the thought of it makes me cringe. And not because Declan asked me to be discreet. It makes me cringe because . . . well, I'm not sure why. It just does.

I hurry down the steps—*tap*, *tap*, *tap*, *tap*—then open the door to the bright sunshine casting blanched-white rays into the parking lot. I see Mike and Kyle drive off together, and I wave at them. Then I walk toward Declan's truck and . . .

And he's leaving. I'm facing the back of his truck, so I'm not sure if he sees me or not, but he's already backing out of his parking spot. I slow my steps, then stop altogether, wondering what he's doing.

Then I roll my eyes at my stupidity.

It's no mystery. He's just leaving. I'm still not sure if he sees me out here in the parking lot, but regardless, he's leaving me in the dust. Just like the other night. For just a moment, my mind does a replay to try to make sense of it. Maybe he misunderstood and thought I wanted to meet him at the pizza joint? But then I squeeze my nails into my palms to jolt myself back to sanity.

He's leaving because he wants to leave. There's no misunderstanding, no dissembling, no retracing of steps necessary. He's leaving because he doesn't want to be with me. He doesn't consider me a girlfriend (God, had I really allowed myself to think that?), and he's not interested in anything other than occasional lip-locking sessions when it absolutely suits him. Maybe last night at Bristow Point, when he realized our one-on-one time would be less, um, *carnal* than he probably hoped, the buzzer sounded on his attention span. He's a player, just like Sara said.

What a fool I am.

I swallow hard and blink back tears.

"*Stop* it," I say out loud, hating myself for caring.

I hoist my gig bag higher on my back and head to my bike. I am *so* outta here.

But just as I'm mounting my bike, I see Zach walking out the door.

I hesitate for a second, then go for it:

"Hey," I call to him. "Can I bum a ride after all?"

• • •

"Sorry it took me so long to get my part right on your new song."

Zach waves away my concern as he backs out of the parking lot. "You sounded great," he tells me.

"What's it called again?"

" 'Fall Apart,' " he says. "Glad you like it."

"It's amazing. You're incredibly talented. When do you write?"

"Um," he says, pulling into traffic, "every morning from 3 to 6 a.m."

My jaw drops, and he glances at me. "I'm kidding."

I laugh. "I could totally see you doing that," I say.

He smiles, his deep-brown eyes crinkling as he squints into the glare.

"Hey, I heard your mom was in the hospital yesterday," I say. "I'm so sorry."

"Thank you. She's okay, though. She was just there for a few hours."

I lick my lips. "You never talk about her, you know. Your mom, I mean."

He contemplates my words, then glances at me quizzically. "O-*kay*," he says.

"I mean it," I persist.

He rubs the back of his neck, still looking confused, then asks, "How often do you talk about *your* mom?"

I sweep my hair behind my back. "You know what I mean. I'm not trying to pry, but I know you're going through a lot. I just want you to know that you can talk to me. I mean, the way you listened the other night when I was telling you about Liam? That was . . . amazing. I want you to know . . . I'm here for you."

He smiles at me and opens his mouth to respond when his phone rings over the car's Bluetooth. He presses a button on his steering wheel to accept the call, and a man's voice comes through over the speakers:

"Zach?"

"Yeah, Dad."

"Can you meet me at the emergency room?"

CHAPTER EIGHTEEN

"So Claire's okay?"

Zach's dad nods quickly as we join him in the waiting room.

My heart's still pounding. When Zach got the call, we assumed his mom had been rushed to the hospital. It took only a second for his dad to assure him that his sister was the one in the emergency room, and only because of a broken ankle, but my adrenaline's still on overdrive from imagining the worst. I'm sure Zach's is, too. He must spend his entire life on high alert, poor guy.

I insisted that he drive straight to the hospital rather than drop me off first, so now I'm trailing behind him.

"She's fine. They're putting the cast on now," says his dad, who, with his chocolaty eyes and lanky frame, looks just like Zach but with thinning, gray-flecked hair. He's wearing jogging shorts, a T-shirt, and sneakers. He looks exhausted, but his face is kind, like his son's.

"Dad, I don't think you've met Scarlett," Zach says, and his dad warmly shakes my hand.

"The new guitarist in the band?" he asks, and I nod. "Great to meet you, Scarlett. I've heard so much about you. We plan to come hear you guys play really soon. Things have just been a little hectic lately . . ."

I nod. "Yes, I understand," I say. "I'm just glad everything's all right."

I glance down at Zach's mom, sitting beside him in her wheelchair. "And it's so nice to see you again, Mrs. Spencer—I mean, *Dr*. Spencer."

"Please, call me Madelyn."

I offer her my hand, and she smiles as she shakes it. "We're thinking they'll name a wing after us any day now," she quips. "Either that, or give us a buy-one-get-one-free emergency visit."

I laugh. "So how did Claire break her ankle?" I ask.

"Well, you didn't hear it from me, but she tripped in the kitchen," Zach's mom says. "I think she plans to spread around a much more exciting version of the story, so mum's the word. In her defense, though, the construction workers have turned our house into something of an obstacle course."

She glances up at her son. "I hated to bother you, honey, but I thought Dad would have his hands full trying to pile two invalids into the car on the way home."

Zach smiles, but he clearly looks pained at his mom's description of herself as an invalid. "No problem," he says softly. "Can I go back and say hello to Claire? We gotta get our stories straight before people start asking me what happened."

"Yeah, I'll take you back," Zach's dad says. He looks at me. "Scarlett, would you like to join us?"

"No, no," I say, feeling self-conscious about horning in on a family moment. "You two go ahead."

As they start walking out of the waiting room, Zach turns around at the last minute and tells me, "Don't believe any of my mom's stories."

I give him and his dad a fluttery wave as they disappear down the hall.

"So how are you doing?" I say, sitting on a vinyl-upholstered couch by Madelyn's wheelchair.

"I'm good," she says. "I've heard so much about you."

"My mom knows you," I say. "Celeste Stiles? Well, it used to be O'Malley."

"Yes, yes! She was in school a year or two behind me. Please give her my best. Oh, and Scarlett . . . I was so sorry to hear about your brother."

I nod and lower my eyes.

"Heart failure, was it?"

I pull a wisp of hair from my eyes. "Drug overdose," I correct her. "Grandpa tells people heart failure. I'm not sure if he's trying to fool them or himself."

Her eyes ooze compassion. "I understand," she says. "I'm so sorry your brother struggled. And I'm so sorry for your loss."

I hold her gaze a moment and nod, suddenly too choked up to speak. "I don't think Grandpa's ashamed," I say when my voice is steady again. "I think he just doesn't want Liam to be defined by the way he died."

Madelyn nods. "I totally understand that."

"And he doesn't want people to think Liam was irresponsible," I continue quickly, too quickly. I'm not sure why I'm so interested in this woman's opinion of me and my family, but I am. "He got hooked on the opiates a doctor prescribed after a basketball injury. He was the most responsible person I knew. He just couldn't kick his addiction."

Madelyn folds her hands in her lap. "It happens far more often than you might think," she says softly. "If anyone should be ashamed, it's the medical community. And the drug companies.

I wish I could say there's no greed in my profession, but unfortunately, I know better."

I twist my fingers together. "I wish I could have helped him," I say, lowering my eyes.

Madelyn reaches over and pats my leg. "You did. You loved him. That's how you helped him. Trust me, that's enough. In the end, that's all that really matters."

I sneak a glance at her. "I'm sorry you had to close your practice. I'm sorry you're sick."

She waves a hand through the air. "I've had way more blessings than I deserve. Life is good. Hey, actually . . ."

"Yes?"

She laughs. "Today is my twenty-fifth wedding anniversary. That just occurred to me! I guess we've been a little distracted lately . . ."

"Happy anniversary!"

"Thanks."

I lean closer from my chair and rest my chin on my knuckles. "So how did you and your husband meet?"

"We met in college," she says. "I really liked him, but I knew med school would be a grind, and I wanted to stay focused. Plus, I didn't want to drag him through the craziness." She holds up her palms and nods toward her wheelchair-bound legs. "The best-laid plans, right?"

I offer a sad smile, then say, "But he wore you down?"

"We'd been spending some time together for a few months—just as friends, I kept stressing to him—and we were scheduled to play Ultimate Frisbee one Saturday afternoon. But I got sick and couldn't make it. So," her eyes shimmer at the memory, "he showed up at my doorstep with a bunch of groceries. He had all my favorites: weird things that normal people hate, like vegetable juice and unsalted Saltines. He'd noticed. All those months since I'd met him, he'd noticed things about me that even *I* didn't pay any attention to. He said he wasn't going to stay, that he knew I needed my rest and he just wanted to make sure I was well-stocked, so he dropped off the groceries, and he left."

She smiles wistfully. "That's when he won me over."

I smile back, then say, "Are you going to do anything fun for your anniversary?"

I wince a little, realizing what a stupid question it is.

But Madelyn is unfazed. She shrugs. "I'm not very interested in *stuff*," she says. "I've never worn jewelry, and I don't care about clothes, so I'm hard to shop for. I like the beach, so maybe we could take a trip, but . . . I'd rather just enjoy my family. You know, watch movies with Claire or listen to Zach play the guitar . . ."

"He wrote a new song that we practiced today," I tell her enthusiastically. "It's beautiful."

" 'Fall Apart'?" she asks, and when I nod, she says, "I love that one. He really is talented, isn't he?"

"Crazy talented. Like, the most talented person I know. I think he—"

Zach and his dad walk back into the waiting room.

"Everything okay?" I ask them, and they nod.

"Claire actually asked if she could talk to you for a minute," Zach tells me.

My eyebrows weave together, and he shrugs.

"She's in the second room on the right, if you don't mind popping your head in," his dad says.

"Sure, sure . . ."

I stand up, then look back down at Madelyn. "I'm glad we had a chance to talk."

"Me, too, honey."

I smooth my shirt, then walk out the door and down the hall. When I reach the second room on the right, I poke my head in tentatively.

"Come in, come in," Claire says, sitting on an exam table and waving me inside.

"Sorry about your ankle," I say, creeping into the room and glancing at her cast. Her injured leg is stretched out on the table while her other leg dangles over the side.

"Can you believe it?" she says, tightening her blonde ponytail. "And it's my parents' twenty-fifth anniversary. This may be the most inconsiderate injury I've ever had."

"Your mom had forgotten that it's their anniversary," I say. "She told me it had slipped her mind until just now."

Claire leans closer. "We haven't reminded her because Dad's planning a surprise party next Saturday night," she says conspiratorially. "No big deal, just a few friends and family. Hey, you should come! Zach said you guys are playing at Sheehan's that night but that he'll try to slip away as soon as he can."

A smile spreads across my face. "I'd love to."

"Speaking of which . . ." Claire raises an eyebrow. "I've got a little surprise of my own up my sleeve, but my stupid ankle is screwing up my plans. I was hoping you could help."

"Yeah?"

Claire glances toward the door, ensuring our privacy. "A new friend of mine is coming to Sheehan's on Saturday," she says in a lowered voice. "I met her yesterday at a health fair. We were both volunteering. She starts med school in the fall . . ."

"Uh-huh?"

"And I think she'd be perfect for Zach."

I fumble with my fingers. "Oh."

"I showed her his picture—I think Zach's the only person on the planet who's not on Facebook or Instagram—and she thinks he's really cute . . ."

"Yeah, definitely . . ."

"And they have *so* much in common."

"Mmhmm," I murmur, staring at my hands.

"He really needs some fun in his life," Claire says. "Her name is Meg, and she's going to med school in Athens, so if they hit it off, he'll have more motivation to go back to college in the fall."

"Yeah, that'd be great . . ."

"Zach would kill me if he knew I was trying to fix him up," she says, wrinkling her nose, "so I was gonna be super chill about it. You know, I'd just show up at Sheehan's with Meg, then introduce them when you guys take a break. Then I'd suggest that Meg drop by for the surprise party . . ."

"Great idea," I say, still staring down.

"But I don't think I'll be able to make it to Sheehan's with this stupid cast on my foot. The place isn't exactly designed for people on crutches, you know?" Claire says. "I texted Meg, and she said she can come whether I'm there or not. She said she'll bring a couple of friends. But . . ."

Claire bites her lower lip and looks at me warily. "I need you to introduce them. Would that be okay?"

I twist a ring on my finger. "Yeah, totally . . ."

"I know it'll be weird, introducing him to somebody you don't know yourself, but I can show you her picture, and maybe you guys can pretend you met at the pool or something."

"Mmhmm."

Claire studies my face, forcing me to look at her. "You're sure you don't mind?"

"No, no, I don't mind."

"I just think it would be so good for Zach, you know?"

"Yeah, yeah. I'd be happy to do that."

Except that, suddenly, my stomach is clenching. My hands are clammy as I twist my fingers into pretzels. My heart feels like it might actually crumble.

Because I'm finally acknowledging to myself what I'm really thinking: I wouldn't be happy at all to introduce Zach to another girl. That's actually the least happy thing I could ever imagine doing.

I know it now as urgently, as fiercely, and as passionately as anything I've ever known in my life. I don't want Zach with someone else; I want him with *me*.

Oh my God, what an idiot I've been! I've been so star-struck by the sketchiest guy in the band that I didn't bother to glance to my left at the awesomely sweet and talented Strat player who writes songs that make me weak in the knees. The guy who happily accompanies his sick mom to the pool, or drops everything to be by his sister's side when she breaks her ankle, or comes to my rescue when a drunk hits on me in a bar, or patiently walks me through a complicated chorus for the zillionth time . . .

It's so clear to me now. Hell, it was clear to Sara the first time she met him. "All you seem to be talking about," she told me when I was ready to throw Declan a parade for buying me a lousy burger, "is Zach."

I cringe as I picture myself trying to impress Declan last night in my stupid skirt and heels or lip-locking with him in the stairwell or Grandpa's Mercury. *Ew*. Times infinity.

Did it really take the thought of Zach being set up with a nice girl to wake me up? Maybe so. That doesn't make me feel exactly proud of myself right now. But I've never been more clear about my feelings for Zach.

"*Thank* you, Scarlett," Claire says, jolting me back into the moment. "Zach really likes you. I know if you put in a good word for Meg, it'll help. And hey, since you're coming to the anniversary party, too, it won't look weird that Meg comes along."

"Right. That works." I can barely look at Claire. I can barely stand the thought of Zach with this girl, Meg. I can barely believe it's taken me this long to realize that Zach is the person who makes me feel warmer and happier than any guy I've ever known.

Claire moves her injured leg slightly and winces.

"Are you okay?" I ask.

"Yeah," she says. "Stupid ankle. Anyway, here's Meg's picture."

Claire scrolls through her phone, then produces a picture of a pretty brunette with curly hair and a sunny smile. She looks natural and friendly in the photo as she playfully mugs for Claire's camera beside a banner for the health fair.

"Isn't she cute?" Claire says.

My stomach tightens. "Uh-huh. Really cute."

"They have so much in common."

Step up, Scarlett, I tell myself. *Quit being selfish. Do what's right for Zach.*

Yes. That's what I need to do. The world's sweetest guy deserves a med student who volunteers at health fairs and looks pretty without makeup and doesn't fall for tools like Declan.

I take a deep breath. "Well . . . I better go. Glad you're gonna be okay."

"Thanks," Claire says. "It was good to see you."

"You, too," I say.

I start walking out, then turn back. I may have blown my chance with Zach, but I might as well seize this opportunity to get a question answered that I've been wondering about for a long time. "Hey, Claire?"

"Yeah?"

"Um," I say.

I stare at my folded fingers, then shake my head. "Never mind."

"No, go ahead," Claire prods.

"It's just . . . um . . ."

Sigh. Now that I'm seeing Zach clearly, I'm seeing Declan clearly, as well. Might as well confirm my suspicions and come to terms with what a clueless fool I've been for the past few weeks.

"Um," I say, "I don't know how tight you are with the other guys in the band, but do you know anything about Mike and his girlfriend?"

"Mia?" Claire asks, and I nod.

"Yeah," Claire says. "I've met her a few times. She's nice. I think she and Mike are really tight—maybe even engaged."

I shake my head. "No, they've broken up."

Her eyebrows arch. "*Really*?"

I nod. "I thought you might have heard and that maybe you'd know why they broke up."

Claire shakes her head. "No, I haven't heard anything. I'm shocked. They dated forever. I wonder what happened."

I glance down. "I think Declan may have had something to do with it," I say.

Claire rolls her eyes. "Figures," she says. "That jerk. He's the kind of guy who . . . well, let's put it this way: he doesn't want every girl, but he wants every girl to want him. So Declan and Mia are together?"

"Oh, I don't know," I answer quickly. "I don't really know anything about it. I just know there's a lot of tension in the band, and I was trying to put two and two together . . ."

"It wouldn't surprise me," Claire says. "But I sure hope Mia didn't break up with Mike over Declan. He has the attention span of a gnat. If Declan and Mia have something going on, I'm guessing it won't last for long."

My heart sinks. On the one hand, it helps that the picture is growing clearer by the minute. On the other, I can't quite process how blind I've been.

"Yeah," I say softly. "But hey, I don't want to start any rumors. I was just wondering what you'd heard."

"I can ask Zach—"

"No, no!" I feel my face flush as I cut Claire off. "I don't want Zach to think I go around gossiping about the band." Or that I give a shit about Declan, which I'm now crystal clear on: I do *not*.

Claire studies me for a moment. How ridiculously transparent do I look? Does she sense that Declan and I have something going on? *Had* something going on? God, I hope not.

"Well," she finally says, "I really appreciate your help in getting Zach and Meg together. I think he's long overdue for some romance."

"Yeah."

I think so, too. But not with Meg.

"Claire, I need to tell you something." I've blurted it out so fast that I didn't have time to stop myself.

She looks at me quizzically. "Yeah?"

I take a deep breath, exhale through puffed-out cheeks, then just say it.

"I don't want to introduce Zach to your friend."

She holds her gaze, an eyebrow arching.

"Because . . . ?"

I pause and take another deep breath. Okay, here goes: "Because I really like him."

• • •

"You're sure you're okay?"

I glance at Zach, nibbling the nail of my pinkie. "Yeah," I assure him as he drives me home from the hospital, silently agonizing that I've selfishly screwed Zach over by dousing Claire's matchmaking plans. "I'm fine. Long day, huh?"

"I'm really sorry about the detour," he says.

"No, that's not what I meant," I say earnestly. "I loved talking to your mom. She's amazing."

"Yeah, she is," Zach says, his eyes focused on the road.

I peer at him cautiously. "I'm so sorry for what she's going through."

He gives me a stoic smile. "Thank you."

I contemplate whether or not to utter my next sentence, but it comes tumbling out without my permission. "Are you scared about losing her?"

He considers my words as stars twinkle in a velvety sky. "I just don't want *her* to be scared," he finally says. "That's the only thing that keeps me up at night."

I swallow hard. "I know what you mean. My brother . . . I hope so badly he didn't suffer . . . and that he wasn't scared."

Crickets chirp rhythmically in the night air as Zach drives.

"You know, my mom told me," he says, "that she imagines dying is like being born. You go through a long, dark tunnel by yourself, but light and love are waiting on the other end. I hope that's true."

We cross the bridge in the darkness, the river glistening beneath the stars.

"Did you write that song about her?" I ask. "The one we practiced today?"

He smiles at me. "So you paid attention to the lyrics?"

"Of course I did," I say, singing them again in my head:

I see the sorrow in your face,
And I don't know just where to start.
But all the pieces are in place,
And I won't let you fall apart.

"It's beautiful," I tell him.

Zach squints bashfully. "Confession?"

"Sure," I say. "What?"

"Um . . ." He taps his steering wheel nervously as he continues driving. "I'm sure my mom was in my thoughts when I came up with that song. But at the risk of completely creeping you out . . ."

"Yeah?" I prod.

Zach sneaks a glance at me. "I kinda wrote that one about you."

• • •

I don't trust my voice not to catch as I absorb his words, so I'm silent as Zach rounds the curve and turns into Grandpa's neighborhood. Pine trees sway lazily overhead as we drive down the street. Zach turns into Grandpa's driveway and switches off the engine, the crickets still chirping in the bushes. A gauzy moon hangs overhead.

"So I *did* creep you out," he finally says, avoiding my gaze as his hands stay rested on the steering wheel.

"*No*," I assure him, taking off my seat belt and leaning closer. "That's the nicest thing anybody's ever told me."

"I just," he says, still not quite meeting my eye, "I saw the pain in your eyes when I met you. I *knew* the pain in your eyes. And I couldn't stand it. I wanted to make it better."

I swallow hard to dislodge the lump in my throat.

"I'm so touched," I whisper, and he finally meets my gaze. "You're the most incredible person I know."

He lowers his chin and smiles.

"I love that the song is hopeful," I say softly, my voice still slightly trembling.

"Absolutely," he says, stealing glances but staring mostly at his hands as they dangle on the steering wheel. "That's how you make me feel: hopeful. You're sad, but you're . . . vibrant. You inspire me."

Nearby branches sway languidly in a breeze. "The lyrics . . . lifting each other up when we're down and putting each other back together—they melt my heart."

I stop short of saying what I actually mean: that the song is about *his* lifting me up, about *his* putting me back together. The comfort of this thought makes my heart soar.

"You inspire me, too," I tell him, and he smiles at me.

A long moment passes, then I say, "You know, Liam and I tried writing a few songs together."

"Yeah? I'd love to hear them some time."

"No, you wouldn't," I say dismissively. "We were kind of

a work in progress. But the potential was definitely there. At least, that's what my mom said."

We laugh lightly, then I add, "I think we'd have eventually made an awesome team."

I snuggle deeper into my seat, hugging my knees against my chest and gazing straight ahead. "Liam and I really got each other, you know?" I say wistfully. "Our sense of humor, our taste in music . . . everything. He and my sister were close, too, but it wasn't the same. When David Bowie died, Liam and I walked around in a daze for a solid month. 'Ziggy Stardust' *still* makes me cry. Sara didn't even know who Bowie was."

"*Pfft*. Sounds like a loser," Zach deadpans.

I laugh and turn to face him. "Zach Spencer, that's the first time I've ever heard you insult somebody."

"I was *kidding*."

I study his face. "You have dimples when you smile," I say dreamily. "Not all the time, but sometimes." I touch my finger lightly against his cheek. "You have them now."

He blushes. "So noted."

I keep smiling, and a quiet moment passes.

"Hey," I say, leaning closer, "your sister mentioned to me that you were thinking about dropping out of school . . . or at least taking a break."

He clears his throat uneasily.

"I hope you don't mind that she told me," I say. "She's just worried about you. She really wants you to finish school. She said that's what your mom wants, too."

"So that's what she wanted to talk to you about in the hospital?"

I squirm slightly. "Yeah . . ."

"Well," he says, "I'll definitely finish. Just maybe from

home. I might take online courses or even commute. It's not that far."

I shake my head. "Claire said your mom really hates the thought of your life getting disrupted because of her."

He ponders my words, then says, "We'll see."

"I'm not trying to tell you what to do," I stress. "I'm just passing along what Claire told me. But, Zach?"

"Yeah?"

"I want you to know, what you do for your mom? It's enough. I've lost a lot of sleep, thinking I could have saved my brother—that if I hadn't been in so much denial, I could have made a difference. I kept thinking *I* was the one who could have saved him; I was the one who *should* have saved him. But I was talking to your mom in the hospital, and . . . I dunno . . . I'm starting to think . . ."

"Yeah?" Zach prods.

"I think what I did was enough. I loved him. I'd have done anything in the world for him. He knew that. I think it was enough."

A cloud drifts away from the moon.

"And to be perfectly honest," I tell Zach, twirling a lock of hair, "I have an ulterior motive for wanting you back in school."

He smiles. "Yeah?"

I give him a sideways glance. "I want you back," I say, "because I'll be there."

• • •

I smile. "Hi, Grandpa."

He closes his book and stands up to greet me. "How was practice?" he asks.

I smile wearily. "Practice was fine, but Zach got called to

the emergency room when he was driving me home. His sister broke her ankle. I went with him to the hospital."

Grandpa shakes his head. "That poor family . . ."

"She'll be okay," I assure him.

"Still, they've had more than their share of problems lately. And such nice people. Harold's grandson . . . he's an awfully nice boy, don't you think?"

I contemplate my response, feeling suddenly exposed. Does Grandpa sense that my heart is about to burst out of my chest after spending time with Zach? Nothing happened; he just walked me to the door and said good night. And I didn't even *want* anything to happen; I'm so ashamed that I was lip-locking Douchebag Declan just a few hours earlier. Thank God things never went farther than a kiss with him, despite his best efforts. I'd have died of shame. I'm dying of shame *now*. What was I thinking, falling for that player? Sure, I came to my senses, but not soon enough. I wish I could erase those kisses from my past. All I can think about now is Zach. Does he know, or guess, that Declan and I have hung out a few times? The thought makes me nauseated. I want to wipe the slate clean. I want to touch Zach's dimple again.

"Yeah, Grandpa, Zach's a really nice guy," I say, then sigh and plop onto the couch. Grandpa sits next to me, placing his glasses on the end table.

"You know," he says, "I was flipping through your graduation pictures again tonight."

"Yeah?"

He nods. "Made me think about myself when I was your age."

I hug a throw pillow against my stomach. "What were you like?" I ask.

He peers into space. "A lot like you. Independent and confident, but deep down a little scared, a little overwhelmed."

A clock on the wall ticks rhythmically.

"Why 'overwhelmed'?"

He shrugs. "I was conscientious to a fault. I thought I had to have everything figured out all at once. I'd graduated, so that meant I was officially an adult. Well, adults have plans, don't they? I wasn't sure what I wanted in life; I tried to enlist in the Army, but my asthma kept me from qualifying, and I'd have loved to go to college, but I couldn't afford it. Still, I knew I needed a plan. And I thought the plan was supposed to be the blueprint for the rest of my life. So I tried to make a plan. I even wrote it down. Might even still have it."

My finger lightly traces the contours of the pillow. "I'd love to see that," I say. "Do you remember what it said?"

His fingers fold together. "Trust me, there were no delusions of grandeur. I was practical above all else. Everybody coming out of the Depression was. I already had a job, so I think I outlined the stages I'd need to go through to work my way into management. And I came up with a budget—how much I'd spend on bills, how much I'd save, how much I'd give my mother and sisters . . ."

I smile. "Was I part of the plan?"

His eyes sparkle as he gazes at me. "You sure were. Nothing was more important to me than family. But, well, I wasn't going steady at the time—"

I giggle at his retro-speak.

"And I didn't have a lot of prospects."

"But Grandpa, you were so handsome. You *are* so handsome."

He waves away my compliment. "Oh, I had some dates

here and there. But I knew none of those gals were the one for me. And that frustrated me, because—"

"Because of your plan."

He chuckles. "Right. Because of my plan."

He leans closer, then says, "But I wish I hadn't worried so much. I wish I hadn't felt like I had to have my whole life figured out at eighteen. Because you know what?"

"What?"

"Everything worked out fine. Your grandma coming along, returning that scarf? That wasn't part of the plan. I'd had no idea when I went to work that morning that I was about to meet the love of my life. It just happened. I wish I'd had more faith that my life would unfold in its own way, in its own time, and that everything would work out just fine."

I lower my chin and raise an eyebrow. "Grandpa, why do I get the feeling you're sneaking a life lesson into this conversation?"

"No, no!" he insists unconvincingly. "Like I said, your graduation photos got me thinking about—"

"It's okay, Grandpa," I assure him, leaning in to kiss him on the cheek. "I love your stories, whether you're sneaking in life lessons or not."

He hugs me tightly. "You're a wonderful person, Scarlett," he whispers into my ear, and I swallow a lump in my throat as he strokes my hair. I'm not sure why I suddenly feel so emotional, but a couple of reasons stand out as prime contenders. For one thing, Grandpa's calling me by my real name, which he only does during Highly Significant Times. For another, I feel a desperate urge to call him out on his glaring miscalculation, to assure him I'm as *un*-wonderful as a person can be, as evidenced by my horrible judgment six hours earlier in the stairwell with Declan.

But I want more than anything in the world to be who Grandpa thinks I am.

I tell him good night and walk to my bedroom when my cellphone chirps. I gaze down at the screen and read a text from Varun:

I wanna come see you tomorrow and take you out to dinner. Sixish?

My brows weave together. Fer reals? I'd love it. What's the occasion?

See you tomorrow.

That's it? No explanation? No random emoji for a signoff? That's weird.

I study the screen for a long moment.

I wonder what's up . . .

CHAPTER NINETEEN

I arrive at the pizza place fifteen minutes early and walk up to the counter.

"I called in an order for Scarlett?" I say to the girl with thick dark hair who is manning the cash register.

She does a subtle double take, then says, "It'll be ready in a few minutes. Eat-in or takeout?"

"Eat-in," I say.

"Okay. Sit wherever you'd like, and your waitress will bring it to you when it's ready. Just one?"

"Um, one person will be joining me." I glance around at the tables. "But he's not here yet. I'm a little early."

"Okay," she says. "The waitress will bring two sets of silverware."

"Thanks."

I start to walk away, but the girl is still looking at me. I pause. Does she have something else to say? But she lowers her eyes.

Weird.

I walk to the table, bouncing lightly on the balls of my feet. This is shaping up as the greatest Monday ever. When I was at the pool earlier in the day, Zach texted me, telling me that he wouldn't be able to swim his laps today but that he was listening to David Bowie in my honor.

Plus, I'm just about to see Varun. I'm still puzzled about why he's coming. He said he wanted to visit, but I figured he'd come on a night when the band was playing. Why tonight? He's probably worked all day in the lab, and now he's driving over eighty miles to see me. I'm psyched . . . just confused.

But it's all good. My best friend is on his way, our pizza is in the oven, and the phone displaying Zach's text is nestled tightly in my hand.

I'm reading it again when the girl from the cash register walks up to me.

"Yes?" I say.

"Um . . ." She smooths her shirt with the pizza logo on it. "I couldn't help but notice your name. *Scarlett.* That's a pretty unusual name."

I crinkle my eyes. "Yeah?"

"I was wondering: are you the Scarlett who plays with the Beastings?"

"Yeah, I am."

She steals a glance, then sucks in her lips. "Could I possibly join you for just a minute?"

I stare at her for a moment, too disoriented to answer. The girl who mans the cash register at the pizza place wants to join me? This day just keeps getting stranger.

"Uh . . . sure," I finally say, gesturing toward the empty seat in the booth.

"Sorry," she says as she slips into the booth. "I know you don't even know me. But . . . my name is Mia. I used to date Mike."

I process her words, then my eyes widen. "Oh, right. Nice to meet you."

"Thanks. You, too."

"Mike's great," I tell her. "He slays the bass."

"Yeah, he's good."

Mia clears her throat. "Um," she finally says, "I'm not even sure what I want to say. I just . . . I want to make sure Mike's doing okay. He's blocked my number, so I can't call or text him."

A couple and two small kids walk past us. I wait for them to move out of earshot, then say, "He's fine."

Mia folds her hands on the table and stares at her fingers. "I was really stupid," she says in a small voice. "I broke up with him, and I . . . I just feel really stupid."

I study her closer. "Did Declan have anything to do with it?"

She blushes and her eyes widen. "How'd you know?"

I shrug noncommittally.

"Declan and I are together now," Mia continues. "I know that sounds sketchy—and I guess it is—but I never meant to hurt Mike. It's just . . . Declan and I had been getting closer, just as friends, then one thing kinda led to another. He was really persistent, and I guess I wanted to see where it would lead."

I eye her coolly. "So you and Declan are a couple."

She frowns. "Well, technically. But I think he's already stepping out on me. I have my suspicions. It wouldn't exactly be out of character. He was dating somebody else when we started going out." She laughs ruefully. "Maybe Mike should date *that* girl."

I rest an elbow on the vinyl tabletop. "How long have you and Declan been together?"

"Just a couple of weeks," Mia says. "I mean, like I said, our friendship had been building for a while, but it was a couple of Saturdays ago that I told Mike we needed to take a break." Her eyes fall. "I really hurt him."

My brain thrums through its database to do the math. A couple of Saturdays ago is when I invited Declan to the Bixleys' cookout. He kept checking his texts, then ducked out early. After he'd finished flirting with my sister, he'd no doubt rushed off to keep his date with his new girlfriend, Mia. Then, just a few days later, he and I were making out in Grandpa's Mercury. I feel queasy.

"Did you guys go out on Saturday?" I ask her in a tight voice, recalling our one actual date. If you can call a burger joint a date.

"This past Saturday?"

I nod stiffly.

"We went out late," Mia says. "He was supposed to take me out to dinner, but he said something came up. Like I said, he's already acting shady. I've been a world-class idiot lately. I think I'm gonna break it off."

I purse my lips. "I think that's probably a good idea," I say quietly.

Mia's eyes search mine. "What do you know?" she asks slowly.

I sigh. Do I owe her an explanation?

No, I don't think I do. I didn't know she was in the picture when I hooked up with Declan, and I don't want to risk having the information get back to the band. Get back to Zach. So I decide to repeat to Mia what Sara said to me: "Declan just seems like a player."

I can't believe I actually got pissed when Sara pointed that out to me a couple of weeks ago. I can't believe I needed to have it pointed out. Maybe I fell on my head after I moved in with Grandpa. There's got to be a logical explanation for my temporary insanity, for my utter lack of judgment.

Mia leans closer. "Would you mind telling Mike I asked about him?"

I open my mouth to respond when I feel a tap on my shoulder. I spin my head around, excited not only to see Varun but to have a graceful way to cut short my conversation with Mia.

And yes, just as I assumed, there stands Varun, looking neatly groomed in khaki pants and a plaid button-up shirt.

But he's not alone.

I blink hard, then stand to face the person he's with. "Sara?" I say, wide-eyed. "What are you doing here?"

• • •

As Mia slips out of the booth to resume her post behind the cash register, Varun and my sister slide into the seat, averting their eyes while explaining that Sara just happened to hear about Varun's plan and decided to tag along.

But that makes no sense. How would Sara "just happen" to have heard about it? I didn't mention it, and she and Varun don't talk . . . do they? Of course they don't. They barely could be bothered to grunt greetings to each other when Varun came to our house. They got along fine, but Sara was no more interested in my BFF than I was in her boyfriend *du jour.*

I'm not buying it. Something is definitely up.

I narrow my eyes as I examine their studiously neutral expressions. "How did you know Varun was coming?" I ask Sara.

A waitress carrying a large pizza breezes past us, the aroma of oregano and freshly baked dough wafting through the air.

"You *guys*," I say through clenched teeth, "tell me what is going on."

A waitress comes to the table carrying three plates and three sets of napkin-wrapped utensils. She arranges them hastily, then disappears as a guy behind her sets three plastic glasses of ice water in front of us. I'm too busy staring down Sara and Varun to glance in the servers' direction.

Varun leans into his folded hands on the table, pumping them nervously, and gives Sara a sideways glance. "We came here to tell you something," he says.

The moment hangs in the air.

"Tell me what?" I say in slow motion, not moving a muscle.

"Here ya go!"

We glance up at the waitress delivering our pizza, setting a stand on the table and centering it on top. "It's real hot," she tells us in a thick Southern accent, then assesses our untouched water glasses. "Oh, and did you guys want anything else to drink?"

All three of us seem frozen in our seats. "We're good," I finally tell the waitress without taking my eyes off Varun.

"Ya sher? We've got Coke, beer, tea, lemonade—"

"We're good, thanks," Varun says, then gives her a brief, apologetic smile.

"Well, y'all just let me know if you need anything."

Varun nods at her, and she slips away.

A hurricane is roiling through my brain as I try to imagine what Varun and Sara want to tell me.

Oh God . . . is it possible? Are they seeing each other? Every other guy I've ever known has salivated over my sister. Well, every guy who isn't gay. And Varun *is* gay, right? True, he's still being cagey with his parents, but that's just because he's scared of disappointing them, not because he isn't really gay . . . right? Or maybe he's bi? I couldn't care less about his sexual orientation, but the thought of my sister once again upstaging me—and with *Varun* of all people—makes me dizzy.

"Scarlett," Varun says, freaking me out by using my real name, "there's something I've been keeping from you for a while. And I'm very, very sorry."

I'm still frozen in place, not sure if I want to hear more.

"The only reason we didn't tell you," he continues, his ebony eyes locking with mine, "is that . . . well, I'm not sure why we didn't tell you, except that it would have felt weird. Neither of us were ashamed or anything. I guess we just didn't want you to feel like our friendship—yours and mine—was being overshadowed. Because nothing could ever overshadow our friendship, Scarlett. But we should have told you."

I absorb his words, then lift my index finger limply and point from Varun to Sara, then back again. "You two . . . ?"

They crinkle their brows. Sara's eyebrows arch. "*Oh,*" she says. "You think Varun and I . . . ? *No,* Scarlett."

I lean sharply into the table, a shot of adrenaline now jolting me into action. "Then what?" I snap at Varun.

Varun and Sara steal glances at each other as if fortifying their will to keep talking. After a long moment, Varun answers quietly:

"I was seeing Liam."

• • •

"Scarlett, please eat something."

Yeah. That's the answer to my utter sense of betrayal: *pizza.*

I'm not the only one who isn't eating. The pizza has gone untouched since the waitress set it on the table.

I have so many questions that I don't even know where to begin.

Varun is blathering a stream of information: he's the one who approached Liam, and Liam resisted at first, but then last summer, they decided to go for it, and they didn't really make a conscious decision not to tell me, they just never got around to actually doing it, and when Liam died, well, as devastated as Varun was, all of his energy went into holding me together, and then . . . then he texted me and asked if we could meet for pizza.

But whereas the information sounds chronological, my mind is bouncing around all over the place. First of all, Liam was gay? How could I not know something so basic about him?

"Why didn't he tell us he was gay?" I ask Sara, but the look on her face is all the answer I need. *I'm* the one he didn't tell. Sara knew.

"And Mom and Dad?"

Sara lowers her chin and nods, staring at her lap.

I toss my head back. "So everybody knew except me." I'm saying it to myself, not them, because, you know, *duh.*

Tears spring to my eyes. "He could have told me anything," I say in barely a whisper, still more to myself than them. "He knew he could have told me anything."

"Of course he did," Sara says, reaching over to take my hand. I feel like pulling it away, but I'm too numb to move.

"How long did everybody else know?" I ask her.

She squeezes my hand gently. "Just a couple of years. I think Liam wasn't really sure himself until he went to college. He was still figuring things out."

I glare at her through tear-stained eyes and reclaim my hand with a jerk. "But once he figured it out, then it was time to tell everybody but me."

Sara closes her eyes and shakes her head. "It wasn't like that."

"*I* was the one he talked to," I say, realizing even as I say it how ridiculous I sound. "He only told me because I asked," Sara says.

"How did you know to ask?"

She considers the question, then shrugs. "I guessed."

I blink hard. Why didn't *I* guess? Just precisely how clueless *am* I?

"I'd heard a couple of rumors at school," Sara says, "and I knew Liam wasn't doing the conventional dating thing, so . . ."

"Oh, great. So everybody in school knew, too."

"Of course not," Sara says. "You know what a private person Liam was. It's not like he went around telling—"

"You know what's weird?" I interject bitterly. "I was stupid enough to think *I* was part of his private life."

Sara's eyebrows weave together. "It's *because* you and Liam were so close that he had a hard time telling you. You were his baby sister. He was so protective of you. He didn't really know how any of us would handle the gay thing. I mean, Mom and Dad are chill, but they're Catholic. And once he and Varun were together, he was terrified that you'd think he was trying to take away your best friend."

Varun leans closer. "Scarlett, he adored you. He talked about you all the time."

I shake my head slowly, my arms squeezed around my chest. "Liam barely even paid any attention to you when we hung out."

"I know," Varun stresses. "That's how it was up until last summer. I was just some kid he barely noticed." Varun squirms, then continues, his ebony eyes downcast. "But I noticed *him*.

When I'd come see your band, I remember feeling like he was singing right to my soul. I was just an awkward kid, though; I knew that even if Liam was gay, he'd have zero interest in me. Except, right before he went back to school in the fall . . ."

"Yes?" I prod, my curiosity overriding my hurt.

"It was when we were painting his bedroom," Varun says. "Remember how I came by that morning? You and I had planned to go running in the park, but you decided to go shopping with your mom and sister instead? So I offered to stick around and help Liam paint?"

"Yeah," I concede.

"We were alone for hours that day," Varun says, "and we started talking."

My fingers squeeze into my arms. "What did you talk about?"

Varun shrugs. "I dunno . . . baseball, music, movies . . . then we started talking about a David Sedaris book we both really liked, and, you know, Sedaris is gay, so we started talking about that, and . . ."

"So you were setting him up?" I say, my eyes steely. "You offered to help him paint so you could hit on him?"

"*Scarlett*!" Sara says, but Varun touches her arm, letting her know he can handle it, that he's willing to endure a volley of insults for my sake.

"It wasn't like that at all," Varun answers calmly. "Even when we realized we were both interested, Liam still resisted. He said I was too young, and that I was *your* friend, and that he'd be headed back to college soon . . ."

"Did you visit him there?" I ask, suddenly intent on ferreting out what I perceive as individual acts of betrayal. "Did you go see him in Athens?"

Varun blinks several times, his long, dark lashes fluttering. "Yeah," he finally says. "Once we decided that our relationship was worth pursuing, I visited him a few times."

"And what lies would you tell me to cover your tracks?"

His eyes fall. "I never lied to you," he says. "I just wouldn't necessarily volunteer any information."

"And when Liam was home, you'd sneak around behind my back?"

"*Scarlett—*"

I whip around to silence Sara. "I deserve to know," I tell her. "*I'm* the one who was lied to, thinking I was having authentic relationships with both my brother and my best friend when they were actually living in a parallel universe."

I stare at my lap, a tear trickling down my cheek, and squeeze my hands together. "Did everybody sit around and laugh about what an idiot I was?" I say, my voice trembling.

"Of course not," Sara says.

"We were going to tell you really soon," Varun says. "We didn't know at first how serious we were. What if we'd told you right away, then our relationship fizzled, and we'd made things weird between me and you for no reason? Neither of us wanted that."

"Well, as long as both of you got what you wanted," I say, spitting the words. "I'd hate it if things were weird for *you*. Because there's nothing weird about finding out that the two people I thought I knew best in the world are the two people I didn't really know at all."

Varun looks at me evenly. "You know that's not true."

"I don't know it!" I say, my brimming eyes beginning to overflow.

I glance over at the hostess stand, where Mia and another

girl are talking. I brush my cheeks roughly with the heels of my hands, anticipating the added humiliation of having people notice I'm crying in public.

I lean in closer and lower my voice. "How could you have let me talk to you about Liam, knowing I was making a fool of myself with every word I uttered? And how could Liam have let me talk about *you*?"

There are so many dimensions, and my head is spinning.

Varun shakes his head sadly.

"Did you know about the pills?" I ask him. "I mean, before Liam died?"

Varun looks at me wearily with his ebony eyes. "You'd mentioned them to me a couple of times," he says, "so, sure, I asked him about them. But he said everything was under control. And, you know, the pills came from the goddamn *pharmacy*. They were *prescribed*. Liam said he was weaning himself off, and I thought it was getting better instead of worse. I thought . . ."

My eyes fill with tears and so do Varun's.

"He was gonna be off the pills by Christmas—he'd promised—and that's when we were going to tell you about . . . about us," he says, his chin quivering.

He pauses, squeezing his eyes shut. "We thought we had all the time in the world," Varun says, choking on the words. "I'm sorry, Scarlett. I'm just so sorry."

CHAPTER TWENTY

"You know what's weird?"

I gaze at Sara in the twin bed next to mine, leaning up on an elbow and hugging the one-eyed bear against my chest.

She sits up and faces me, her silhouette gauzy in the moonlight as her loose bun topples to one side. We've been talking for two hours and had finally started drifting off to sleep. But I'm apparently not quite talked out. Sara, who insisted on spending the night with me even though it means she'll miss a day of work tomorrow, doesn't seem to mind the disruption. I'm still mad—mad, hurt, confused—but I'm too drained to pull off my customary big chill. And before Varun dropped his bombshell, I'd been dying to talk to my sister about the last couple of days.

"What?" she asks, pressing her knees against her chest.

"Right before you and Varun got to the pizza place, something happened that I was pretty sure at the time would qualify as the most interesting part of my day."

Sara leans closer. "Details, please."

So I find myself blurting out two weeks' worth of information in a single sitting.

I tell Sara how I let Declan kiss me that night in the parking lot, and how I let him kiss me again, and how we'd gone out on an actual date (sorta), but that I kept hearing warning bells in my head the whole time. I feel a silly smile spread on my face when the story moves to Zach: his patience and encouragement in the band, his visits to the pool with his mom, his weekend trips to the emergency room, the song he wrote for me . . .

"*Aw*," Sara says, her brows forming an inverted V. "He wrote a *song* for you?"

"Yeah," I say dreamily. "You'll have to come hear us play it."

"I *love* Zach!" she says. "I *told* you he's your type."

I smile. "We'll see. I'm not even sure what kind of signals I'm getting from him. I mean, he's so sweet to *every*body, so it might just be that he—"

"Scarlett. He wrote a song for you."

I wrinkle my nose. "Yeah. He did."

Sara bounces lightly on the bed, then squeals, "I love this!"

"Except that . . ."

"Except that what?"

I wince. "I'd die if Zach found out about me and Declan. I don't want him to think I'm some flake who hooks up with anybody who comes along."

"So you don't think he knows?" Sara asks.

I shrug. "I hope not. Declan said he didn't want the band finding out, oh, which is what I started to tell you: right before you and Varun got to the restaurant, a girl who works there came up and introduced herself—as Declan's *girlfriend*. He stole her away from Mike, the bass player in the band, and they started going out, like, the exact same time he started hitting on me."

"Classy," Sara says, her lip curled in disgust. "What did she say?"

"That she thinks Declan is already stepping out on her. That she regrets breaking up with Mike."

"Did you tell her about you and Declan?"

I shake my head. "Nah. Just that I think he's a player."

"Now, who else do I know who uttered those words of wisdom?" she teases, cocking her head and resting an index finger against her chin.

I smile ruefully, then lower my head and bite my bottom lip. "What I want more than anything," I tell her, "is to hit the reset button and pretend the past two weeks never even happened. The Declan parts, that is."

Sara sits up straighter. "Except that they did happen."

I roll my eyes. "Don't lecture me, or I'll be mad at you again."

She presents a palm as a stop sign. "No lectures. Not even any advice, even though I *am* the one who warned you about Declan. Just a little reality check, that's all."

I rub the bear's mangy fur. "I guess I'm due for one of those."

"Well," Sara says, eyeing me warily, "maybe I do have *one* piece of advice."

I roll my eyes. "What?"

She squeezes her lips together. "Make things okay with Varun," she says. "Scarlett, he loves you so much. And I love him. I didn't really know him well until Liam died—I was worried about him, especially after you left town, so I reached out to him a few times—and I'm just amazed at how *together* he is. But he's really, really hurting. And it would crush him if you let this come between you."

My back stiffens slightly. "So now you're gonna school me about Varun, like Varun schooled me about Liam?"

"Stop being an ice queen," Sara says. "And a drama queen, while you're at it."

"Stop being a priss. And an ass, while you're at it."

"Ooh, burn!"

We giggle, and I throw the mangy bear at her.

"Now throw him back," I say with a pout, and she obliges.

I hug him close.

"There," I say contentedly. "Now I can sleep."

CHAPTER TWENTY-ONE

"Aw, leaving already?"

I glance up at Zach, startled.

Since Sara is in town, Julie, the second-shift lifeguard, offered to clock in early so Sara and I can grab lunch before she heads back to Atlanta. Sara joined me at the pool a few minutes before my shift ended so she could swim a few laps before we eat. She's squeezing water out of her long brown hair as she pads behind me in flip flops on our way out of the gate. But considering that Zach is walking in as I'm walking out, I may be rethinking our plans.

"Hi," I say, adjusting my sunglasses as I stand there in my razor-back Speedo, dodging the squealing kids zipping past us. "Zach, you remember my sister, Sara . . ."

They smile at each other. "Hey, Zach. Good to see you," Sara says.

"Yeah, you too." He rubs his chin. "Too bad about our timing."

I glance over his shoulder and see Mike and Kyle approaching the gate in their swim trunks.

"Hi, guys," I say, giving a wave. "Your timing sucks. My sister and I were just leaving."

"You can't go!" Kyle says cheerfully as they catch up with Zach. "Who's gonna rein in our horseplay?"

"And I was seriously considering a noodle assault," Zach quips.

I grin. "This is Sara," I tell them, nodding toward my sister. "We were gonna grab lunch."

"Hi," Sara tells them. "I heard you play at Sheehan's a couple of weeks ago."

"Yeah, yeah," Mike says enthusiastically. "Did you like what you heard? If you stay, we can sing *a cappella* for you."

We laugh, but Sara folds her hands together and says with a playful lilt in her voice, "Or you guys could join us for lunch."

Zach holds out his arms and stares at his torso. "Not sure how presentable I am," he says. "Maybe we could swing by my house so I could change?"

"Clothes are overrated," I respond. "How 'bout we go to Taco Loco? Sara and I have shorts and T-shirts in the car. She and I can order, then we can sit outside and eat."

"Sold, to the lady in the Speedo," Kyle says.

It's as we're walking out the gate into the parking lot that I find a chance to subtly pull Mike aside.

"Hey, Mike?" I say, lowering my voice.

"Yeah?" he says.

"Um . . . I met Mia yesterday."

He ponders my words as we slow our pace. "Okay."

"I'd gone out for pizza, and she introduced herself," I explain. "She told me what happened between you two."

"Well, shit happens, right?"

He's looking straight ahead as we walk, his voice tight.

"She asked how you were doing. I think she has a lot of regrets."

"Yeah, regrets," Mike says. "They're a bitch."

"Well . . . she asked me to tell you that she's thinking about you."

He nods sharply, still looking ahead as we walk. "So noted. Thanks, Scarlett."

We walk a few more steps, then I say casually, "For what it's worth, I think she made the biggest mistake of her life. You're a great guy."

He finally smiles. "Thanks."

After a few more steps, he says, "You've got a fan of your own, you know."

I furrow my brow. "Who?"

Mike nods at the back of Zach's head. He's outpaced us by several steps and is out of earshot. "Just between you and me," Mike says quietly.

I give him a sideways smile. "Yeah?"

He smiles back. "Yeah," he says, pumping heart-shaped hands against his chest. We keep walking, and I suddenly feel like I'm skipping on top of a cloud.

I like having Zach for a fan.

I like it more than just about anything else in the world.

• • •

"*Pet Sounds*, hands down."

Mike groans as Zach weighs in on his vote for best album ever.

"You're livin' in the past, man," he teases. "*Dark Side of the Moon* gets my vote."

Zach snorts. "Yeah, that's current."

"*Revolver*," I say. "I like it even better than *Abbey Road*."

Sara sips her Coke as we sit outside Taco Loco under an umbrella and pouts. "Are you guys gonna geek out on music the whole time we're here?"

"We're a band," Kyle says faux-solemnly. "That's what we do."

We bite into our tacos beneath a cloudless sky.

"You know what I don't get?" Sara says. "I don't get how you play without music. I play piano, and sure, I can play a few things by ear, but a whole night's worth of songs with no music to follow? I might as well be trying to speak Latin or something."

"Just because we *play* doesn't mean we play *well*," Mike qualifies, and we laugh.

"Rock 'n roll isn't like Mozart," I explain. "It's organic. You don't *play* it; you *feel* it."

"Deep," Kyle deadpans. "Either that, or we just kinda mess around without really knowing what we're doing."

"Although we could definitely consider adding some Mozart to the set list," Zach suggests.

A breeze makes the umbrella over our heads rustle lazily.

"I'm less interested in what we *add* to the band than what we *subtract* from it," Mike says, still sounding lighthearted but casting the guys a knowing look.

"Aw, Dec's been on his best behavior lately," Kyle replies. "And he's keeping up with his hair appointments—those streaks are looking fierce lately. That's what really matters."

He and Mike laugh, but I steal an uneasy glance at Sara. I feel confident now that none of the guys know about Declan and me. Surely they wouldn't be this unguarded if they did . . .

right? Plus, if Mike knew, he'd have mentioned it when I talked to him about Mia . . . right?

I take a deep breath. I'll have to face Declan at practice tomorrow night, but I'm almost home free. Once we endure our first post-couple encounter, the awkwardness will be out of the way, right? Plus, he's no doubt moved on to some other girl by now, so he's not likely to be distracted by my awesomeness anymore.

"Guys, I hate to cut things short, but I've got to get home," Zach says, tossing a crumpled napkin on top of his empty tray.

"Right, right," Mike says. "Tell your mom we said hello. Oh, and Claire. I hope she's feeling better. Try to stay out of the emergency room for a day or two, okay?"

"Sounds like a plan to me," Zach says as he rises from his chair.

My eyebrows suddenly arch. "Oh, Zach, I left my bag in your car the other night," I say, "the one with my spare strings and picks. Can I grab it?"

He extends his arm, then helps me with my chair.

"Be right back, guys," I tell the others.

As Zach and I walk to his car, he asks, "Any special occasion for Sara being here?"

My muscles tense. I haven't thought about Liam and Varun since I saw Zach walk through the gate at the pool. I'm still processing the news. That's fair, right? Yes, I know Varun is suffering, and I know now why he's cried along with me for the past six months. I get that he needs a friend now more than ever. But I'm entitled to feel betrayed. I'm gonna need a while.

"Long story," I tell Zach quietly.

We reach his car, and he studies my face. "You okay?" he asks.

"Yeah, yeah. I'm fine." I take a deep breath.

He looks unconvinced, but he eventually nods, then opens his car door, reaches inside, and pulls out my bag.

"I would've brought it to practice tomorrow," he tells me.

I flick my hair off my shoulder. "Yeah, but then I wouldn't have had a reason to walk with you to your car."

He smiles at my response, and we stand silently for a moment, gazing into each other's eyes. *Whoa*, his eyes are beautiful . . . so warm and silky and chocolaty and. . .

. . . and he kisses me.

Just like that.

He just leans in and kisses me. It's a soft, gentle kiss, as natural and effortless as the summer breeze.

As he pulls away, his face suddenly brightens. "Hey, my dad is making tacos tonight. Want to join us?"

I raise an eyebrow. "Tacos."

He hesitates for a beat, then lightly whaps the side of his head. "Tacos," he repeats.

I laugh, extending my arm toward the taco place we've just left.

"But you know what?" I say. "I loved our lunch so much that there's nothing I'd rather do than recreate the experience."

"You're sure?" he says, squinting shyly as he lowers his head to look me in the eye.

I smile. "*Si, señor.*"

• • •

"Play your ballad," Zach's mom calls from the kitchen.

As his dad finishes up the dishes, Zach and I have walked into the adjoining den and, per his mom's request, start strumming some tunes. Zach's playing his acoustic guitar and singing, with me joining in on harmony.

"Gonna need to get a little more specific than that, Mom," Zach calls back.

"Um," she says, "the new one. I mean, not the *new* new one. The one about being new."

" 'New to Me'?" Zach queries.

"Yes!" Madelyn responds. "I love that one."

Zach wrinkles his nose at me. "She loves all of 'em," he says breezily. "No accounting for taste, right?"

I smile. "I love them, too."

"Well, in that case . . ."

He strums the intro on his guitar, then begins the first verse: "I had some lessons left to learn. I had some bridges to unburn . . ."

Madelyn joins us after a couple of minutes, tapping the rhythm on her walker and singing along on the chorus: "I'm waking up. I feel the sunlight shining through. My eyes are open; now I see . . ."

When Zach drove me to his house a little after seven, I was surprised to see Madelyn out of her wheelchair. She explained, while apologizing for the construction mess all around us and reminding me to watch my step, that she tries to stay on her feet as much as possible at home. And she looks great—relaxed, content, youthful . . . it's so hard to comprehend that she's sick.

Zach's dad walks into the den, pulls his wife away from her walker, and sweeps her into his arms, doing a little dance with one hand on the small of her back, the other holding hers lightly in midair. A candle on the end table casts an amber glow in the room, and the scent of our taco dinner lingers in the air.

"You knew all along, but it's new to me," Zach sings as his dad gives Madelyn a dip.

I swallow to dislodge a sudden lump in my throat, then resume the lyrics, pushing past the melancholy undercurrent as Zach's parents glide across the floor: "I shook the shackles from my past. I left behind the pain at last . . ."

By the final chorus, my eyes are teary: "Your love has finally set me free. You knew all along, but it's new to me."

As we applaud ourselves, Zach's dad takes a little bow.

"Play 'Crazy,' " Madelyn tells Zach as his dad eases her onto the overstuffed couch, trying to look nonchalant.

"The Gnarls Barkley 'Crazy'?" Zach asks, then grins mischievously at me to signal that he's just messing with her. He laughs at his mom's blank expression and mutters playfully, "Okay, fine. *Geez.* How deep into the former millennium do you intend to go?"

"Can't beat the classics," she responds.

He starts strumming the Patsy Cline ballad, and his mom taps the languid beat on her thigh, her husband hovering protectively while acting like he's not. He's enjoying the music, standing two inches to his wife's right so he can just happen to help her back on her feet whenever she's ready.

Claire hobbles in on her crutches to join Zach on vocals, going full pathos on the chorus.

We're all swaying by the end of the song.

"Hey, you're really good," I tell Claire. "You should join the band."

"One superstar in the family is plenty," she teases, and Zach tosses her a scrunched-up smile.

Theirs is the same kind of banter Liam and I used to share. When he picked me up for dinner tonight, I was tempted to tell

Zach about Varun's revelation, but I didn't want to spoil the vibe that's saturated my soul since Zach kissed me in the Taco Loco parking lot. I can't help but feel that I'll have lots more chances to have heavy conversations with him. I sure hope so.

After a couple more songs, I tell the family that I better be getting home.

"Scarlett, we're so glad you could join us," Madelyn says. "Please come back soon."

"I'd love that," I say, then sneak a glance at Zach, who's smiling.

He hops up, sets his guitar aside, and pats the empty pockets of his cargo shorts. "Left my keys in my room," he says. "Be right back."

I say good night to his parents and walk with Claire to the foyer. "I thought the chemistry between you two was going to make the den spontaneously combust," she says.

I giggle. "Hey, that friend you wanted to set Zach up with? Meg? She should still come hear us play," I say. "Mike and Kyle are both single, and they're such sweet guys . . ."

"And there's always Declan," Claire adds, then does a double take at my expression. "I was kidding," she clarifies.

"Yeah, I know," I say, averting my eyes.

Declan. Even the name makes my skin crawl. I want more than anything to forget my temporary bout of insanity and move on, with Zach never being the wiser.

That's doable. I'm almost home free.

Right?

CHAPTER TWENTY-TWO

Declan breezes into the loft and studies our faces, one at a time.

"What?" he asks defensively.

"You're half an hour late," Zach says, his voice measured but firm.

"Sorry." He runs his fingers through damp hair. Mike and Kyle exchange glances, and I avert my eyes, squeezing the neck of my guitar.

"We need every spare minute of practice," Zach tells him, "especially with two performances coming up this weekend, not to mention the new material we're—"

"Two?" Declan says. "I thought we were just playing Friday night at Sheehan's."

"Friday and Saturday this week," Zach says. "We talked about it Sunday at practice."

"Yeah, yeah," Declan mumbles, walking toward his guitar. "I remember now. But sorry. Saturday night's not gonna work for me."

He straps on his guitar and plugs it into an amp.

"It's not gonna work?" Kyle repeats in a clipped voice.

"I'm busy Saturday," Declan says. "So where were you guys? Just pick up where you left off, and I'll jump in . . ."

"How about jumping in to Saturday night's gig?" Kyle says. "You gotta step up, man."

Declan narrows his eyes. "I said I'm busy."

The moment hangs in the air.

"You told us Sunday you'd be there," Zach says.

Declan exhales dramatically and rolls his eyes. "I said I can't make it. Sue me."

"I've got a better idea," Mike says. "I say we fire your ass."

Declan drops his head back and gives a sharp laugh. "Because of one gig?"

Then he turns back to Zach, tilting his head. "It's just one night, man. Cut me some slack."

"He's half an hour late tonight, and he's blowing us off Saturday," Mike tells Zach. "I vote we cut him loose."

"I second that, man," Kyle says from behind his drum set. "It's happened too many times."

It feels like the oxygen has been sucked from the room.

Declan scans the room, looking at all of our faces. Finally, his eyes lock on me. "How about you, Scarlett?" he says.

I push a lock of hair behind my ear and shift my weight.

"I agree with the others," I murmur, my eyes downcast. "I think it's best if we make a change."

"Make a change," he repeats, glowering at me.

I nod, still staring at my feet.

Declan plants a hand on his hip. "I seemed to suit you just fine the other night at Bristow Point."

I feel my cheeks flush as a hurricane of mortification swirls through my head.

I don't move a muscle as four sets of eyes settle on me.

It's out there now. There's nothing I can say. Every one of these guys—guys I have mad respect for—knows I've been hooking up with Declan after hours. Zach knows. Oh God.

The seconds tick away like hours as the guys process this breaking news. I glance at Declan just long enough to see a look of smug satisfaction on his face, then avert my eyes again.

It's Zach who finally breaks the tension.

"It's unanimous, man," he finally says to Declan. "I'm sorry. You're voted out."

"Yeah?" Declan says defiantly. "Well, I vote that you kiss my ass."

He unplugs his guitar, roughly unstraps it, and grips it by the neck as he storms out of the loft.

The four of us are frozen in our spots for a moment.

I'm gripping my guitar with a clammy palm, wondering if I'll throw up. I still can't bear to look up, to meet their gazes. Will I ever be able to look Zach in the eye again? Would he want me to?

"Um, Scarlett," Zach finally says tersely, avoiding my gaze, "if you could take the lead vocal this weekend on the songs you've already practiced, I'll take Declan's part on the other stuff. Work for you?"

"Yeah," I manage to mumble. "That works."

The moment hangs in the air, then Zach busies himself retuning his guitar. I try to meet his eyes a couple of times. God, how desperate I am to connect with him, to apologize, to explain, just to feel the warmth of his eyes . . . but he's looking at nothing but his guitar.

Finally, he glances over his shoulder at Kyle and says in a muted voice, "Count us off on 'Shamblin',' will you?"

Kyle clears his throat awkwardly, then nods and whacks his

drumsticks together four times. After the opening bars, Zach leans into his mic and begins the first verse:

You're crying as you're telling me goodbye.
I never meant to make our love a lie.
Wish I could stop you now, but I just don't know how.

My tattered heart is hanging by a thread.
So many of my words have gone unsaid.
I'd tell them to you now . . . but I just don't know how . . .

I move into my mic to join in on the chorus, but my throat won't open up. I swallow the lump but still can't unleash my vocal chords. Zach is singing the chorus now without my harmony, so surely he'll glance at me to prod me along . . . right?

Wrong. His eyes are closed as he croons into his mic:

You left my life in shambles,
And my words are only rambles.
I guess I lost the gamble, yeah, I'm shamblin'.

I've never heard him sound so hurt. I feel utterly alone . . . ashamed . . . shattered. Then I feel my stomach lurch.

I raise my arm to signal the band to stop.

"Guys," I say, tossing the guitar strap off my neck, "I . . . I feel sick. I'm so sorry. I've gotta go."

I prop my guitar against the amp and bolt out of the room.

CHAPTER TWENTY-THREE

It's all good. See you Friday.

That's it. That's all Zach writes back in response to my text explaining how Declan and I had met up a couple of times after band practice, but that I'd realized quickly what a mistake it was. Hanging out with Declan, I wrote, was nothing but a once-off, a temporary lapse of sanity.

I left out the part that's ripping my heart out: that the reason I'm so embarrassed for Zach to know about Declan and me is that I care so much about *Zach*.

A tear trickles down my cheek as I read his text again, and again, and again.

What does it mean? Does it mean, "Wow, now I totally understand, and I'm dying to scoop you in my arms again?" Or does it mean, "I'm too decent to be rude, so I'll muster the minimal amount of feedback required to be polite and hopefully keep you from bothering me again?"

I don't know, I don't know, I don't know . . .

Should I call him? I know it's late—I'd been tossing and turning for over an hour before I got the nerve to text him—but

I'd chop off my arm right now for the chance to connect with him.

But of course I can't call him. He knows the situation now, and he's either okay with it or he's not. But the thought of him *not* being okay with it—not being okay with *me*—is twisting my heart into a suffocating knot. I've never valued anyone's opinion more than his, and I've never wanted so badly to keep someone from hurting.

I don't know what to do. I'm tempted to call Sara, but I really can't bear any *tsk-tsking*. I'm aching to call Varun, but even though I know I'll forgive him (hell, I already have), I can't know for sure if things will ever be normal for us again . . . and I can't bear to find out. Because if I've lost that, too, well, then my life is just shit.

So I lie still in the moonlight, crying salty tears on the one-eyed bear and making his fur even mangier than it was before.

CHAPTER TWENTY-FOUR

A thunderclap jolts me awake.

I glance out the window and see rain pouring. I check the time on my phone. It's almost sunrise, but the cloud-filled sky is dusky and swollen.

I see a seven-minute-old text on my phone—how did I miss the *ding*?—and read: Pool closed. Enjoy your soggy day off.

Great. Now I won't even have my job to distract me.

And there was a chance, just a chance, Zach would have come to the pool. Now there's no way I'll see him today.

I smash my pillow with my fist. This would have been the perfect day to sleep in, but all I've done all night is toss and turn, and that's all I foresee in the future. I'm so desperate to hear from Zach: a call, a text, an *anything* to give me a glimmer of hope that I can gaze into his eyes one more time.

I sigh heavily, pull my covers tighter under my chin, toss them off, then pull them tight again. The rain thrums hypnotically on the roof. I remember visiting Grandma and Grandpa one weekend when a thunderstorm chased us away from the pool, and Liam and Sara and I came back here, changing into our shorts and flopping around like fish for the rest of the day.

We'd lie in bed reading for a while, then pad to the kitchen for Moon Pies, then collapse onto the couch for a *Star Trek* rerun, then start the whole process over again. I remember feeling lazy and bored that day, but I was also content.

I wish I were still twelve. I wish Sara were in the bed next to mine, and that Liam was one bedroom over, and that Varun was an uncomplicated nerd who was waiting for me to get home from my grandparents' house so we could binge-watch Netflix.

I sigh again, then impulsively grab my phone.

Awake? I ask Varun.

Yep, he responds almost right away. What's up?

I pause, then type, I think you better ask me about my like life.

He signs off with a slice-of-cake emoji, then my phone rings.

• • •

"You did the right thing."

I stare at my oscillating ceiling fan as I lie on my wrinkled sheets, my hair splayed on the pillow. "You think?"

"Yeah," Varun says. "You were right to come clean to Zach and own it."

I press my phone tighter against my ear, the rain still pounding on the ceiling. "It's not like I had any choice. God. What if Zach never wants to see me again?"

"Doing the right thing and getting the result you want are two different things," Varun says. "Although, in this case, I'm guessing they're not mutually exclusive."

I sit up on the bed, crossing my feet at the ankles. "You don't think Zach will hate me and never want to see me again?"

"Nah," he says.

I moan. "So what do I do?" I ask. "Do I call him? Send him another text? Go to his house?"

"No," Varun responds. "You said what you had to say. Now give him some space."

"But I need to know where we stand," I moan.

"Have faith, Scarletta," he says. "I gave you some space, and three days later we're talking on the phone."

I smile. "I'm still mad at you."

"I know."

"But I'm sad for you, too," I add wistfully, my pinkie nail dangling by my lip. "I didn't know you were going through hell when Liam died. I thought you were just sad because I was sad."

"That too. But I'm okay."

I lightly trace the plaid pattern on my flannel pajama pants with my index finger. "Did your parents know?" I ask. "Did they know about Liam?"

"Noooo. They barely know about *me*."

"Yeah, you're really gonna have to spell out the gay thing for them," I say. "Maybe then they'll stop treating me like your girlfriend."

"I've strongly hinted," Varun says.

"Yeah, well, they've strongly disregarded your hints."

"I think they prefer happy and clueless to devastated and up to speed."

I huff. "You're not giving them enough credit," I say.

Varun sighs heavily. "I know I'm a coward. But . . . I dunno . . . I can't stand feeling like I've failed them, or disappointed them, or . . ."

"If they've made you feel like you can't talk to them about one of the most basic parts of your being," I say firmly, "then *they're* the ones failing *you*. Which is why I'm so sad I didn't know about Liam. Did he think he was going to disappoint me?"

"No," Varun says gently. "He just thought it would be awkward to talk about."

"Still . . ." I twirl a piece of hair. "I wish he'd known there's nothing he could have told me that would have made me love him less."

The ceiling fan clicks lightly with every rotation, adding a heartbeat to the rain on the roof.

"You know," I say, "it might be kinda nice to compare notes about Liam. I like thinking there will still be some new things to learn about him."

"God, I'd love to be able to talk about him," Varun says, relief pouring from his voice. "Thank you, Scarletta. Thank you for that."

I wrinkle my nose. "Sorry I was mean to you the other night."

"You were brutal," he teases.

I squeeze my pillow against my chest. "Varun, how unobservant am I?" I muse. "I mean, I overlook a million red flags about Declan, I'm clueless about my own brother's like life, and I clearly know nothing about you . . ."

He laughs.

"Seriously," I say. "Am I a completely self-absorbed moron?"

"No," Varun replies. "You're the most 'ingenuous' girl I know."

I laugh, then he laughs, too.

"Tell me I stand a chance with Zach," I say.

"You stand a chance with Zach."

I cross my fingers. "Wish me luck."

"You don't need luck," he assures me. "You've got awesomeness."

I smile. "I feel a teeny bit more awesome now than I did before you called me."

"Well," Varun says, "that's what friends are for."

CHAPTER TWENTY-FIVE

"Hey, how's it going?" Zach asks.

It's going shitty, that's how.

I'm stepping onto the stage at Sheehan's just as Zach is hopping off of it, attending to one of the many details involved in setting up for tonight's performance. I've just arrived, and it's the first time I've seen him since Declan ratted me out. Zach and I haven't communicated since his "It's all good" text.

Now that he has no choice but to be around me, he's barely making eye contact or asking how it's going as he brushes past me. His greeting is the kind you give a plumber fixing your pipes when you pass him in the hall.

I walk over to our equipment and set down my gig bag by a mic.

"Hi, Mike," I say quietly as he adjusts the settings on an amplifier.

"Hey, Scarlett."

"Hey, Mike?" I say, glancing around to make sure no one else is in earshot.

"Yeah?"

"Um . . ." I shift my weight, staring at my shoes. "I . . . want you to know something. When Declan mentioned that we'd hung out after practice? It's true. Unfortunately. But it was only a couple of times. And I had no idea he was seeing Mia."

Mike rubs his stubble-covered chin. "You're entitled to see whoever you want to see."

"*I'm not seeing Declan*. I can barely stand him. It took me longer than it should have to realize that, but it should never have happened, especially with all the tension that was going on in the band. I feel like I misled you guys, and . . ."

"Yeah?" Mike prods.

"And I don't want anyone thinking I'm interested in Declan, because the person I'm interested in . . ."

I hold his gaze, then squeeze my eyes shut and say it out loud:

". . . is Zach."

Mike ponders my words, nods, then puts his hand on his hip and says, "Look, Scarlett, I—"

"Hi, guys."

I look up and feel my cheeks flush as Kyle joins us on the stage.

"Hi," I murmur.

"'Sup, Kyle," Zach says as he walks back, carrying a couple of guitar cables.

I stand motionless for a moment, then retrieve my guitar from the gig bag.

Our first set will start soon, and we'll be busy between now and then tuning up and going over whatever last-minute revisions Zach made to the set list—a bigger deal than usual since Declan is out of the band.

So that's it. I've said what I needed to say. I'm fully exposed.

My soul is laid bare. Whatever happens from this point on is out of my hands. I just have to have faith, like Varun said.

But what if I've screwed up potentially the best thing to ever happen to me?

I can't think about that now. We've got work to do.

• • •

The Sheehan's crowd is extra stoked tonight.

They're loving our music, and a few of the regulars have heard Zach's original songs enough by now to sing along on the choruses. What a high it must be to have your own words rushing back to you.

I think the added spark of magic tonight is that Zach, rather than Declan, is singing his own songs. Yes, Declan is showier than Zach and maybe even a slightly better singer. But Zach's heartfelt renderings of his lyrics feel intense, profound, authentic. Whether he's melting into the sultry blues of "Shamblin' " or cranking up the unrestrained energy on "Back It Up," the crowd is totally loving it—some even dancing by their seats, holding half-eaten chicken wings aloft as their arms sway over their heads.

I've tried to catch Zach's eye several times, but it's not happening. He's been perfectly polite to me all night, but polite makes me even sadder than pissed. At least pissed is something I can push back against. The thought of our relationship being reduced to *cordial* makes my heart hurt.

We play a few more covers, all fun crowd-pleasers, then get to the last song of our first set.

I swallow hard as I realize Zach is about to sing "Fall Apart," the song he wrote for me. My hands feel clammy, and my heartbeat quickens as we play the opening bars. I force down a lump in my throat as he begins the first verse:

You say that life has shook you up and knocked you down a time or two.
And I can see it in your eyes: you think I haven't got a clue.
Your heart is heavy, and the phantoms of your past have seared your soul.
But hold on tight, 'cause hope's in sight, and I'm about to make you whole.

Despite my best effort, tears spring to my eyes as he begins the chorus:

I see the sorrow in your face,
And I don't know just where to start.
But all the pieces are in place,
And I won't let you fall apart.

I was supposed to sing harmony on the chorus, but my throat won't unlock. So I just strum along, gazing at Zach's face. As sad as I am, I'm lulled by the tenderness in his voice.

He still won't meet my eye.

He moves on to the second verse:

I'll pick you up and gather all the shattered parts you left behind.
There's nothing missing from your bruised and broken heart that I can't find.

As we play a bridge leading to the last chorus, he finally glances my way, signaling that he noticed I sat out the harmony on the first chorus. This is my cue to do what I'm supposed to do.

My throat is still tight and my eyes are misty, but I've got to do my job. As we begin the first line—"I see the sorrow in your face"—I realize my voice is shaky. I'm doing more harm than good. I need to stop singing.

Except that suddenly, Zach has moved from his mic to mine. He's singing with me, his eyes coaxing me along. I ease back in on the second line of the chorus:

And I don't know just where to start.
But all the pieces are in place,
And I won't let you fall apart.

By the end of the verse, our voices are perfectly synchronized. Zach's eye contact is pulling me through, and our voices are blending so beautifully that my heart is swelling.

But as we lean into the mic to repeat the chorus and finish the song, I realize tears are welling in my eyes. Zach is still gazing at me, looking so sweet and caring and gentle, and . . .

And I can't do this. I'm about to crumble in sadness, contemplating the words he wrote for me. Even the kindness in his eyes can't pull me back in. I can't finish this song.

I cast Zach a frantic, apologetic glance, then pull the guitar strap off my shoulder. I let my guitar thunk against an amp, then run off the stage and into the restroom. I hear the band finish the song, Zach singing alone, as I let the restroom door shut behind me and cover my face with my hands:

I see the hope back in your face,
'Cause now I know just where to start.
Yeah, all the pieces are in place,
And I won't let you fall apart.

Yeah, all the pieces are in place,
And I won't let you fall apart.

Tears are flowing down my cheeks when I hear Zach promise the crowd the band will be back soon for a second set. He's trying to sound buoyant—you always want a crowd to stay psyched for the second set, and I'm sure it doesn't help that I bailed halfway through a song—but his voice sounds pinched, distracted.

A girl walks in the restroom and studies my blurry eyes uneasily.

"You okay?" she asks, and I manage to nod.

"I'm fine, thanks," I say.

"You guys sound great," she says, and I laugh ruefully. Thank God she quickly cuts me loose and dashes into a stall. I'm wiping more tears from my eyes when I hear an urgent knock on the door.

"Scarlett? Are you in there?"

It's Zach.

I glance at my blotchy face in the mirror and cringe.

"I'm okay, Zach," I call back, trying to sound steadier than I feel.

"Scarlett, can you open the door?"

No, thanks. I think I'll just crawl into a corner and die.

"Really, I'm fine," I call back. "Sorry I bolted. I . . . had something in my eye."

"*Scarlett.*"

I put my hand on the sink to steady myself. I've got to face him sooner or later, and he's way too decent to leave me like this. I've got to open the door.

I do.

Then I fall into his arms.

• • •

"I'm just so sorry."

I'm murmuring into Zach's shoulder as he whispers into my ear that everything's okay.

I haven't disentangled from his arms since he wrapped them around me, but he's somehow managed to inch us over to a discreet spot down the hall from the restrooms. I don't think anyone's around, but even if everybody in the restaurant was gawking at us, I'm not sure I'd care. It feels so good to be in his arms.

"I'm such an idiot," I say, my voice muffled against his T-shirt.

"Scarlett," he says, then pulls me back so he can look me in the eye, holding on to my shoulders. "You didn't do anything wrong. You're entitled to see whoever you want to see."

"Declan is the last person I want to see! The only person I'm interested in is you. But God, what an idiot I am. You know who's a perfect fit for you? Meg."

Zach narrows his eyes quizzically. "Who?"

"Her name is Meg. I was supposed to introduce her to you."

"*What*?"

"It was Claire's idea. And Meg is great! She's about to start med school, and she volunteers at health fairs, and she's really pretty in this totally natural way, and—"

"Now, *who* are we talking about?"

"That's exactly what I should do," I say, talking more to myself than him. "I should introduce you to Meg."

"Okay, do I get a vote?"

"No. You don't get a vote. All you need to know is she's not some immature, superficial moron. She's perfect for you."

Zach smiles sweetly. “I’m thinking perfection is overrated.”

“Well, you’re wrong.”

He laughs, and now I’m laughing, too. Through my tears.

Then I stare at my hands as I twist my fingers together. “I’m sorry I ruined your song.”

He lifts up my chin with his index finger. “You *inspired* my song.”

The moment hangs in the air, then Zach leans in and kisses me. I’m tentative at first, but then I kiss him back, wrapping my arms around his neck. I can’t press him close enough. I don’t think I’ve ever felt this safe, this content, this elated.

When he finally pulls away, I stare into his chocolaty eyes and say, “I guess we’ve got another set to finish.”

“Are you gonna cry through the sad songs?”

I laugh again and shake my head. “No more crying,” I promise.

“We can bring tissues to the stage with us, you know . . .”

“I’m good,” I say, still laughing. “Just promise me you’ll stay by my side, you know . . . in case I fall apart again.”

He smiles at me. “That’s a promise.”

CHAPTER TWENTY-SIX

"You guys! I'm going to spend the whole night crying!"

The guests at the anniversary party have complied with Zach's father's request to each bring a photo of Madelyn, then tell the story behind the picture.

She got teary-eyed at the very first photo—one of her mother, Mrs. Carver, kissing the top of her daughter's head as Madelyn held newborn Zach in her arms—and she's gotten progressively weepier with every new picture she unwraps.

Some of the photos are poignant, others funny, but even the funny ones are prompting tears of laughter.

I squeeze Zach's hand, fighting tears myself. This anniversary party may be the last one his mom will ever have, and it definitely has the potential to be the world's most heartbreaking event. Here's this young, beautiful, vibrant woman who has everything to live for, yet precious little time left to enjoy it. But Madelyn is setting the tone by reveling in every single moment.

"And who is this one from?" she asks, holding up a package in silver wrapping paper.

"That one's from me," I say. "I know I haven't known you long, but . . ."

"Scarlett, how thoughtful," she says.

Zach looks at me quizzically, no doubt wondering when I managed to take a photo (during taco night Tuesday) and how I knew about the gift request (Claire tipped me off).

Madelyn unwraps the gift and gazes at the framed photo, a smile spreading across her face. She strokes it for a moment, then turns it around for everyone to see.

It's a photo I surreptitiously took when she and her husband were dancing while Zach played his ballad, "New to Me," on his guitar.

Everyone oohs and aahs as Zach smiles at me.

"The story behind it," I say after clearing my throat nervously, "is that my very first visit to your home was all it took to know how much love fills these walls."

"Oh, Scarlett," Madelyn says. "Thank you. Thank you so much."

I nod, smiling, as Zach puts an arm around me and squeezes me close to his side.

The look on Madelyn's face in the photo?

That's how Zach makes me feel.

CHAPTER TWENTY-SEVEN

We've just finished the first set at Sheehan's, and I'm coming back from the restroom when I see Grandpa walking toward me.

The people milling around us are wearing shorts and flip flops, so Grandpa stands out in his striped tie, looking dignified as hell.

He takes my hands. "Doing okay, Scarlina?" he asks gently.

I smile and nod.

Mom, Dad, Sara, and Varun have all driven down for our performance, the Beastings' summer finale. Zach's parents and sister are here, too, and both families are sitting together outside on the deck, cheering us on. Even from her wheelchair, Zach's mom is all smiles tonight, looking totally carefree. That goes for my family, too, in spite of the circumstances. We're just happy to be together, I guess. Today would have been Liam's twenty-second birthday.

"Your brother sure would be proud of you," Grandpa says.

I swallow a lump and nod. "He taught me everything I know," I say softly.

Grandpa leans closer. "*You've* taught *me* a lot this summer," he tells me. "I learned a lot about resilience."

I hold his gaze. "No, Grandpa. I learned that from you." My voice breaks slightly as I add, "I don't think I could have made it through these past few months without you."

He shakes his head. "You can make it through anything. I've seen that firsthand. Look at everything you've accomplished this summer: You worked hard at the pool. You joined a band. You made fine new friends. I know you were hurting, but you didn't let that stop you. That's just what Liam would have wanted."

Now I'm the one to squeeze *his* hands. "I learned from the master. We're tough cookies, aren't we?"

"Damn straight," he says, and I laugh at his salty language. "I sure am gonna miss you when you head to college."

"Grandpa, I am totally coming back every weekend to visit you."

"You most certainly are not," he says, raising his snow-white eyebrows. "You're going to live it up in Athens with all your friends."

I laugh. "Nobody's more fun to live it up with than you."

He puts an arm around me and hugs me close to his side. "Well, if we've accomplished nothing else this summer," he says, guiding me slowly back to the deck, "I hope we've put your mother's mind at ease."

My brow furrows. "About what?"

"About my needing a designated driver."

"You weren't supposed to know about that," I say cheerfully, swishing my ponytail off my shoulder. "The official story was that *you* were supposed to be helping *me*. And remember, Mom still thinks I've been doing all the driving this summer."

"Time to set her straight?" he asks.

My index finger flies to my lips. "Our little secret, Grandpa," I say, smiling. "She's surprisingly uncool with me mowing down people in parking lots."

"Well, when *I* mow somebody down," he grumbles, "then they can talk about taking away my car keys."

Grandpa opens the back door, and as we step onto the deck, a dusky sunset washes over us. It looks amazing—shades of peach and coral bleeding into a sun-bleached sky.

"I've never had so much as a parking ticket my entire life," Grandpa grouses, more to himself than anyone, and I laugh lightly.

He straightens his tie as we near our table, and a cardinal swoops past us gracefully.

Happy birthday, Liam, I say to myself.

• • •

"Wow, you sound incredible! Wish I had a lighter for the second half."

I laugh at Mom's lameness as Grandpa and I rejoin the group. "Nobody's used lighters since your Metallica concerts in 1984," I tell her.

"So what do people use instead of lighters?" Mom asks.

"They rub sticks together until sparks fly," Zach's dad responds, and we laugh.

"If you guys get it started, we'll add 'Burning Down the House' to our second set," Zach offers, and we nod our endorsement.

"Ooh, I know that song!" Mom says. "See? I'm not so lame."

But even as she's saying it, I'm mouthing "lame" to the group, adding L-shaped fingers for emphasis.

I feel Zach's hand settle on the small of my back as a waitress hands us soft drinks.

"So how often will you guys regroup once school starts next week?" my dad asks.

"We can squeeze in some weekends and holidays. The money's too good to walk away from," Zach quips with a grin. "With everything I've saved from this summer alone, I'm closing in on a down payment for a mini-fridge." We laugh.

"I'm buying a private island with my share," I say.

Claire's eyes glisten. "Can you believe we'll be in Athens in five days?" she tells me.

Zach steals a glance at his mom, and she smiles.

Yes, this is what she wants: both of her kids living their lives without hitting any pause buttons on her account.

"Varun," I say, "you gotta wash the smell of formaldehyde out of your pores before we move into our dorms. Maybe full-strength Clorox?"

He cocks his head and grins. We're still feeling our way back to our old connection, but in some ways, we've never been closer. My parents have practically adopted him. I've been home a couple of times since his bombshell, and it feels so good for everybody to be able to talk openly about Liam around the dinner table or sitting on the front-porch swing. I love that Varun has given me new things to learn about Liam. Right before our set started tonight, he sent me a text requesting that we play "Open Up My Heart." Their song. He ended the text with a cardinal emoji, I guess figuring it was random. Weird, huh? Yeah, Varun and I will be just fine. Provided he bathes in Clorox by next Wednesday.

"Evening, folks," Kyle says as he and Mike walk up to our table.

"Hi, guys. You sound awesome, per usual," Claire tells them. "Wanna sit?"

"Naw, we're signing autographs at the bar," Mike quips.

"You boys get better every time I hear you," Zach's grandmother says, and Mike takes a little bow. He and Mia have seen each other a few times in the past few weeks—she's here tonight—but they're taking it slow. Maybe they'll pick up where they left off when fall semester starts. Who knows?

Kyle has started dating, too. He actually met a nice girl at Frosty's. It may not last—she's a junior at a community college here in town, and he'll be in the thick of his brutal last year of pre-med this year—but it's great to see him so light on his feet.

And it's not just Kyle. The whole Beastings vibe feels easier, more relaxed, more natural since Declan bounced. I've seen him around town a few times, usually with his arm around some random girl, and I'd be glad to wave or say hello, but he won't make eye contact. Zach keeps in touch with him; after all, they've been friends since first grade, and Zach's always felt protective of him, knowing Declan's swagger is just a front. Or at least that's Zach's take. I'm less charitable, but at least I can see him on a sidewalk without wanting to hurl. Maybe everybody needs one Declan in their past to make them appreciate the Zachs in their present.

And their future.

That's what I'm banking on.

ACKNOWLEDGMENTS

I am forever grateful to my wonderful parents, Gregory and Jane Hurley, for filling my world with love, literature, and music since the day I was born.

When Mom died in 2013, the "unofficial editor" torch was passed along to my daughter, Julianne. Thank you, Julianne, for being my first and best reader—for filling my words with heart and my heart with joy. I see Mima in you every time you smile. And the resemblance of your poetry-filled and razor-sharp brains is uncanny.

To my *actual* editors, Mari Kesselring, Kelsy Thompson, and the rest of the wonderful crew at Flux, thank you for the most exhilarating and TLC-infused publishing process I've ever had. And to Andrea Somberg, my wonderfully kind, diligent, and supportive literary agent, thank you for setting it in motion.

I offer more appreciation than I can put into words to John Hurley, the musician/producer extraordinaire who lovingly vetted my music scenes and inspired me to create music of my own. Our songwriting collaboration has been more fun and enriching than I could ever have imagined.

Thanks also to my songwriting teacher, Craig Carothers, an unbelievably talented lyricist and composer who loaded my toolkit with the lessons and wisdom he's accumulated over a lifetime. He also produced the *All the Wrong Chords* trailer, which exceeded my loftiest expectations. Oh, and both he and John perfectionism-ed the heck out of this project. Thanks for that.

A shout-out also to Jeff Cook, a brilliant and world-class musician whose expertise is worlds out of my league but who, as my nephew, is stuck taking my calls.

Thanks so much to the incredibly talented Adrian Kothman for my beautifully redesigned website (chderiso.com).

To Steve, Cecilia, Anne, and John (youngest to oldest for a change), thank you for providing so much fodder for my family scenes and for always cheering me on.

To Graham III, Greg, Taylor, and the rest of my family and friends, thank you for being the most bountifully loving support group I could ever wish for. I'm eternally grateful.

And to Graham, always.

To access the music featured in *All the Wrong Chords*, visit itunes.com/allthewrongchords

ABOUT THE AUTHOR

Christine Hurley Deriso is an award-winning young adult author who loves putting interesting characters in character-defining situations. Her novels include *Then I Met My Sister*, *Thirty Sunsets,* and *Tragedy Girl.* Visit her at www.chderiso.com.